CANNIBALS
IN LOVE

CANNIBALS IN LOVE

MIKE ROBERTS

FARRAR, STRAUS AND GIROUX   NEW YORK

Farrar, Straus and Giroux
18 West 18th Street, New York 10011

Printed in the United States of America
First edition, 2016

Library of Congress Cataloging-in-Publication Data
Names: Roberts, Mike, 1980– author.
Title: Cannibals in love : a novel / Mike Roberts.
Description: First edition. | New York : Farrar, Straus and Giroux, 2016.
Identifiers: LCCN 2015048946 | ISBN 9780374536633 (paperback) |
    ISBN 9780374715113 (e-book)
Subjects: | BISAC: FICTION / Literary. | FICTION / Urban Life. |
    GSAFD: Love stories.
Classification: LCC PS3618.O316795 C36 2016 | DDC 813/.6—dc23
LC record available at http://lccn.loc.gov/2015048946

Designed by Jo Anne Metsch

Our books may be purchased in bulk for promotional, educational,
or business use. Please contact your local bookseller or the Macmillan
Corporate and Premium Sales Department at 1-800-221-7945, extension
5442, or by e-mail at MacmillanSpecialMarkets@macmillan.com.

www.fsgbooks.com • www.fsgoriginals.com
www.twitter.com/fsgbooks • www.facebook.com/fsgbooks

1 3 5 7 9 10 8 6 4 2

FOR MY
MOTHER AND FATHER

CONTENTS

CANNIBALS
IN LOVE

A DAY AT THE RACES

My father said I was living in his house *persona non grata* and that I needed to find myself a job. I asked why he wouldn't just buy me a baseball team like the president's daddy. He thought about this a second and offered me a ride to the temp agency instead. I liked that, though. The Latin.

This was how I ended up working with Don, counting lampposts for the city of Lockport. A *field audit*, they called it. The temp agency told us they'd had trouble finding a team who could execute this task with consistency. Don and I got a kick out of that, all these anonymous flameouts going down counting lampposts.

But Don was late this morning, and I couldn't help imagining an accident. I'd driven around with the old guy enough to picture him doing something ill-advised. Reaching under his seat, or behind him, or into the glove box like I'd watched him do a thousand times before. Letting his head drop below the dashboard as he blew the red light so that eyewitnesses would claim that there *was* no driver in the 1991 Honda Civic at the time of the accident. Not an accident at all, really, but a crash. And maybe even a pileup. Dozens of cars slamming into each other behind Don. Heads hitting steering wheels; coffees bursting into laps. I imagined trucks jumping curbs and bending themselves around lampposts, *our* lampposts. Tires blowing out. Glass shattering. Women screaming. This caterwaul of brakes and impacted metal in the street. And Don's car, in the middle of everything, sparking and bursting into flames as it flipped and rolled over on itself.

Why else would he be a half hour late?

But eventually I picked out the sound of his little Honda growling up the block. A hundred and fifty-four thousand miles, he liked to brag as he punched the dashboard. Don had total faith in his machine and he showed it no mercy, taking us through every pothole in the city, almost willfully. In a funny way the Honda matched his own shambling presence, perpetually overburdened by found and collected objects. Every morning involved a clearing off of the passenger seat anew, just to make room for me.

The car boasted a series of laminated icons who were the saints, I supposed. Led on high by Jesus on the Cross, swinging from the rearview. *Bless this mess*, Don would always say with a chortle, and I liked him for that. He was unmistakably a man in search of a calling, and yet it surprised me to find out he was a volunteer chaplain with the fire department. A couple times a week Don's police radio would start twitching and crackling on the nightstand, and he would get out of bed and drive to the awful scene of some burning building. Watching and waiting; standing out in the street. Talking to the people there; looking to make himself useful. Don would never give me any real details, just some mornings he looked tired. I would ask if there had been a fire and he would exhale and nod. "Mm-hm. A pretty big one."

But there was something off about Don this morning, something almost melancholy. We liked to start slow as a rule, but this was different. Usually we turned on sports talk radio, but Don was playing music at a whisper. I asked if there had been a fire and he said no. We drove on, past blocks of lampposts: *five, ten, fifteen, twenty*. I asked where we were going and Don said a circle. Letting it hang there.

"This isn't really coffee," he said, picking up his mug.

"Uh-huh."

"I figure you have a right to know. I'm thinking about not working today."

"Uh-huh," I said, not following this at all.

"You up for something like that?" Don smiled. "Hooky?"

"Sure, I guess. I don't care." I shrugged and looked away.

Don swished the dregs of his coffee mug before finishing it. "Good. We better switch to beer, then, if we're gonna be driving around."

Don stopped at a gas station and cut the engine. I sat in the car watching him limp across the parking lot. He was a giant man with a clubfoot, which was inescapable. Lamed by birth or life, I had no idea. We weren't brought up to talk about how something like a sixty-year-old man's clubfoot could make you feel numb and self-conscious. It was easy enough to forget the thing entirely. But there were always moments like these when I'd see him lumbering on it, dead-asleep for all time.

Don was constantly shifting his weight as we drove around, tucking the crippled foot under the good one to streamline operation. I wish I could say that it was Don's wonky feet that made us drive around in circles, but that was really just the job. Ostensibly this was a city audit, but that didn't make the fact of counting lampposts feel any less absurd. Every lamppost was a near-identical copy. Even between decades the models stayed remarkably the same.

Don would pull the Civic up to a curb and start craning his turkey-neck under the windshield. "Thirty-foot post . . . wooden . . . ten-foot truss . . . cobra-head fixture . . . Wait, wait, it's flickering . . . Yep, this one's a dayburner."

"Tag?" I would ask, looking up from the boxy laptop with the city serial number burned across its bottom, as I locked in our GPS coordinates.

"Charlie-four-one-seven."

"Cee-four-one-seven. Got it."

And Don would pull up to the next post. All day long like this, over and over. It was fantastically boring, tedious work. Some days we would spend ten hours in the car this way, driving in circles, professionally lost. I had come to know Don as a meticulous micromanager of our days. He hated to backtrack, and he hated to put the Honda into park. When possible, Don preferred to ease off the pedal entirely, letting the car coast. This was how we missed the majority of our stop signs. Me on the computer and Don making a blind spot with the map. Rolling, to be inevitably jerked up by the sound of some angry horn. It was in the residential areas where Don felt most above the law. Driving up the wrong side of the street; going backward down an alley or a one-way. He thought nothing of wheeling right onto somebody's front lawn in a hasty U-turn, if necessary. After all, we were working.

People often stared openly as we drove through the city with our hazards on. Don said the blinking lights made our work self-evident, but I thought it just invited cops to stop and ask us stupid questions. Smiling along like assholes. *Yessir, we're working out here. Yessir, counting the lampposts, har-har-har.*

On a lucky day the girls from the high school cross-country team might run by in their short-shorts. This huddle of pumping arms and legs, with flushed cheeks and glistening skin. Shiny hair pulled back into ponytails, swinging and bobbing. They smiled and laughed as they ran, like they could keep it up exactly this way forever. These girls were a forest of young trees to me. I would stare out the window openly, trying to will eye contact with one of them. Any of them. Somehow, the fact that I was twenty years old now made them all suddenly too young for me. It didn't matter anyway. I was invisible inside of Don's little Honda. Even with the blinking lights.

Don actually took our job seriously, though, and I appreciated that he cared enough to set that tone. He liked talking to the cops and answering questions. He liked being out in the city where we might run into a mailman or a guy up on a power line. Clearly Don included us in their great Civic Brotherhood, and I could tell that he'd begun to consider himself some kind of authority on counting lampposts. It was fine with me. I was happy to let him play the boss if that's what he wanted. I'm sure it's the reason that we lasted so long.

Don came out of the gas-station store cradling a twelve-pack of Stroh's. This was a beer I'd seen my entire life but never thought to try. It made me smile to suddenly know what Don drank. And all at once this day began to seem like fun. Two guys skipping work; driving around; drinking beers. I couldn't decide if this was some kind of last stand for Don, and I didn't really care. I was just going to go with it now.

I had gotten used to Don's physical presence, but I could see in the reactions of others that he was creepy in some non-descript way. Always snuffing his nose and clearing his throat, or chortling unexpectedly when he laughed. He wore an uneven beard and glasses that tinted in the sunlight. It was not untrue to say that Don bore some vague resemblance to the Unabomber, and I tried to imagine him living in an iso-lated shack, which was easy. The Civic suggested a certain kind of house. Some old shackle falling in on itself, held up at pressure points by load-bearing columns of newspapers. Dusty cans of food lined up in the cupboards, bomb-shelter-style. A harem of cats straight out of central casting, even. And maybe Don was living off the land and fertilizing a garden with his own shit, like the real Unabomber did. Tinkering with complicated math by candlelight, and writing his mani-festo longhand. Clearly the simple mechanics of a pipe bomb would appeal to a character like Don. *The Clubfoot Killer*, they

would call him in the newspapers. And I would be inter-
viewed on television as the blank-faced schmuck who worked
with the madman. But instead of saying that I never saw it
coming, I would say, with total earnestness, that all the warning signs were there. Everything Don did was a red herring
to me. It was all so very, very obvious, and I was terribly sorry
that I had not said something earlier.

But that was not really Don, either. He was too gentle for
all of that stuff. Especially now, pouring a beer into his coffee
mug. I was reminded that I did not really know this man at all.
I didn't know who he was or how he spent the four decades
that separated his age from mine. I didn't know what brought
him to the world of temp work or why he couldn't hold a real
job. None of it. All I knew was that Don was in a great mood
now, informing me that we were headed to the OTB.

"*Off-Track Betting?* Is that even open?" It was eight thirty
in the morning and I was sipping the foam off my first-ever
Stroh's.

"Of course it's open. Have you never been?"

I shrugged. Not only had I never been to the OTB, I
couldn't even tell you what they bet on in there. Sports? Dogs?
Horses? Those rickshaw-chariots you always used to see on
Wide World of Sports? The only thing the layperson knows
about the OTB is that it's probably not for them. Like a bingo
hall or a dirty movie house. Someone must be having fun in
there, but we were sure we'd never met them in the daylight.

"The OTB." Don flashed a toothy grin. "Where the magic
of the racetrack meets the charm of the bus station."

I couldn't help laughing with him. I wanted to remember to write that one down.

It made sense to think of Don as a gambler. He bought scratch-off tickets compulsively throughout the week. Forcing me to participate in his ritual of losing, making me a party to it. Not only that, but Don would pick up other people's discards. Even out of the tops of trash cans. *Just to be sure*, he always said.

Admittedly, there was a kind of scattered brilliance about Don's disordered way of thinking. Don was a talker and he always had a theory. And he always had a theory for why his original theory was always so flawed. He reminded me of those Y2K doomsayers who changed their money into gold and talked endlessly about airplanes falling out of the sky. I imagined the old guy holed up in a dark house with a clock and a shotgun, waiting for the New Year, waiting for the End Times. That's how it felt playing captive audience to Don in the passenger seat of the Civic sometimes. Still, there were certain tics that I enjoyed. Like the sports conspiracies.

Don insisted, for instance, that *Monday Night Football* was dreamed up by ABC Television and the Mob, back in 1970, as a way of hooking all these poor assholes who'd lost their shirts on Sunday afternoon. Don said they'd all come running back to their bookies, double-or-nothing, trying to salvage the weekend. But by that point, luck had already sailed on them.

"Less than a third of all double-or-nothing bets pay out. Did you know that?"

"Holy shit," I said. "Is that true?"

Don would raise his eyebrows and nod solemnly. "Oh, yeah."

Even more damning was his takedown of the NBA. Don hated the NBA. "The most crooked sport by far," he told me. "Don't ever gamble on the NBA."

"What's wrong with the NBA?" I wanted to know.

"It's the referees, for one. They have too much power over the pace of play. More than any other sport. They literally blow the whistle and take away baskets, if they want to. Baskets we all watched go in. In front of you and God and David Stern himself. Gone! Or the opposite, right? Guy misses at the rim and here comes the whistle again. *Free throws*," Don said cryptically. "More than one-third of all NBA points are scored at the free throw line, with the clock turned off. Heh?"

I nodded blankly, knowing Don was winding himself up for something big.

"Did you know they've actually lowered the rim a quarter of an inch since 1987 to bring more dunking into the game? Do you even understand what that means!"

I laughed out loud when he went on this way. I was sure that Don was fucking with me. Either that or the NBA had burned him pretty bad. But this was really just the way he talked. After a while, I'd have to roll the window down and let the crush of wind into my ear instead.

I couldn't help wanting a different life for Don somehow. Something steadier, more middle-class. Counting lampposts was a lark for me; I was headed back to school at the end of the summer. But there was something sad about Don really needing to do it. I tried to imagine how many different jobs a guy like this must have in a lifetime. All these different versions of the man I didn't know. I wondered if he'd ever served in the military or tried college or been trained in a vocation. Don could be funny and scholarly, in his own cracked way. He had a strange way with expressions and I pictured him up on a stage, in a dark theater, in a play. I imagined him reading the Beats and hitchhiking across the West. We had a running joke that Don was in training to become Lockport's only full-time taxi driver.

"We could put a shingle up right now and call ourselves a gypsy cab," he told me with a wink. "Make ourselves a few extra shekels, heh?"

Whenever I thought of Don, I thought of him in motion, driving around in circles. I tried to imagine him driving a school bus, or a tow truck, or an armored car. Maybe he could've been a great paperboy, or an ice-cream man, or a dogcatcher, even. And then I'd always remember his clubfoot, and it was hard to even picture him five years younger. Somebody should buy Don a baseball team, I thought.

We parked the Civic behind the Off-Track Betting and got out. Don clearly had a spring in his step now, floating on that broken foot. The back door, and main entrance, of the OTB was tinted a kind of privacy-black. There was a handwritten sign, threatening: "Positively no alcohol or firearms allowed on the premises." Don was holding the door as I realized I was carrying our box of Stroh's.

"C'mon, c'mon . . ." He hustled me inside.

I walked in, glancing at his waistband, hoping we were

following the stricture on firearms, at least. It was barely 9:00 a.m., but there was already a good crowd. Men sipping coffees and ashing cigarettes and ruffling newspapers. All eyes were fixed on a bay of television screens—everybody always watching the screens. They jotted down notes, and ripped up slips, and traded around some kind of track newsletter. I felt a weird charge just being here, suddenly feeling underage. It was like wandering into some secret Gentlemen's Club, or a Meeting of Divorced Men. It struck me then that I didn't know Don's status on that front. He didn't wear a ring. If he had a wife and kids bouncing around I figured he would've brought them up by now. Who knows?

Don got to yakking and joking with a couple of the guys right away, to prove he was a regular. I shook a few hands on cue and set our beers up on the big center counter. As Don and I settled onto our stools, I could see we were the only ones drinking. Still, I felt happy to have it, somehow. The Stroh's was like a prop in my hand. I was certainly an odd presence in this Hall of Men, but I didn't care. I was too taken up in the watching. Mesmerized by this wall of televisions and its hold over the gamblers. Endless fuzzy satellite feeds of horse racing.

"Where are all these races coming from?" I asked Don.

He smiled and spread his arms grandly. "All over the world. Mostly Florida."

A bell went off on a corner set, and the men all turned like they'd been waiting for this race to start. A few got onto their feet and moved right up under the screen. A young man with a mustache was shouting at his horse to run.

"Go, Alimony! Go!"

He cursed it around the turns as the lady ticket-taker shook her head behind a wall of Plexiglas. The young man cracked the whip against his thigh, willing his TV horse to run faster.

"Go, Alimony! Run, you fucker! Run!"

And he did. Alimony raced his way around the track to an easy victory, which was strangely thrilling. The young gambler turned back to the room, looking vindicated, and I couldn't help but wonder what his stake in the race had been. There was some polite applause and a chuckle as he strutted back to the window to collect his winnings.

"Well," he said, "time for work, then." And he disappeared out the front door with a swagger.

This was enough to make me want to gamble, too. I picked out a horse called Helter Skelter and Don showed me how to fill it out on the slip. I gave my money to the sexless woman behind the counter and promptly lost. I felt like a sucker. That five dollars was supposed to buy my lunch.

Races kept going, one after another across the bay of televisions, to decidedly little fanfare. I had no idea what distinguished one race from another, a good one from a bad one. I was looking for patterns in the men, but they were giving off something else, something worse. Lucklessness, I thought.

We'd slowed to a perceptible lull since Alimony first paid out, well over an hour ago. The OTB held the sad air of a waiting room, or a holding cell, maybe. Everybody carried a ticket, but no one's name was called. I couldn't help imagining some of the more stalwart characters coming here as a proxy to real employment. Telling the wife some lie about day labor or construction, before working banker's hours at the OTB, desperately trying to reanimate luck.

Don was still going strong, however. Betting and losing, though I could tell he had some system underneath it. Don was not casting into the current haphazardly. He knew exactly where he wanted to drop his line. It was all a matter of time, he said. Losing didn't seem to faze him as he sat there, stiller than a Buddha, sipping from his Stroh's like it was hot coffee. He mooned at the televisions expectantly. Waiting.

I tried to keep following the races in earnest, but the whole thing had lost its appeal. I wanted to tell him to play it double-or-nothing already so we could get the hell out of here. Just that quickly, though, Don stood up with a ticket in hand. "See that?" he said, and I tried to find his winning horse on one of the screens.

Don took his money back to the counter and started winning compulsively then. This feeling was contagious, and he was suddenly a sage among the men. Explaining his bets and doling out racetrack maxims. I was surprised to find how much time could pass in the winning. Don made a big show of peeling off a twenty and asking me to go buy lunch down the street.

"What do you want?" I asked.

"Anything but peanuts."

"What?" The guys all laughed like this was funny.

"It's an old superstition," one of them said.

"No peanuts in the barn," Don added with a grin.

"Uh-huh," I said, without comprehension.

"Just some chicken wings or something. Whatever you want."

Don was playing the Big Man now, showing off for his friends, but I didn't care. I was happy to run this errand just to go outside. The low ceiling and the still air had begun to wear on me. The OTB smelled of cigarettes and sweat and aftershave.

I drank down the warm bottom of my beer and walked out the door.

I actually thought about ditching Don then. Not to screw him over, but just because I had a couple beers in me. What the hell were we doing at the OTB anyway? I might as well have stayed home in bed.

The sad part was that no one was ever going to catch us blowing off the day, either. We did have a boss—this schlubby middle manager down in an off-wing of City Hall. He had red hair and pink skin and yellow teeth, and he was always calling Don and me *guy* or *fella*, no idea what our real names might be. He also had no idea how long it actually took to count a lamppost. He was just thrilled to see we'd made it through another week together. It was a good situation for everyone, really.

Don and I would show up in his office, every other Friday, with a 3.5-inch floppy disk filled with everything you'd ever want to know about a lamppost. Don loved being down in City Hall, and he'd try anything he could to prolong these visits with our faithful bureaucrat. Unfolding our maps and trying to talk inside baseball with the poor guy. It was pretty clear to me that this man did not give a shit about lampposts. We were just one more thing that landed on his desk.

I did wonder what happened to our disks after we left, though. Who's to say they weren't just putting them into a drawer, or a garbage can? I'd had a job once, in elementary school, helping the janitors collect recycling. I imagined a big truck that took our old tests and book reports to a processing plant, where they were cooked down and rolled out into wide, clean sheets of new paper. What I ended up finding out instead was that the janitors were just throwing it all into the dumpster behind the school with the rest of the trash. There was no truck, and I didn't know how to feel about that.

When I came back with the food I was surprised to find that most of the men were gone. It was darker and warmer than I'd remembered, too. But Don was still there, sitting in the same seat, going through discarded slips and checking for a stray winner. I invited him to come outside and eat, thinking he could use the sunshine, hoping I could get him back into the car. But Don declined my invitation.

I sat outside alone, at a graying picnic table, throwing chicken bones at a menace of seagulls sunning themselves in the parking lot. It felt strange to watch these birds fighting over their own meat. Or close enough anyway. The warm beer and greasy wings weren't helping me any, either. I sat there, feeling bloated and lethargic, unsure what to do.

"Don't eat those," I said tersely, scattering the birds.

Back inside, several of the sets had been switched off, and Plain Jane behind the Plexiglas window had been replaced by a man who could've been her brother. Don was still hunkered over his slips, but his face was blank and chalky now. I could see him crossing and uncrossing his fingers under the table, which was a thing I'd never seen a grown man do before, except as a joke. The Stroh's was gone, too, and I decided this would be my last try.

"How's it going, huh? Almost done? I'm thinking we should make a move soon. Go count some lampposts, maybe."

But Don wasn't listening. Something had gone wrong here today, and I wondered the extent to which he thought of me as a jinx. He grumbled without looking up, and mumbled something about *holding my horses*. I smiled and waited for the wink. But Don hadn't meant it that way.

I went back out to the Civic and got the laptop and the GPS (which they tell you never to leave in an unlocked car), and I decided to work. Fuck it. There were lampposts out here, so why not just count them.

I walked around the lot and grabbed three or four quickly: thirty-foot posts; ten-foot trusses; cobra-head fixtures, all of them. I tried to use my body to shade the sun off of the computer, but the whole thing was demoralizing. Some kids on skateboards had stopped to stare at me, and I was already losing the point of my protestation.

I sat down in a bus shelter and gave all four lampposts a single GPS location. And then I didn't move. I didn't know where to go, really. I stared out across the buzzing traffic, feeling shipwrecked. I didn't care about Don's suffering. I was thinking about myself, which is the only thing you know how to do when you're young.

All of a sudden the back door opened and my bolt-necked partner came limping out to the car, like he'd forgotten all about me. Forgotten everything. I grabbed my things and hurried back to the Civic, worried I was watching him leave me here.

"Ho, Don, wait up, man. What're you doing?"

But Don didn't answer, opening the door and closing it behind him. I let myself in, expecting him to fire it right up. But he didn't. He just sat there with his hands on the wheel, not moving.

"What's going on?" I asked defensively.

But Don didn't look at me. He started to speak, but I couldn't hear him. Something about his inner voice shouting at him, he said. Something telling him it was all shit and meaningless. The fallacy of doing good. The impossibility of trying to see God in the world. Everything was temporary. People don't care. Everything we do goes for naught in the end.

"The less you expect of the world, the less it lights you on fire and consumes you whole," he said in one scary, lucid beat.

I nodded blankly, trying to measure this. "I think a lot of people probably feel that way sometimes . . ." But I stopped myself, knowing I was way over my head. I wasn't even sure that he could hear me.

And without wanting to, I saw Don as some hackneyed drunk, falling off the wagon today. Letting it all go at once and hitting the concrete ground like a brick. One last act of futility after years of piety and sobriety and love. But that was all so stupidly easy for me to swallow, and I was sure it had to be much, much worse. Don's real life had come wailing to the surface now and I couldn't understand a goddamn thing. I was suffering a profound inability to actually imagine being Don in this moment. To really be this sixty-year-old man with this life and these problems. I was struck dumb by my total and utter lack of imagination. It scared me. I wanted to shut him up, to stop him. I wanted to shout in his face, *Hey! Don't look at me, old man. I'm just a kid.*

Bang! He hit the steering wheel with his fist, and the tears finally dropped. It jarred me back to the present. Trapped in this car, with its religious icons hanging so limply. I knew I had to go. I knew I had to leave Don here, abandoned. We were just strangers, after all. What do you owe a man you hardly know? How do you stop yourself from fleeing another man's suffering?

"I won't tell anyone about today," I said. "No one will even know we didn't work." I immediately regretted saying this, but I couldn't stop. "We can make it up tomorrow. I'll be ready in the morning like always, if you wanna pick me up."

But Don didn't answer. He didn't do anything. He just stared out the windshield for a thousand empty yards. And when I saw he really wasn't going to start the car, I finally let myself out. Leaving Don there, exactly that way.

I walked away from the Civic and crossed the busy street at a jag, not willing to wait for the light. I hurried across the open parking lot to a block of pay phones outside the Tops. I needed the space between. I needed to move away from the OTB. I didn't want to have to say that I was there. I didn't want to have to talk about Don. I didn't want to make up a story about these things yet.

THE SUMMIT

It was the limbo week between Christmas and the New Year, and the Sabres had just lost. They really should've won, too, but they didn't. Up two goals in the third period, with ten minutes to go, but they lost. And now the whole night was fucked.

Louis stood up and booed at the television in a horsey, exaggerated way until Cullen told him to stop. Louis sat back down and I could see that he was actually angry about this: one midseason hockey loss.

"Bad teams lose these games," Cullen announced, almost smirkingly.

"Bad teams? Be serious. We were one game away from winning the Cup two years ago."

"Two years! Time to flip your calendar, little guy. Those days are done."

Cullen was enjoying himself, taking it out on Louis, pretending he didn't care just as much. For the last three days I'd felt this strange thing happening here. We'd always acted this way, but suddenly I was on the outside of it. It wasn't that I was made to feel unwelcome so much as they just weren't interested in crucifying me anymore. I was just a guest.

"You gotta be fisting me," Louis grumbled to no one. "Every goddamn year. How does this shit keep happening to us?"

I couldn't help smiling. I'd barely been gone four months, yet somehow they'd invented a whole new way of speaking. Filthier, funnier, more oblivious.

"You see," Cullen said to me drunkenly the night before. "Because instead of saying *kidding me* he's saying—"

"Yeah, yeah, I get it," I said, and Cullen smiled.

To be honest, I was still a little shaky from flying. I'd told my mother not to count on me for Christmas. They'd only just started rerouting flights over my house, in Washington, D.C., and the sound alone made my chest tight. I told her I was looking into bus tickets, or train schedules, or a ride share, maybe, but I wasn't really planning on anything. I couldn't care less about the school's winter break. My idea was to just stay put: to remain in my own city; in my own neighborhood; inside my house.

Then she sent me a plane ticket, and that was that.

I took some comfort in the long lines at the airport. I'd never really seen that before. But when the line stopped for me, I was shocked. Shocked when they found a bike wrench in my backpack. Shocked by the way the TSA lady held it up. Even the man behind me turned away in embarrassment. I raised my hands and tried to accept the crowd's guilt. I had forgotten it was there; I really didn't know. I was very, very sorry.

I barely protested when she moved to throw the wrench away. I stood still as she waved her magnetic wand over me one more time. And finally, when she was satisfied, she nodded, and I thanked her for letting me fly in spite of my crimes against National Security. I bowed and I genuflected, and I tried to reorient myself on the other side of the metal detector. I sort of expected not to understand what was going on here.

We stood in Cullen's driveway, kicking ice and passing our last two cans of beer. A snowplow went by in a cloud of silted exhaust that stained the snowbanks brown. We watched its orange and yellow lights flicker as it dropped the blade with a harsh metal scrape, before gathering, and running cleanly along the snow again.

The stinging cold was sobering in small doses, and not entirely unpleasant. I always found myself more sensitive to the weather coming back to it. The low-watt sunshine and the sharp, leafless trees. The frozen, invisible smells of cordite and gasoline in the air. And the cool, continuous quiet of nighttime. These long, gray, birdless winters. Buffalo, a girl once told me, was where clouds went to die. I always liked that.

We'd decided to go out to a bar and someone said something about a taxi. Louis and Cullen were bickering about *dooeys*, which was a term I didn't know. Louis was saying who had what dooeys and when.

"Dooeys?" I asked. "Do both of you have *DUIs*?"

"Just *one*," Louis said with a scowl, and I nodded dumbly.

The taxi was an old yellow minivan with a peeling checkered stripe. Cullen pulled back the door and held it, like a gentleman, as I slid across the bench seat next to Louis. I could feel the heater on blast, buffeting us with the smell of sweat and smoke and Febreze. Our driver turned his head toward the dome light as he waited: an impossibly fat young man in a Santa hat.

"Ho, ho, ho. Where to?"

"We wanna get drunk at the Summit Street Saloon, Santa," Louis said.

"Right-o."

He popped the minivan into gear and began eyeballing me in the rearview. I held my face down in a frown, which was a plea not to speak. Santa had big clay ears and tiny marble eyes, and greasy skin that duffled around the neck. He wore a pencil sketch of a mustache that was marred, in all directions, by violent constellations of acne, running off his cheeks and into his collar.

This was the guy I pictured when someone said the word *lardass*.

"I was just thinking," he finally said. "You boys look like you could use a little ganja tonight. Am I right? Santa's running a special New Year's deal."

None of us said anything, not a word. We just left the poor kid hanging there, which seemed to depress and demoralize him all out of proportion. Santa was not much of a pusher, which was too bad for him.

"Nobody?" he said.

I was actually sort of relieved that Louis and Cullen weren't interested, but it was too late. Santa gave up, right there on the spot, and offered to smoke us out for free. No one was strong enough to say no to free drugs, and this made Santa fat and jolly again.

I watched as he let his belly out into the wheel and took both hands away. A lighter flickered in the dark and he inhaled asthmatically, slowing the car down with him. I took the glass bowl over his shoulder, and I passed it away to Louis. Everything about this made me anxious, and I reached behind me for my seat belt then. Santa struck me as a guy with a couple dooeys at least.

That first hit seemed to liven him up, too, and he started telling us racist jokes about *ragheads* and *sand niggers*. I was inhaling deeply and not following how this began. But Cullen was *hee-hawing* in a way meant to mimic Louis's laughter. Leaning across me with a big, shit-eating smile. But Louis wouldn't bite.

"No, dude, that's not funny," Louis said to Santa, in total seriousness. "You're telling it wrong. You're stepping all over the joke."

And suddenly Louis was telling his own racist joke.

Out the window the taxi dollied through illuminated cones of static as my body flushed with heat. My fingers tingled and the capillaries in my head locked. I didn't like this at all. This was all really happening where I lived. Terrorism was not some abstraction on the television. It was the promise of endless war. It was the fear of people and buildings. It was the suspicion of strangers and foreigners. It was the avoidance of crowds and public transportation. It was the brand-new paranoid connections that bloomed inside our heads with no clues for how they got there, or what to do next.

After a full month of waiting on death, I went back down into the Metro, where a Muslim man got onto my train and began reciting loudly from the Koran. This deep, impenetrable monotone issuing down the long car. Incanting life, incanting death, I didn't know. I watched as people found him in the rabble—this wraith in white cloth—and the tidal way that they backed up and emptied out at each next stop. Looking for a new train. Looking for the stairs. Looking for a police officer, perhaps.

But I decided to stay. I would not be scared off by this boogeyman in his ghutra and his robes, because I wanted to know what he was saying. I wanted him to see me watching, too. I wanted him to know that I was paying witness. One more stop, I thought, exhilarated; and one more, I thought, terrified. What was this that was happening now? And could it be a thing that was happening to me?

When the man finished his prayer, he sat and closed his book. Staring down the empty aisle, utterly expressionless. But as we pulled through the dark tunnel into the high-ceilinged station, he turned to watch the crowds on the platform. The car stopped and the doors opened, and a crush of new bodies pressed in all around. I stood up to keep watching the man. Thumbing his pages right to left, preparing himself again. The bell chimed, and the hydraulics released, and I suddenly found myself reaching out to catch the closing doors.

"Because his goat *is* his wife!" Louis said loudly, and the three of them snorted with laughter. Louis laughed the loudest, elbowing me. "You get it?"

I didn't say anything. I was staring out the windshield with the perfect sensation of landing through a cloud. Searching for the absent ground, and waiting for the wheels to touch. I looked up at Louis with the scenery coming back again. Christmas lights blinking madly; American flags frozen to their poles. Just like everywhere else.

"That was stupid," Cullen said. "And not funny. And offensive toward goats." The cabdriver snorted again.

"Why did you laugh, then?" Louis asked indignantly.

"I was still laughing at Santa's joke. It was like a little aftershock. I just got another part of it, ha-ha."

Louis glared at him, and I felt my ears begin to ring. I had the sudden need for this taxi ride to stop. And almost as suddenly, it did.

Outside the bar, I felt Louis's hand on my shoulder. "Santa anagrams to Satan, dude. Think about that. I didn't see any registration on the dashboard. Who *was* that guy?"

"Be serious!" Cullen berated him loudly.

"I'm just saying, I don't feel so good. I think there was something bad in the pot." Louis was licking his lips and staring at Cullen. "Don't you think it tasted a little anthraxy?"

Cullen didn't say anything.

"My mailman died of anthrax," I said absently. Louis turned to me and squealed with laughter, like he couldn't even help himself.

"I'm serious. I haven't picked up a single piece of mail in over three months."

"Jesus. Both of you, fuck off!" Cullen said tersely, as he opened the door to the bar and let it slam shut behind him.

The Summit Street Saloon was a wash of neon beer lights, and wood-paneled walls, and shiny linoleum floors. There were balding pool tables, and ripped leather stools, and water stains on the ceiling. Red and white Christmas lights hung heavy over every pipe and beam. They really overdid it, which you had to give them credit for.

Highlights of the Sabres game were playing on the televisions, and everybody stopped to watch. Mesmerized; horrified. Laughing because they all really cared. I heard Cullen tell somebody that we should've won. And someone else said, "Yeah, but we didn't."

"The Baby Boomers have fucked us."

I said this out loud, at the dinner table on Christmas. In front of my Baby Boomer parents and their Baby Boomer friends.

"How do you mean?" my Boomer uncle asked with a quizzical smile.

"I mean in the corrosive, soul-sucking way . . . fucked." This hung over the table like a bad smell, as people wiped their mouths and set their forks down. I took another sip of wine as my sister scowled at me.

"That's called righteous indignation," she sneered.

"And whose side are you on?"

"The side of not being a rude, boorish asshole."

"All right, all right," my mother said, but I didn't care. This was the point. They were all talking about everything without really talking about any of it, and it was pissing me off.

"I hardly think that the role of each generation is to decide what is and is not—" my father began, but I cut him off.

"And George Bush is the president that you all deserve. I hate to say it, but he is your worst selves come home to roost. And none of you seem to give a good goddamn fuck about it." I paused to look at my uncle again, with my own quizzical smile. "Fucked . . ." I said. "That's how I mean it, totally *fucked*."

Throats were cleared and glasses tinked together, before my uncle broke the tension with a laugh. Wagging his finger at me, like he just got the joke.

"You've been in the Big Apple too long, kid. Har-har-har."

Everyone chuckled and moved on happily. It wasn't even worth correcting him. This had been happening all week. They all seemed to think I lived in New York City for some reason. Weren't they paying any attention? Didn't anyone care that a military target had been hit in Washington, D.C.? Didn't that fucking mean anything?

My mother frowned at me across the table in a sad way, and I did feel bad then. I'd been doing this a lot. I was finding it hard to just sit still and relax here. In three days, I'd argued with my brother that 9/11 proved Buffalo was in the Midwest. I'd ruined a perfectly nice dinner by explaining some revolting fact I'd read about turkey farms. And I cited widespread pederasty in the Catholic Church as the reason I would not attend Midnight Mass (or any church services) with the family.

My mother said she was afraid I was losing my sense of humor.

We tried to do simple things together, as a family. My parents wanted us to go to the movies, but we couldn't agree on anything to see. My sister accused me of trying to make them watch "cerebral movies," which made me laugh, because it was true. I knew exactly what an insufferable ass I was being, and I didn't care. I wanted to have a real fight with somebody about something, but no one would engage me in any way. Everyone just sort of shrugged and put up with me, and it was making me crazy.

I looked out over the bar at all these disappointing and disrespectful children, and I felt myself slipping into inebriation. Everyone was still talking about the Sabres, and I couldn't blame them. I'd watched the game, too. I saw the same thing. Up two goals in the third period. Bad teams lose those games.

Right on cue, the clip started over on the televisions, and we all stopped our conversations to watch these last three goals play out like deaths in a Greek tragedy. People groaned and heckled. Someone asked if *this* was what we paid them for.

I heard Louis tell somebody that it was un-American not to grow up in a dump, and I turned back around to face him.

"Are you talking about here?" I asked.

"Sure. Here, there, everywhere, man. God Bless America."

I sort of liked this cracked sentiment. I couldn't deny that I did feel safer in Lockport somehow. After all, this was the place where clouds came to die.

We ended up sitting down at a table in the back, where we could all stop talking, finally. I noticed Cullen staring at a girl near the bar, and I understood immediately that he was going to ditch us.

"Uh-oh." Louis smiled. "Looks like somebody's about to get a dick suck."

"Are you fisting me?" Cullen scowled. "Cut the fucking shit, already."

"What?" Louis said, pretending not to understand.

Cullen turned away again, and succeeded in inviting this girl to join us at our table, in some nonverbal way. I nodded hello, trying not to smile at what Louis had said. I'd never heard it put quite that way before.

"Which one of us do you think will die first?"

Louis asked this, obviously. His face was blank, and I wasn't sure I'd heard him right, until I looked at Cullen. Louis turned more generally to the girl and me.

"Because I think there's a better than even chance that it might be Cullen. Cullen could die really young. Really, really young."

"I said, fuck off, idiot." Cullen pushed out his chair and took the girl by the hand, disappearing for real. Apparently

Cullen was even more afraid of death than I was. Or, at least, I was glad that Louis thought so.

Louis sank into his chair and brooded. There would be no consolations in this bar for us tonight, and certainly not sex. I slunk back, too, and watched in disbelief as the Sabres game started over on the televisions. This was the late-night replay, and I smiled, remembering how we got an early one somewhere. I looked around the bar and saw others thinking the same thing. Here comes a goal.

I'd watched infinite amounts of television in the last week. I'd forgotten how much time we spent shut up indoors here. Sitting on the couch with my brother and sister. There were all these new shows on the food channels about eating as a kind of masochism. All the shows were like this now, and we were surprised, and slightly embarrassed, to admit how much we liked them. They were short and colorful and took great pains to disguise themselves as travelogues and situation comedies. They were careful to never explain what was really going on, or why our faithful host was always doing this to himself.

"Bad economy," my sister said, and we laughed.

"Violent narcissism," I added.

There was a strange bonding happening as we watched the fat man flagellate himself with food. We marveled as he showed up in each new town with his sweaty arms around the locals. A prelude to the gluttony. Short-order cooks fixed him novelty plates and troughs. *Let's add a dozen eggs; let's add a hundred peppers; now let's melt the cheese.* His face choked and his arteries bulged as his pancake makeup began to drip. He suffered as he told us how delicious it was. Mooning and mugging as he kept on eating. Every half hour brought him closer to the brink of vomiting and heart attack and death. He was laughing and making a joke of death. Always laughing.

We were sickened and exhilarated by these new shows. We couldn't stop watching them. We said we wanted the host to stop, but that was a lie. We wanted to see him get the thing he had coming. We wanted to see him buckle and hit the floor unexpectedly. Would they show that on television if it happened? Would that be going too far? Was that too real? Was anything on TV real anymore?

"Jesus Christ," my brother said with a kind of awe. "The terrorists' heads must explode when they watch this shit."

I looked back over the bar at all these bleary kids I went to high school with. Bodies reduced to frosted tips, and upturned collars, and terrifying eye makeup. They were a sea of leather jackets and boot-cut jeans. I was definitely drunk tonight, I thought. Time had gotten away from me, or they were closing the bar down early. Either way, it was last call and everyone was being hustled out the doors.

But Louis and I continued to sit at our table, watching the Sabres play on. We were winning now, and besides, there was nowhere else to go. But they weren't really going to let us watch the whole game over again. And eventually the bartender came over with two unopened cans of Genny and told us to hit the bricks.

In a weird way I sympathized with the Baby Boomers. They grew up thinking that the Soviet Union was going to drop the *Big One* on them at any moment. They went to sleep at night dreaming of atom bombs and radioactive cities. And not without good reason. This was a penance for the bombs of their fathers. So who could really blame them for buying Walkmans and doing cocaine and fetishizing Wall Street? They had cable TV and porno on VHS tapes, so what if they were raping the planet? Maybe they really did think these were End Times.

My uncle put his hand on my shoulder before he left to drive home drunk on Christmas night. "Don't kill yourself worrying so much, kid. You just need to get laid more." He winked, and I nodded solemnly because I thought that he was right.

Outside the bar, people stood around in huddles. Someone asked us if we wanted a ride and Louis spoke up to say no. We were staring at an empty car left idling with its lights on. Louis said that we could ghost-ride it into the canal. I smiled and told him we could drive ourselves home instead. But Louis said that it was a long way, and we had better start walking.

We opened our beers and packed through the dead field behind the bar, under a dull scrim of snow. I realized for the first time that Louis wasn't wearing a jacket. He said he'd left it in the bar and it didn't matter anyway. I asked if he was cold and he said no. I asked again after a hundred yards, and he said yes, but he didn't care. I thought Louis might have taken some pills or something inside the bar, but I didn't ask. I just kept my feet moving in front of me: feeling the cold, and watching it billow out as my breath.

I felt like I was sleepwalking now. I used to do that when I was young. Waking up in the shower, or out in the yard, even. Feeling startled and embarrassed, even though I was alone. I could still remember the way the dark trees looked just like a stage set to me. Tacked up against the unmoving sky. I would blink until I really saw them there, jarring in their three dimensions. It struck me then that this was *not like TV*, where something is always happening. This was real life, where you could stop and freeze endless stretches of nothing at all. Everything in its right place, and all of it made real.

I would go back inside the house and never speak a word of it. Lying down in bed, with my wet hair, and counting up the sleep I'd lost.

Louis bent down and picked up a horseshoe, and I could tell how much it pleased him. He kept swinging the thing in his hand, back and forth, back and forth, while we walked. It was so rusty and old, but it was beautiful just the same. It must have been so cold in his hand that it felt like fire. Louis finally let the horseshoe go and we watched it sail away into the darkness.

I laughed and threw my beer can out into the night after it, and we sleepwalked on. It was easy to enjoy the way that impossible things always happened in a dream to move the plot along. Like walking home with Louis, and waiting on the first light of day. Watching the scenery come wheeling off the stage. Hearing the invisible snow machines humming in the rafters. Blinking my eyes on the red numbers of the clock. Waiting to fall out of bed, onto the floor, out of the dream. Just waiting.

TOMBOYS

One summer I started falling madly in love with all the Tomboys in the city. These rough, noisy girls with their square jaws and their angular haircuts. They had tattoos and chipped fingernails. They had tight jeans and loose shirts. The Tomboys liked to ride bikes and drink beers, and go out into the night looking for trouble. They had bruises on their knees and cuts at their elbows. They had dirty jokes and tremendous cascading laughs. The Tomboys had health and sex and danger. These girls knew something you didn't know, and it was the reason they could indulge in being simply and purely young.

Once I knew all these girls were out there in the city, I started seeing them everywhere. At a grocery store; outside a post office; passing through a crosswalk. They intimidated me with the ease with which they did these simple things. All

these beautiful Tomboys that I walked right past and never
said a word to.

Until, one night, I was leaving the bar when Lauren and
Cokie walked in. I felt myself hesitate at the door. I was a
little drunk, but not enough to know how to begin. I walked
back into the room and I turned my back to their table. I suddenly started to stretch, folding myself in half and touching
my toes. I didn't actually think that they were watching me,
and I was only vaguely aware that I might be making a scene.

"What are you doing?" one of them asked.

"Nothing," I said, arching my back as I turned to face
them.

"Stop showing off," Lauren said, not unkindly.

"In a minute," I said, putting my leg up on a chair. "I'm
almost done."

"Don't you think those jeans are a little tight for stretch-
ing?" Cokie smirked. "I mean, I'd hate to see you rip them
right here in the bar, in front of everybody."

Both girls snickered and I came a little closer.

"Oh, don't worry about the jeans," I said. "I have a very
pompous ass."

Lauren practically went into a fit of squealing, but Cokie
frowned. "I'm pretty sure you're misusing that word, dude."

"No, I don't think so. Look at it." I turned and stuck my
ass out, smiling with my teeth. "Go ahead. I'm not shy about
it. Look."

Lauren laughed and grabbed my back pocket, guiding
me down into the empty chair. "Shut up and sit down already,"
she said. And that was that.

The night ended with a suitably awkward goodbye as we unlocked our bikes outside the bar. "You have poison ivy," I said, pointing at Lauren's arm, surprised I hadn't noticed it earlier.

"Yeah. You better hope it's not catching."

She smiled wickedly and touched her forearm to my neck. It surprised her, I think, that I didn't pull away. I liked the damp smell of sweat, and the sticky feeling of Lauren's skin touching mine. This was a test, I thought. A strangely intimate gesture of initiation. I would take Lauren's poison ivy now if this was how it passed.

"We should all have it," I said, as I pressed the girls' arms together. "Blood brothers."

This was how I became one of the Tomboys.

I was not trying to sleep with Lauren and Cokie, really. I just wanted to be there in the moment with them. They were always together, and I wanted to be together, too. We were supposed to find each other, we said. We were supposed to laugh and break each other's backs and make trouble, because we were more fun than fun. Lauren and Cokie opened up the city and made it feel new. They took me around to the places they liked to eat, the places they liked to drink. They introduced me to kids who had never heard my boring stories and jokes before. And, all at once, I stopped waiting on death and started having real fun again.

We would meet up after work and sit out on our porches

drinking tall cans of beer, laughing and talking shit. Our friendship was a flirtation, of course. We would stay out late, dancing at bars or an apartment that belonged to friends of friends. There was something loose and joyful in it that we didn't need to question. Something unselfconscious that was beyond sex. Because sex could come from somewhere else, and it should, I thought. And we could even share that, too. All our little trysts and hookups laid bare.

And yet, Lauren and Cokie could be cruel about the girls I talked to at the bars, which was confusing. In small ways we were all becoming possessive of the group. There was power in the moments we were together, and it could feel strange if I was left alone with one or the other too long. Especially with Lauren. There was something charged about the way that she would smirk and snarl at me, and it made me guilty because I knew I had picked a favorite. Lauren, whose flirtations were so alien and wonderful to me. She was always reaching out to grab hold, touching my head or my neck. Taking my hand too long and squeezing as she released me. Lauren would smile wickedly, sometimes for no reason at all.

One day we were talking in her kitchen when she climbed up onto the counter and put her feet into the sink.

"What are you doing?" I asked.

"I need to shave my legs quick. Is that weird? I could go upstairs, but I just figured we were talking . . ."

"Oh. No, it's fine," I said. "Are you gonna let me watch?"

Lauren smiled crookedly as she pulled off her jeans and dropped them onto the floor. "You can watch."

I hopped up onto the counter across the sink, as she played with the water. She tossed me a brand-new lady razor that I'd watched her buy an hour before.

"Be a sweetheart and crack that open for me."

I nodded and did this, watching Lauren sheen her legs with a drop of lemon dish soap. The short hairs standing on end, almost invisibly, as her legs glistened. I stole glances at her thighs and the black cotton panties that I could not see through. Lauren reached out and took the razor and began trolling it up from the ankle, in long, clean swaths. She rinsed it under the faucet and smiled at how quiet this could make me.

"I've never seen a thing like this," I said, smiling back at her. "I've never watched a girl do this before."

"Yeah, we've got all kinds of secrets." Lauren laughed, and I felt her go even slower then. Torturing me.

"It's nice," I said, pushing down off the counter. I walked back across the room to the table where I'd left my can of Coke. I was suddenly aware that Lauren was in control, and I didn't know what to do with that. I had a feeling that I was supposed to resist, and so I did.

But there were other nights, too. Lauren and I closed out the bar slow-dancing to "Jesus Doesn't Want Me for a Sunbeam" on the jukebox. With the lady bartender taking pity on us, waiting for our song to end. Lauren clasped her arms around my neck and told me it was our middle school dance. We were drunk and laughing, and she even gave me a little pop on the mouth before the song was through. And then, *click*, the lights went up, and Lauren skittered out the door, leaving me no choice but to follow her out into the sidewalk night.

There was a heat wave that summer that killed a homeless man and a couple elderly women. It was a heavy heat that never really lifted, not even at night. The air was thick and wet, and tasted metallic, like smog. It was that oppressive heat that makes your clothes, and even your hair, feel heavy. People got lethargic and cranky, and there was a spike in domestic crimes and traffic accidents all around the city.

One night, Cokie's friend Patrick Serf showed up at the bar and told us about a swimming pool. We got excited and decided to go right then. Following Patrick through the downtown canyons that the businessmen deserted each night. The hot air flushed our faces as we ran the red lights. It felt good to have some movement again. It was important to go out riding bikes through the city at night sometimes.

Patrick turned down an alleyway and stopped beside a wall. "This is it," he said, and we smiled because this wasn't anything.

"Where?" Cokie asked.

"Over the other side." Patrick held his bicycle steady, against the bricks, for Cokie to climb up onto the crossbar.

"Whoa," she said, turning back with her face aglow. "It's a bomb-ass pool."

We locked our bikes in a knot, and helped each other over the wall, into the courtyard of some nameless luxury apartment. Buzzing around like little children, we stripped down to our underwear and tried to keep our voices low. I looked up at the silent building, wondering where all the people could be. And then I dove in.

In the water I could just barely see through the girls' underwear and it made me happy. Lauren caught me staring and she didn't flinch. Daring me to keep on looking.

"How do you know about this?" I turned to ask Patrick.

"I work as a bike messenger," he said, with his feet dangling in the water. "Sometimes I deliver packages to a doctor who lives here."

Cokie snorted. "Patrick's not a bike messenger. He's a *marijuana courier.*"

We laughed, and Patrick frowned, but good-naturedly. Something effortless that I didn't have, and it made me like him all the more.

"What?" Cokie gleamed. "It's true."

He reached out and grabbed her by the calf, and she squealed and begged for mercy. There was a familiarity about the way that they behaved together, and I wondered why I'd never met Patrick Serf before.

I floated on my back and listened to the hum of unseen air-conditioning pulsing off the building. I was astonished that we could be the only ones swimming on a night like this. I waited for someone to join us, or at least kick us out, but the buzzing only added to the building's air of quietude and sleep.

Lauren suddenly crashed her weight down on top of me, pinning me under in a game of murder. We wrestled this way, while Cokie and Patrick got out of the pool and back into their clothes. I saw them kiss once, and I could tell that they were planning their escape. They invited us to come to the next bar, but it was obvious enough where they were really headed. Lauren and I laughed childishly, as Cokie flipped us off behind her back. And then we really were alone in the big pool.

I felt the quiet tension of getting what I wanted, and I hesitated. Lauren went underwater and came up at the far end, looking back at me. I followed and it made me calm. There was nothing left but the physical need to touch. I kissed Lauren and she kissed me back. And then she pulled away, which was thrilling and confusing.

"What's wrong?" I said, almost soundlessly.

"What if this ruins everything?"

"Ruins what? This is what I want. I thought you—"

"I do," she said. "I do, it's just . . . Cokie."

I looked at Lauren and tried not to blink.

"I don't want it to feel like we've abandoned her, or pushed her out, you know? I don't want us to lose the thing we have right now."

I nodded, staring at her this close. Lauren radiated something bigger than confidence, bigger than sex. There was a line we must not cross now, and I tried to understand it. I agreed with her, even. Everything would have to change after this.

We got out of the pool and we didn't kiss again that night. We stayed up and rode around for hours, not to go home. I left Lauren at her doorstep, giddy with sleeplessness and not making sense. And then I didn't see her again for three days.

The first day was mine. I had spent every day of the last four weeks with Lauren and Cokie, and it scared me a little. I felt like I'd lost my equilibrium. There's something incestuous in that kind of platonic closeness: brothers and sisters left alone too long.

The second day was Lauren's. I eventually gave up and tried to call her, but she never called me back. I didn't really understand what was happening then. Had I rejected Lauren, or was she rejecting me? I brooded over this at work, the whole third day, until Cokie called and said to meet them out at the bar.

I felt stupid for worrying so much. Everything was fine. I thought I wanted Lauren to say something about it to me, but she didn't. We were out in a larger group, and she seemed to float at the fringes. And maybe this was the right thing, too.

Later, after people started to leave, she slid beside me in the booth, which was nice. We began to talk, but there was tension there, and we stopped. It was in this silence that she started doing something false—pulling at my hair and telling me it was too long. She jagged her fingers through, trying to make it hurt.

"I just think you should cut it," she said.

"I don't wanna cut it," I told her. "Why are you being so weird?"

"I'm not being *weird*," Lauren said with a laugh. "I just wanna cut it. I'm good, too. You would like it." She smiled at the other people around the table. "I promise."

I looked at her and tried to figure out what this was. "All right," I said, "If that's what you want. I'll take the *Rachel*-cut. Do you still do that one?"

"Or the George Clooney!" Cokie snarked. "God, remember how stupid the *George Clooney* one was?" People laughed, and Lauren smirked, and we all let it go.

But outside the bar, she tried to hold me to it. She was really going to cut my hair, she said. I didn't know what to say to this, and finally just gave up. We said goodbye to Cokie and the kids, and we rode our bikes to Lauren's house.

We sat in the kitchen with her roommate, drinking beer, and I really expected this to be the end of it. But Lauren tipped her can over in the sink, and smiled at me all over again. So I followed her up the stairs to the bathroom, where she set out a chair. And, all at once, as I looked at us in the mirror, I did want her to cut my hair.

"Okay," I said. "I trust you."

"Shut up," she said. "You'll be fine, I swear."

Lauren got very serious then, as she combed through my hair with her fingers and pulled away pieces to cut. Snip, snip, pull, pull, we caught each other's eyes in the reflection. There was something charged and intimate happening. Lauren touched my neck and pressed her chest to the back of my head as she worked. We stared at each other in the glass, without speaking, and she laughed.

"What?"

"Nothing."

"So keep cutting."

"You just have really nice hair, you know that? It's soft and thick," she said, smiling at me in the mirror.

"Then why won't you let me grow it out?"

"Just hold still." Lauren snarled and took a big swatch off

the top of my head, without hesitating. The pieces fell across my shoulders and onto the floor. The inexactness of this cut made my neck tingle. She stopped again, considering the flying hair.

"Maybe you should take your shirt off," she said.

And I did, and that was it. The dam broke for real this time. Something beautiful and unavoidable happened, and we were suddenly kissing. Tasting lips and tongues and the smoothness of each other's teeth. The rush of feeling in taking hold and pressing our hips together. I felt her hands and her fingers moving over me. I felt the female softness of her body give inside my grip. We pulled each other's clothes off and tumbled around the bathroom, ending up in the tub briefly. We laughed at the stupidity of the whole thing, the waiting. Reveling in each other's sex, and making ourselves naked. We kissed close and hushed ourselves as we really started to screw. Right there on the bathroom floor. Giving over to the wild, ineffable energy of it all. We smashed through the waiting and it released us.

Why we didn't just go into her bedroom, I never asked. This was how it happened, and this was the only way I could imagine it now. Acting it out in secret, as her roommate cooked her dinner, one floor below. We were already a secret. *This is a thing which I am following Lauren into,* I thought.

That weekend Cokie went home to see her parents, and Lauren and I lay around naked in bed. Eating and fucking and watching bad movies. It is a small but infinite happiness to share a bed this way. Standing in the shower after, I would let her clean my face and wash my hair, and I began to think of Lauren brand-new. There was a swelling feeling attached to her love. If she shone it on you, it became a force of nature with the danger of swallowing you whole and making you forget. Lauren and I had a secret, and it drove everything else.

But Lauren agonized over whether or not to keep it all from Cokie. I would laugh because we talked about the whole thing like it was some shocking affair. And in a way, I guess, it was. If this was a thing I didn't fully understand, then I didn't need to understand it, I thought. Everything felt exactly right. Stealing kisses in the bar, or right there in Cokie's house as she walked out of the room. We got off on our own ridiculous efforts of subterfuge and denial. All these transparent acts of holding back in public, before we'd meet up again, on a doorstep or in a park. Throwing our bikes down and kissing in the dark.

And somewhere in the middle of this, Cokie just seemed to disappear. Worse, we couldn't even really find her. I hadn't heard one word from the girl in almost two weeks. And that's when Lauren decided that we finally had to tell her.

But Cokie just laughed at us. "Yeah, thanks, no shit," she said. "I mean, did you really think I didn't know? Jesus! I just got sick of watching you drag it out."

"What do you mean?" Lauren asked.

"I mean, stop being such babies and assholes, and just say that you're fucking! Who cares? *I* don't care. It's not really that interesting, you know? Fuck all you want, for all I care. But stop treating me like I'm stupid."

Lauren didn't say anything.

"Oh," I said. "Sorry, Cokie."

Sadly, everything changed after that. Everything that had been right the week before was now wrong. The sex got bad or boring, or at least less frequent. It was strained and fraught with too many strange concerns. Sex became a thing we did by rote, and then it just stopped altogether.

Lauren and I decided we should take some time apart. But the tension of this made me crazy, and I broke down after a day. Showing up at her house, where we fought and fucked, and kissed good night out on the sidewalk, as she sent me home again. I couldn't shake this new and terrible feeling that she was ignoring me. Lauren seemed to disappear for days at a time now. When we talked at all, it was in rambling ten-minute phone calls. These bursts where we would cover everything except the thing that had happened to us. Lauren wanted to talk about Cokie. She said she needed to repair the things that we'd undone. Lauren acted cavalier about this, saying it had all been childish in the end. We'd had our fun, and now it was over. *C'est la vie.*

But even as I agreed with her, I knew I didn't agree. I didn't want to stop. I felt like Cokie had given us permission to try and make it work, even. But Lauren was adamant that this was about *their* relationship—Lauren and Cokie.

Right, I said, of course. And then I had no choice but to back off.

The Tomboys retreated into their friends. A whole new cast of characters, it seemed to me. These superficial, asshole kids that I hated unreasonably. All boys, too, because Lauren and Cokie didn't seem to have any real girlfriends, outside of each other. They would invite me out, but I found it impossible to sit there listlessly, or join into their conversations about obscure bands and important DJ sets. These dudes who were always laughing but seemed to have no sense of humor at all.

Worse, Lauren was ignoring me again.

I followed her outside the bar one night, where she was smoking a cigarette alone.

"You're smoking now?" I asked her critically.

"Not really," she said, blowing the smoke away from me.

"It's just sort of a disgusting habit, don't you think?"

"Is it?" she asked, looking away.

"I just think it's kind of sad, you know? It seems like you're turning into all of your elitist friends."

"You don't even know them."

"Yeah, I know, right. Thank god for that."

She almost had to laugh then, putting up her hands like it was unbearable to even affect patience with me. "What do you want me to say? Does it even matter? You don't even listen to me."

"I am listening," I said. "And I'm disagreeing with you."

"You're being insanely, abrasively arrogant. And I don't know how to deal with you this way."

"Good," I said. "If we're finally going to talk about real things, we can start with how condescending you've been acting toward me lately."

Lauren sighed patiently. "Your attitude is the cause of my attitude."

"No. That doesn't mean anything. You're not allowed to simply reverse the things that I say."

"Please don't talk down to me."

"I'm not!"

"I can't help the way I feel," she said maddeningly.

This was not how I'd wanted it to go. I was losing ground and making things worse, and I desperately wanted to reset. "I just want us to be together," I said earnestly.

"We tried that."

"No. But we didn't, not really. Okay, because, see . . ." I stopped myself. "I think I might be in love with you. And I didn't think I could say that, but I've said it."

It hung there uncertainly as Lauren's face softened in a way I couldn't read.

"I just think we should try to be friends right now," she said.

"Why are you always trying to pick a fight with me!" I shouted.

That was the end. I felt trampled and manipulated, and I was done with the whole thing. I'd let Lauren turn me into a crushing bore, and I resented her for that. It was exhausting trying to stay so goddamn angry. All I wanted now was for things to stop changing.

I went back to my own friends, where I didn't have to try so hard. I could be sour and sarcastic and drunk, and they didn't even care. They hardly noticed if I was more depressed or belligerent than usual, and I loved them for that.

And then, one day, near the end of the summer, I ran

into Cokie on the street. We got to laughing easily, and it struck me that Cokie had not done anything to me. She was not Lauren, and I seized on this impulse to invite her over to my house for dinner. Cokie seemed charmed by the idea that I might actually try to cook, and she accepted happily.

I started drinking the cheap wine I'd bought as soon as I got home from the grocery store. I felt excited: happy to make this one dinner, happy to save this one relationship. I wanted the gesture to be a kind of apology for myself and all my bad behavior. I wanted to be able to laugh about the summer and move on.

And it was like that, too. The wine had a way of making me come unbound. I knew that I was talking too much, but I didn't care. We sat on the couch listening to records, and I felt lucky just to talk to anyone again. Cokie said she wanted to get out of D.C., and I locked onto this idea with her. Maybe it was the city that had dragged me down, and not Lauren Pinkerton at all. I made some drunken generalizations about the kids here. Insulated. Overeducated. Underemployed. Cokie laughed, and I knew that I was rambling, but I was laughing, too.

There was a kindness in her laughter, I thought. Something loose and free from judgment. And, all at once, a spark flashed in my brain. It was *Cokie* I had been in love with all along, and not Lauren. I had simply picked the wrong girl!

Cokie was talking excitedly now, too, and feeling the wine. She was saying that she wanted to travel, and maybe we could travel together. Yes, I said, not really listening. She was saying that it should be somewhere big, somewhere we would never think to go. I was nodding along, thinking about kissing Cokie; thinking about hurting Lauren. Who could say that Cokie didn't secretly want to hurt her, too?

"The Middle East," Cokie said, and I stopped.

"You want us to travel to the *Middle East*? *Now*?"

"Yeah, yeah, totally, listen . . ."

But I wasn't listening. Even as I saw that Cokie was serious. Talking about flights to Morocco and hitchhiking through Northern Africa. She said we could find jobs as journalists or bloggers, to subsidize the traveling. I was hearing her tell me all of this, and I was trying not to laugh. But this got Cokie laughing, too.

"This all sounds fucking terrifying, Cokie," I said. "I have to tell you, I have no idea what you're talking about." It was making me feel delirious.

"Wait, wait, but no . . . I've actually looked into this. It's not really that dangerous," she said, going on about the Zagros Mountains, and an American professor in Tehran whom she'd been emailing. But none of this mattered anymore. I just wanted Cokie. I suddenly wanted her to stay and sleep with me, in my bed tonight. I couldn't even care that Lauren had told me, in the strictest confidence, that Patrick Serf might have given Cokie herpes that summer. I just needed to kiss her.

And when she stopped talking and turned to me expectantly, I leaned in, in a kind of slow motion. This, not unpredictably, was a spectacular failure. Cokie saw it coming and she dodged my kiss the way you might duck a punch. Moving in and away as she gave me her chin and cheek. She was really very sweet about it, too, almost acting as if it didn't happen. But it did happen, and I was left sitting there, stunned.

Cokie retreated into the kitchen to find her phone, still talking over her shoulder, sounding unfazed. "Patrick and his friends are at the Raven."

She ducked her head back into the living room, where I was sitting motionlessly on the couch. "Do you wanna go with me? You should come."

"Oh," I said. "No. I don't think I'd be much fun tonight."

Cokie smiled sadly and let it go.

We walked out through the front hallway, and I carried her bike down the steps. I could tell that Cokie wanted to give me some kind of parting embrace, but I was far too demoralized for that. I propped the bike between us instead, as we said our goodbyes on the sidewalk. And then I went back up the steps, where I watched Cokie ride out into the night without me. Back into the fun. Gone.

MEN WITH PLAIN NAMES

By October, there was a killer on the loose. Five dead the first day. Several more each day after that. And no one was surprised, either. This was the new normal in late capitalist, pre-revolutionary America.

I was working for a man named Mike, helping him paint a one-story apartment building orange. Working outside on ladders, standing in the open, we were easy targets for a man with a gun. I could've been back in school, but Mike really had to be here. It was his truck, and his paint, and his job. Mike had a girlfriend at home who was pregnant with a baby boy they were thinking of calling Michael. Just like his name. Just like my name. I tried to talk him out of this, of course, but it was no use.

As we worked we listened to the classic rock station where they almost never talked about anything real, and certainly not the Beltway Sniper. These were the radio voices in your nightmares. Upbeat. Impersonal. Commercialized. They were not being maudlin or ironic when they played "(Don't Fear) The Reaper" for the third time in a day. This was just part of another all-new, nonstop, workday rock-block.

We knew that our faithful disc jockeys would not condescend to listing off the totals of the dead or mentioning the manhunt. They didn't pander by offering us any updates or breaking news. They didn't tell us when the Terror Alert level was raised from yellow to orange to red. They just kept their heads down and played the hits: schlocky, feel-good rock and roll.

Things were looking up for me, though. I'd actually inherited my father's car that morning. A blue Toyota Camry. It was just sitting there in front of my house when I came down the steps with my bicycle. I knew the car was my father's because I could see my brother sitting in the front seat.

"Hello, young man," I said cheerfully, as he got out, wearing a necktie. "Are you here to tell me about the Bible?"

"Shut up," he said. "Let me inside the house."

But I was already out in the street, pacing around the Camry. This car was a beautiful thing to me. It never even occurred to me to ask my parents to bring it down.

"Have you had this here the whole time?"

I knew my brother was around, of course. Right there at the end of the Green Line. My parents had driven him down to the University of Maryland at the end of August. The three of them spent the weekend in a hotel, getting him settled. They drove into the city, where I met them for dinner, twice. And that was the last that I saw of my baby brother.

"I meant to come and visit you," I said. "I've just been busy."

He nodded cautiously.

"This is good, though. You've done the right thing bringing this to me." I slapped my palm down on the top of the car. My brother didn't say a word.

"What is all this shit anyway?" I was cupping my hands and peering through the back windows. The seats were filled with boxes and bags. I could see a matte-black stereo and a nineteen-inch television set.

"I got kicked out of the dorms. I need to stay with you."

"You got kicked out of *school*?"

"No. Just the dorms."

"In five weeks? That must be some kind of record."

"I seriously doubt that," he said blankly.

I straightened myself up again to stare at him in judgment. Glaring at his stupid necktie. "What did you do?"

"I didn't do anything."

"Why are you wearing that tie, then?"

"Because I want to. Jesus Christ. Are you gonna let me inside the house or not?" I could hear the strain in his voice now. "Three more people were killed last night. Did you even know that?"

"Yeah, sure . . . I know," I said absently. I was still marveling at the car. "You've really had this here the whole time?"

My brother frowned. Crossing and uncrossing his arms. He was glancing out toward the intersection warily.

"I almost died in this car, you know? I was driving drunk on my birthday and I spun the fucking thing around backward like—"

"Can we please just get off the street," he asked me for the third time. "Please!"

"Sure," I said, passing him my bicycle. "Bring this into the house. I'm taking the car."

"Taking it where?"

"To work," I said. "Where do you think?"

"Don't you have school?"

"Don't you?"

My brother sighed and handed me the car keys.

There was a killer on the loose. These are the plots of horror films. Or crime thrillers. Or just some bad buddy-cop movie. We didn't know what was going on, which is different than being surprised by it. We had grown accustomed to a world of sudden, randomized death. Literally anything might happen next.

The news reported that the Sniper had been seen fleeing in a white van. Strangers would repeat this to you eagerly. We made a game of pointing them out to each other. White vans were everywhere now. Was this a thing that people already knew, or had the Sniper brought this fact to bear? His was a vehicle chosen for its indistinctiveness. Its ubiquity. Its absence of shape and color. It was astonishing to realize just how many people made their living driving white vans through the city.

As often as not, he was killing in broad daylight, too. People died outside strip malls and parking lots. Places they never wanted to go to in the first place. They were killed in front of gas stations and grocery stores. Running errands and waiting at bus stops. Understandably, the whole thing made people crazy. It became harder and harder not to fixate on the white van. It was the only thing we had to go on.

People wanted warnings. They wanted a fighting chance. They wanted signs that they could see and understand. If only a flock of birds would leap out of the treetops, in the seconds before he squeezed the trigger, we would know to hit the ground. Even just the glinting mirror of a rifle sight could count as something.

As a community, we had yet to produce even one credible police sketch of the killer. Who were we supposed to look for? A man? Someone with a story? A person with a past? We were still just looking for a man now, right? Somewhere among the ten thousand white vans was a person with a gun. Feeling the same heat that you felt, breathing in the same air. I imagined him driving with the windows down, his seat belt left dangling at his side. He was just a blank and smiling face. The only truly carefree man in three states.

The white van itself could never have come as much of a surprise, though. Ghosts have always worn white, traditionally. Flashing in the dark. Floating through walls. In gunfire and bloodshed he was there. In everything else, he might as well have never existed. The Sniper was a terror. A cipher. A blank.

I came home from work to find my brother watching CNN. I could tell right away that he'd had it on all day. Staring back at me with this haunted look. Worse, he was still wearing the tie.

As soon as he saw me, he stood up and started following me through the downstairs of the house, telling me that two more people had been shot in the parking lot of a Michaels Craft Store.

"So what?" I asked.

"So isn't that weird? He keeps shooting people in front of these Michaels Craft Stores. Why there?"

"Why anywhere?" I asked, exasperated.

I told him to stop counting deaths. I told him to turn off the TV and go outside. I told him to go back to school now. To go home. To stop hiding. There was no grand conclusion to draw from all of this. It just was.

"And take off that fucking tie."

"No," he said, stepping backward.

"What does it mean?"

"It doesn't mean anything."

"Do you work at a bank?"

"What?"

"Are you a Jehovah's Witness?"

"Shut up."

"Are you now, or have you ever been, a member of the so-called Republican Party?" I asked, getting right up in his face.

"Fuck off."

"Have you ever knowingly *consorted* with any so-called Republicans?"

"It's just a tie!" he snapped as he walked away.

"That's not an answer," I said. "That's evasion. I'm keeping my eye on you."

All in all, I had a car. More than a car, really, I had a birthright. The blue Camry had always been a thing that was rightfully mine, and I was hell-bent on keeping it now. I was the eldest son, of course. Mine was a condition beyond reproof.

Plus, it was fun just to drive. Ripping through the city with the windows down and the radio up. I laid on the horn as I rocketed past every white van I could find. Looking up and laughing at all these startled faces. A young man with a car can do whatever he wants. Go wherever he wants. Even with a killer on the loose. This is the stuff of a thousand classic rock songs. I was going too fast to be killed now.

Mike and I hadn't always listened to this music while we worked, though. Back in August, after I'd quit my data-entry job and joined him painting apartments, we were devoted listeners of NPR. These marathon runs with the radio going eight hours a day, until we could practically recite the news breaks verbatim.

This was on the other side of town—at the yellow apartment—before we'd made the hard switch to classic rock. Mike already had the orange one lined up, too, taking us straight through the Terror Alert color wheel. The joke was not lost on me, but I was serious when I told him I would quit before he found a red one.

Unfortunately, it was this yellow apartment that introduced us to the specter of death. Long before the Sniper started circling the city, Mike fell into a period of distraction. A new and brooding silence that coincided perfectly with the midpoint of his girlfriend's pregnancy. We wouldn't even turn the radio on some days.

It was one of these mornings when Mike climbed the roof with a bucket of yellow paint, only to find the top sealed shut. Painted on and baked hard in the sun. Mike tried to pop it off with a knife, but his foot slipped, and the blade jerked, right through his wrist.

"Fuck!" he yelled.

I stepped back to see what was happening, as the yellow paint came rolling off the roof and nearly struck me. WHAM! The metal can hit the ground and exploded all over my legs. Mike was already coming down the ladder, holding his wrist and cursing.

"What? What happened?"

He took his hand away and the blood squirted four feet across the sidewalk. Mike had severed one of the small blue power lines running up his wrist. Clutching it again, as he stared at me. "I cut myself," he said simply.

"Jesus Christ. No shit," I said, feeling completely scrambled. "What do we do?"

I walked away, looking for something, anything. I took my shirt off and pressed it to his arm. "Hold this," I said, as we watched the dirty white cotton bloom with blood.

"Fuck, fuck." I panicked. "Do we make a tourniquet?"

Mike just smiled dimly and walked away from me, toward his truck. I ran out ahead and opened the passenger side, helping him into the seat. I found the keys in his front pocket and slammed the door closed.

I wanted to call an ambulance, of course, but Mike wouldn't let me. He said that he was fine; he'd insisted on driving, even. He was laughing when he said this to me. That was the thing—the anger was gone, and Mike was nothing if not tickled by the whole situation.

The pickup made a tortured sound and fired right up. With my adrenaline pumping, I found the clutch and scraped it into gear. We lurched forward and I felt insane. I didn't know the first thing about driving a stick shift. I just tried to keep it in a low gear. *Straight lines*, I told myself as I accelerated into traffic. I was terrified of stalling this thing out. I couldn't stop thinking of death. Was I really going to have to tell Mike's girlfriend he was *dead* because I'd never learned how to drive a stick? I mean, Jesus Christ.

Mike leaned forward and flipped on the radio, inexplicably. Van Morrison's "Wild Night" came blaring out of the tiny speakers. Mike smiled and started to sing.

"The wiii-iiii-iiii-iiii-iiiiiild night is calling! The wiii-iiii-iiii-iiii-iiiiiild night is calling!" He turned to me then, sounding insistent. "Sing it!"

"No."

"Sing it, goddammit!"

"Shut the fuck up, Mike. I'm trying to drive!"

"Hurry!"

"I'm going as fast as I can!"

"I'm dying!" Mike screamed theatrically. "Aggghhhh! I'm

fucking dying!" He was cackling and going delirious on me.
I floored it through a red light, with horns screaming out on
both sides. I couldn't even hear myself think.

In the end, of course, we made it. Mike lived. Everything was
different after that, though. Mike became suddenly and un-
remittingly resolved. Resolved in being a father. Resolved in
being alive. Resolved, even, in painting this next apartment
orange. Slitting his wrist had been some kind of come-to-
Jesus moment for Mike. The brooding silences were replaced
by stupid jokes. NPR was overtaken by classic rock. He even
entreated me to play the name game with him. Baiting me
into talking him out of calling his unborn child Michael. One
more thing that he was fully resolved about now.

"What about Tony?" I would ask mildly.

"Too ethnic," he would deadpan.

"How about something modern, like Todd or Chad?"

"What is this, a country club?"

"How about Dave?"

"Too many vees."

"It's one vee," I protested.

"That's too many."

And on and on this way. I couldn't help but laugh with
him. I'd started to wonder what kind of painkillers he was
actually on. But mostly I resisted the urge to psychoanalyze
Mike. I didn't want to think about how the pressure he was
feeling had caused him to cut his wrist and almost die. If he
said that he was happy now, then I was happy for him. He

could play the radio as loud as he wanted, for all I cared. I couldn't even hear it anymore. Classic rock was the sound of orange paint drying.

Slowly, I began to realize that my brother wasn't leaving the house. Not to go back to Maryland, and not even to go outside. He wasn't eating; he wasn't showering. He hadn't even changed his clothes yet. He carried around with him this undertow of dread. You could feel it coming off of him in waves as he stalked from room to room.

"Did you know that the Queen of England is in town?"

"What?" I asked. "Why would I know that?"

He shrugged. "She's here to meet with the president. A state dinner or something."

"Good. That will solve everything."

He leaned against the counter and watched me put my groceries into the fridge. Staring at me, in silence. He was waiting for me to speak. He wanted me to tell him something now, I knew. But I didn't even know what he was doing here.

"Here. Drink this. You're freaking me out."

I pulled a tall can off a six-pack ring and handed it to him. We leaned back against the countertop and drank our beers in silence. I was grateful for the car, of course, but at what cost? Was I really responsible for all of this? And what the hell was this anyway? I mean, how long were we actually going to do this?

"Did you go to school today?"

"No."

"Why not?"

"You had my car."

"You could've taken the subway."

He didn't answer. Sipping from his beer.

"What did you do all day?"

"I didn't do anything. I watched TV."

"Did you eat?"

"Not really."

"Why not?" I asked, feeling exasperated. "What do you do when you're at school? Who cooks for you there?"

"Nobody cooks for me. There's a dining hall."

"You have a meal plan?"

"Yeah. I mean, of course."

"Well, shit." I beamed at him. "Why didn't you say that two days ago? C'mon. Put your shoes on. Let's go eat."

We drove the twenty minutes out to College Park; my brother in the passenger seat, with his shoulders tight around his neck. He used his ID card to swipe us into the dining hall, and there we were: a meal out on Mom and Dad. They would be pleased to know that we were finally spending some real quality time together.

The cafeteria itself was a veritable Valhalla of salts and sugars and fats. Decadent buffet tables lined with gleaming processed foods. These extraordinary foods that you would never actually pay for in a restaurant. Corn dogs and popcorn shrimp. Soft pretzels and shish kebabs. Mexican pizzas and English muffins. We ate potato skins and pigs in a blanket. There were chimichangas and Denver omelets. And we even ate some vegetables, too.

We stayed for nearly three hours, eating this way, in fits and starts. Feeling sickened and exhilarated in turns. We sat in silence, feeling full, feeling soothed. I watched the girls as they crossed the room, back and forth. These lively, pretty state school girls. This dining hall was teeming with blond and buxom cheerleaders. Former field hockey captains and high school prom queens. It was almost enough to make me give up on the orange apartment and go back to my own school.

"Where is your girlfriend?" my brother asked me out of nowhere. I looked up at him, baffled by the question. "The girl I met when—"

"I don't have a girlfriend," I said.

He stared at me blankly, before nodding. I looked away again.

"What about your roommate?"

"What?" Where were all these questions coming from? The kid barely says one word for three days, and now he won't shut up.

"Your roommate," he said again. "I haven't seen him once since I've been there, and I've been there the whole time."

"Okay?"

"So why hasn't he come home?"

"I don't know why. Sometimes he just doesn't." This was met with an anxious pause. "Why?" I smiled. "You think he's been killed by the Sniper?"

"I never said he was killed by the Sniper. I just asked—"

"Why did they kick you out of school?" I interrupted.

"They didn't kick me out of school. I told you, they kicked me out of the dorms."

"What did you do?"

"I didn't do anything."

"Yeah, sure, whatever you say."

I turned and tried to keep watching the girls, but my brother had ruined it. "Are you finished? Let's go," I said, picking up my tray and walking away from the table.

Overnight, it seemed, the city had suddenly become a patchwork of blue and green tarps. Hanging loosely off of awnings. Covering doorways and entrances. Gas stations draped them over their corridors to obscure the innocent pumpers below. This was not diversion. This was an effort made, in earnest, to restore the public safety.

I could hear the cheap plastic rippling overhead as I filled Mike's truck with gas. Staring at the rusted side panels, I tried to imagine the thing riddled with bullets. Mike liked to joke that the pickup never really rode the same after I drove it. There was a rumble, or a cough, somewhere deep down in the guts of the machine, he said. Buried a level below whatever I was hearing.

I looked up and watched a white van go wheeling through the intersection. This was strange, actually. I realized it was the first one I'd seen all day. What had happened to the others? I wondered. Was it possible that white vans were being rounded up and taken off the streets now? Registered? Detained? Disassembled?

I watched the people as they got out of their cars and circled the pumps. I watched their heads snap up as the tarps caught in the wind and shot out like sails. I watched the way they flinched when the nozzle clicked off in their hands. P-pop!

I saw a woman in black tights go scurrying across the street in a zigzag pattern. No one could decide who had told people to do this, but you would see it happening everywhere. The Metro Police were adamant about dismissing their own liability. They called it wanton superstition, and asked that people try to remain calm. But no one cared. It made sense to behave erratically now. I mean, what could it hurt?

Unfortunately, people were cracking up left and right. Something bad had happened that morning. One of our faithful disc jockeys had broken character and mentioned real life. I could hear it happening, too: this quaver in his voice as he started to speak. He was dedicating David Bowie's "Heroes" to all the brave men and women of law enforcement.

"Ugh," I said, getting down off my ladder, dejected. This man had broken through the fourth wall now, and there was no going back. This was not his job, of course. It was like watching a flight attendant start to lose it at thirty thousand feet. This was the moment we were all supposed to panic.

"Did that just really happen?" I asked.

Mike smiled and kept on painting. "Don't worry. I'm sure he'll be taken off the air for a few days."

———

My brother was already putting his shoes on when I walked through the door. With that fucking necktie hanging down in front of him, like a dog's tongue. We didn't even talk about it anymore. This was just our routine. We got into the Camry and drove out to College Park, where we ate our free meal together in silence.

Afterward, walking back out to the car, I gave him the keys. I told him I wanted him to drive now. I pointed out a liquor store with a burning yellow sign, and I told him to stop. My brother pulled the Camry into the parking lot and left it idling, with the doors locked, as I went inside. A minute later, I was back in the car, with a bottle of whiskey in a brown paper bag.

"Okay," I told him. "Drive."

"Where are we going?"

"We're going to Michael's," I said.

"Michael who? *The guy you work with*? I thought you said he has a kid. It's like ten thirty at night."

"Don't worry about his kid. Just drive the car."

My brother sighed and put the Camry into gear.

"Turn up here," I told him.

"Where?"

"Right here. Get onto the Beltway."

He looked at me like I was crazy.

"Just do it."

My brother shook his head and accelerated up the on-ramp and into the sea of red taillights on the westbound lane. Nobody had actually been killed driving on the Capital

Beltway, of course. The Sniper waited till you stopped, till you stood still, till you looked the other way. But it was in the man's name now; it was part of the stigma. And I watched as my brother's grip grew tighter on the wheel.

I knew we weren't far. There was a Home Depot in the suburbs where Mike and I would pick up paint. I could see it in my mind's eye perfectly. Standing in the parking lot and staring across the buzzing traffic at this simple cursive sign.

"Okay, here. This is our exit."

My brother sighed and turned off the Beltway. We were spit out onto an arterial road that funneled us down through an enclave of box stores and strip malls. The night sky was a wash of neon signs and corporate logos. We could've been anywhere in America right then. It was my brother who saw it first, though: the big glowing lights of a Michaels Craft Store. This bloodless hobby chain; the infamous setting of a half-dozen shootings in the spree.

"What the fuck?" my brother said.

"Turn."

"No," he answered as we passed the first entrance.

"What are you doing? I told you to turn!" We were coming up on the second driveway and he was shaking his head. "Park the fucking car!"

"No."

I reached out and grabbed the steering wheel recklessly.

"Stop, stop! All right!" he yelled, and something snapped. As I let go of the wheel my brother made the turn into the craft store parking lot. He eased his foot off the pedal, letting the Camry coast.

"Just stop," I said, and he did then. Turning off the engine.

We sat there in silence, staring out at nothing. I uncapped the whiskey and brought it to my mouth with a wince. "Drink this," I said, pushing the bottle on him. But he wouldn't take it. Leaning his elbow against the window, he looked angry enough to start crying.

"Jesus Christ," he finally whimpered. "Why would you do this to me?"

"Will you relax? I told you to drink this." And, after a minute, he did. Flinching with the first sip. My brother eased back against the headrest and stared out over the blank and empty lot. This was good, I thought. This was what I wanted.

"What are we doing here?"

"We're being brothers."

We sat there in the dark, with no reason and no plan. And in this moment my brother finally stopped asking why. He stopped expecting to get an answer out of me that would make any sense, at all, out of everything that was happening. And in this way the quiet here became infinite.

"Why did you get kicked out of the dorms?" I asked, for the one-thousandth time. But he didn't answer. Taking a sip off the whiskey, he seemed to smile into the bottle.

"Do you trust me?" I asked him.

"What?"

"Are you afraid?"

"I don't know what you're talking about."

"Does this feel like your home?"

"In what way?"

"Do you believe in God?"

"What?" he said, losing patience.

"Have you ever been in love?"

"Fuck you," he scowled.

"Have you ever even had sex?"

There was a long pause here as he opened his mouth to answer me. But he looked away instead. What did that mean?

"I'm going to keep this car, you know."

He didn't answer.

"Are you listening to me? It's mine now. No sense in being mad about it."

When he didn't answer again, I took his necktie in my hand. Turning it over gently. "And take off this fucking tie!" I said, ripping down on it.

My brother came uncoiled in an instant. Shoving my head against the window, hard. I laughed and smiled at him with wet lips as he seethed at me. We sat there, the two of us, trapped in this car. In this parking lot. In this suburb. In a war zone. This had been my idea all along, I supposed.

"I love you," I said, with a sickening smile. "Do you love me?"

He clenched his jaw, not answering.

"I'm your older brother," I barked at him. "You're supposed to worship me the way that Jeb worships George."

"Jeb hates George!"

"Everybody fucking hates George, asshole! You're my brother."

"Fuck you."

There was a long silence again before I took the bottle away from him.

"Why did you get kicked out of the dorms?" I asked.

"I didn't," he said.

"What?"

"I just left." He stared out the windshield, toward the entrance of the Michaels Craft Store, and he started to smile.

I didn't even know what to say to this. I could feel my face begin to burn. I was furious at him for this stupid lie. I was ready to start screaming in his face.

But before I could even get my head around, there was a rap against the glass. My brother and I jumped. This was followed, in short order, by the blinding beam of a flashlight, and a brawny command to roll down the window. My brother did this and we found ourselves squinting into the face of a young police officer. He banked his flashlight around the inside of the Camry, blinding us once again. We stared back at him, waiting. The young cop's face was grim. Nervous. We seemed to catch him in a moment of indecision. He couldn't have been more than twenty-five years old.

I moved the whiskey bottle against the door, knowing full well that the cop had already seen it. But he didn't say a word. We stared straight ahead as he walked around the back of the car, peering through the windows. He studied my brother's boxes in the backseat. I was sure it must've looked like we were living in this vehicle.

"You shouldn't be out here," he said, flicking off the flashlight. "This is a dangerous place."

We nodded dumbly. We could hear the tension in his voice now. The frayed edges of a man who's been drinking coffee to stay awake.

"You don't wanna end up in the newspapers. Believe me," he said. "You don't wanna make yourselves a part of this thing."

He raised his head to look behind him, into the street. Watching an eighteen-wheeler blow by in a flash. The Sniper had yet to pick off a police officer, we knew, but it was hardly out of the question. He turned back to us with a big moony face.

"Where are you boys from?"

"We're from here."

"Not me," my brother spoke up stupidly.

"Uh-huh," the young cop said. "That's how come the New York plates?"

"Right, yes. This is my brother. He drove this car down from Buffalo. He's leaving it for me. It's mine."

My brother didn't say a word.

"Uh-huh," the young cop said again. He didn't seem to know what he was doing out here, I thought. Alone and in the dark. He didn't even ask for our IDs. He just anchored himself there. Holding on to the side of the Camry, as though the whole thing might float away.

"This is some shit," he said absently.

My brother and I nodded, letting him talk. But he stopped again. We waited for him to bust us now, to end all of this, but he didn't. Was this really the guy meant to find and kill the world-famous Sniper? Or, worse, to apprehend him peaceably? How the hell was that going to work? You could practically read the question on his face.

In a blink, the darkness was punctured by a flash at the

far end of the lot. The young cop jerked up and pulled away from the Camry. We saw a pair of headlights dip and bob, as they bounced over a speed bump a hundred feet away. The driver slowed down suddenly as he picked out the police cruiser in the shadows.

The young cop reared up, with a hand on his gun belt, as the vehicle began to veer off in a slow, sweeping turn. And, all at once, it was there: a white van!

"Stop!" the young cop shouted, following this vehicle into the distance. "Stop!" he yelled again, as he ventured out into no-man's-land. My brother didn't hesitate. He turned the key in the ignition, and the Camry fired back up.

"What are you doing?" I asked in a panic.

The cop turned, too, holding out his pistol in a disoriented way. He took his eyes off the van as we pulled away in a rush. The young officer was going to have to shoot out our tires if he wanted to stop us now. I gripped the armrest as my brother floored it through a yellow light and back up the on-ramp. I turned and looked over my shoulder and saw the young cop running into the darkness again. Still chasing the white van.

In the morning, my brother was gone. He had taken the Camry with him, of course. I knew this even before I went outside to look. He was on his way back to my parents' house. This had been his plan all along.

I shouldered my bicycle back down the stairs to the street. Exhaling before I swung my leg over the top bar. I could already feel the heat coming up off the blacktop. Mid-October, and the humidity still hadn't broken. I was miserable; I was hungover; I was aggrieved. I didn't want to do this anymore.

Mike just nodded and climbed up his ladder when I told him I was quitting. I couldn't care less, honestly. Let him be pissed off all he wanted. Let my brother be pissed off, too, for all I cared. That motherfucker stole my car.

It was time for me to go back to school now anyway, to get on with it. This was supposed to be my senior year in college, for fuck's sake. Mike and I both knew that he was perfectly capable of finishing the orange apartment by himself.

At lunchtime, we got into the truck and drove down Georgia Avenue in silence. We were headed downtown to a hardware store where Mike kept a standing account. We made our turn, and cut across the avenues, where we found ourselves suddenly, and unaccountably, stopped. Traffic had come to a dead halt at Fourteenth Street.

"Holy shit," Mike said softly, and I felt my stomach drop.

I knew immediately that I did not want to see this. But when Mike opened his door, I followed him. Everyone was leaving their vehicles now, as the sidewalks filled with people. I walked behind them, feeling anxious. Feeling vulnerable.

There were two motorcycle cops holding traffic in the street as people lined up on the sidewalks, standing shoulder-to-shoulder. Mike and I moved through the crowd, stepping down off the curb, where we were confronted, inexplicably, by *nothing*. We looked across to the other side, where people craned their necks the same way. Looking dumbfounded; looking disappointed. There had been no shooting after all.

No white van. No bodies lying bloodied in the street. There wasn't even a car crash to gawk at.

"What's going on?" Mike asked one of the motorcycle cops.

"Queen of England is coming through," the cop said flatly.

"The Queen of England?" Mike asked indignantly. The words didn't seem to fit in his mouth. Mike turned away and looked at the gathered crowd.

"We have to get through here. You're blocking us in."

"Everybody has to wait," the cop answered.

"The *Queen of England*," Mike said again with disgust. "Look at all these people on the street! You're putting all these people in danger! You realize that, don't you?" But the cop wasn't listening.

The crowd began to titter as the Queen's cavalcade breached the hill. This opulent and imposing show of force; a motorcade running more than a dozen vehicles deep. Motorcycles and police cars and unmarked SUVs formed a pocket of protection around Her Royal Highness. *Look at all of these resources on display,* I thought. *Imagine all of this Sturm und Drang for a doddering old woman. The* Queen of England, *no less!*

But Mike began to boo. Pushing up to the front and booing lustily at the passing cars. "Boooooooooo!" Mike bellowed through his dirty hands. "Boooooooooo!" He was a single voice cutting through the din of our collective bewilderment.

I didn't know what to make of this. The veins were bulging

in his neck as he shook his arms and taunted. I was afraid I was going to have to pull him out of the street now. But, almost as suddenly, people started joining in; picking up Mike's war cry as a chant. This big and brawling noise that started somewhere in their guts. A raucous and spontaneous protest that was suddenly irresistible. People were booing the Queen!

I pushed up to the front, next to Mike, where I could see her limo rocketing past. "Booooooooooo!" I screamed, feeling giddy and alive. To know for a fact that the Queen of England was hearing my voice was a strange thrill. I was smiling like crazy as I heckled with the crowd. Ours was a deep and guttural complaint. It was a thing beyond reason or reproof. I had chills running up my spine.

The whole thing was over before it started, though. The motorcade flashed in the sun and the roar died out. The crowd began to laugh. Where had all of this come from anyway? People felt the urge to look away, to disavow themselves from the noise that they had made. These were not the kinds of people who felt a frenzy in their anger. These were not the good folks who identified with a mob.

I watched as the motorcycle cops who had barred our passage fell into line behind the Queen, and the show was over. People scattered and cars were set in motion. The sidewalks cleared, and it was almost as though it had never happened. And, for all the good it might've done, it hadn't, of course. But what did that have to do with us?

THE AMBULANCE RIDE

I must've fallen asleep at the wheel, as near as I could tell. I was kneeling on a sidewalk in New York, puking my guts out. My hip and elbow were bloodied, and there were two cops standing over me, waiting. I watched one of them prop my bike up against the wrought-iron fence of a park. It didn't look that bad, really, and I tried to remember crashing it. But it was no use. I was fucked up good.

It was dark; it was almost morning; it was a weekday. That was about as much as I could figure out straight off. If it really was a weekday, I had a temp job that I was definitely going to be late for this morning. It hardly mattered. Everyone has nine lives at a temp agency.

I was done vomiting and I decided standing up would make a better presentation for myself. The two cops were smirking, and I tried to play it the same, casual-like. I gave a terse thank-you that may have included some sort of bow, and then I took my bicycle back off the fence.

"Well, anyway," I said. "Thanks for everything."

"Whoa, whoa, whoa. Hang on a sec, Mikey," the big cop said. This familiarity was slightly unsettling until I realized that the other big cop had my driver's license. Again I was struck by the sheer fact of how drunk I was. What day was this now? All these bad nights in New York City, blurring together meaninglessly.

The big cop put his hand on my shoulder in an avuncular way. Apparently he was in charge here. I let go of the bike, missing the fence by a clear three feet. With a series of apologetic head nods we decided to leave it where it was on the ground. And then, with a shallow breath and a deep nod, I was smashed in the head by the powerful feeling of sleep. All these vague disorientations here: the cops in their uniforms; the red, painless bleeding. None of this seemed particularly serious to me, especially after the big cop handed back my license.

"Where do you live?" one of the cops was asking. "Where do you live?" They both kept asking this.

"I live here. This is my neighborhood. Right around the corner," I said, pointing generally. "Thanks for everything."

"Whoa, whoa, whoa," the big cop said again. He tightened his grip on my shoulder, positioning himself between me and the bicycle. "No, no, listen. *Where* do you live?"

"Right here, man. I'm practically home."

"What street?"

"Gates. Franklin and Gates."

Their foreheads dented with this. "Where's that? *Brooklyn?*"

"Yeah," I said, with a little less spit.

The two cops burst into hysterics. "You're in *Manhattan*, Mikey." They were looking at each other, truly tickled by this. And I laughed, too.

"Har-har-har. Very funny. You're wasting all your jokes, man. I'm not some tourist. I'm already half asleep in my bed. I'm on autopilot here. Don't you guys know you're not supposed to wake a sleepwalker?" This was my best crack at New York posturing, and the cops seemed to warm to it a little. They were having fun with me.

The truth was I'd barely been living in New York a couple months at this point. Filing photocopies in some featureless Midtown office building. This qualified as working in the abstract, in the extreme. It had something to do with investment banking, a thing they were very careful never to explain to me. I copied and shredded documents until my left eye began to tic. What did *that* mean? Stress? Guilt? Boredom? It was all a little scary in its formlessness. Time was a drum, beating in my blood, I thought. This was not a life.

I was living in some filthy rattrap apartment with a family of mice and a couple of Pratt kids who smoked cigarettes all day. My bedroom looked out onto an air shaft, and I would lie there and wonder about fire codes. I tried to imagine how many people lived in a building like this. Who even kept track of such things? People lighting burners; ironing shirts; smoking cigarettes, all day long, distracted. Every day was like this. It was surprising how few fires there actually were, when you stopped to think about it. I would go through a kind of morbid checklist each night, wondering if I'd even know how to get out of here when the smoke alarms went off. I walked through it in my head as I lay there in bed: crawling for the front fire escape, or groping for the hallway stairs. Did we even have a smoke alarm? Did it work? What if I jumped down three flights into this air shaft and found out that the doors didn't open? What then?

I already knew I would end up going back to Washington before the end of the year anyway. This was disheartening because I'd been so ready to leave it. I was desperate for a real change of scenery, some actual sense of urgency. To my mind there was a strange logic in moving to New York City at the dawn of the twenty-first century. Some raw desire to live under the volcano. Stress. Congestion. Pollution. Terrorism. I was courting death. This was the modern condition and I was the modern man.

Still, I couldn't believe that the temp agency actually wanted me to work in Midtown Manhattan. This seemed sadistic to me. Wasn't Midtown going to be next? Downtown, Midtown, Uptown: crashing over the island like a tidal wave or a virus. Was it possible to not think about the world this way now?

The woman at the temp agency did not find these sorts of questions amusing. Me neither, I told her. *Me neither.*

Of course, I took the job, and I tried to do it right. Just like everybody else. I rode the subways at rush hour, like a real goddamn New Yorker. Sweating. Claustrophobic. Rushed. This lasted all of one week before I resigned myself to riding my bike the ten miles each way, from Brooklyn to Midtown, through the warm poison clouds of truck exhaust. I locked up under the Chrysler Building and learned to stop looking up for the top. I grew numb, the way that all the people in the business suits acted above fear. Aloof and impersonal. So, so very busy.

If there were windows on the thirty-second floor, I never saw them. It didn't take long for me to get a bit of a reputation in this office, either. Working inside of a storm cloud, I wanted to familiarize myself with the stairways. At first the floor security guard just laughed. When I assured him that I was serious, he creased his brow and told me that the stairs were on alarms.

"I just want to make a test run, though. To time myself," I said.

We suffered each other like this, talking in a circle. Him shaking his head, not understanding me; both of us trying to keep smiling. It just did not compute that I would want to voluntarily walk the thirty-two flights of stairs, for any reason.

"Everybody has to use the elevators, kid . . ." he said, almost apologetically.

I nodded, feeling this a grim proscription. I went back to my desk and put my headphones on: working in isolation; talking to nobody; wandering the floor; hiding photocopies in boxes for money.

I was being detained now, and it was starting to make me restless. I didn't understand why the cops were holding me here.

All this small talk, yakkety-yak. Not answering my questions, not letting me go.

"What's the deal here, guys? Am I under arrest or what?"

This got the big cop smirking again. "Why? You do something tonight you wanna confess to?"

"Yeah, get me a priest," I said. Har-har-har.

There was always this strange rapport with the cops. This joviality. They made it perfectly plain how unthreatened they were by me, and it was starting to piss me off. All these fucking cops: *Yes, Officer. No, Officer.* We were constantly explaining ourselves to the police, which was impossible. They talked to us like we were idiots.

At this point I knew that they were right, too. There was no way I made it back to Brooklyn last night. But why was I still in Manhattan? I hated Manhattan. Not only that, but one of the big cops was loading my bike into the trunk of the cruiser. This was the exact moment when I understood I'd lost control of the situation. And then the big white bus was pulling in on top of me.

There was something impressive about how close they brought the ambulance in on us. How big it really was, with its wheels up on the sidewalk, unnecessarily. They were even running the lights, for chrissake! It was a total overkill, all out of proportion with the way that I was feeling. I was on my third or fourth wind, no problem. I was perfectly ready to finish riding home now. Hungry. Sleepy. All those good things. There was no way I was getting into that truck.

"Aw, c'mon, what the hell is this thing? You guys called for *backup* on me?"

But the cops weren't listening anymore. The jokes had stopped, too. They were talking to the EMTs about me: "Mikey . . . Drinking . . . Mikey . . . Been out drinking. Hey, Mikey, talk to this guy. Tell him how much you been drinking."

I looked up at them with my blankest face. "You're the detective, figure it out."

This was the wrong thing to say, obviously. But I seemed to have a certain genius for saying the wrong things to authority figures. The big cop looked more stunned than angry. Frowning harshly as the other big cop saved me with a deep guffaw.

"*Detective! You?* Har-har-har." And they all shook their heads and turned away again. Taking pity on me. Forgiving me my stupidity.

I sat there on the ground, waiting for a decision to be made. I was depressed. I knew that I was drunk; I knew that I was bleeding; I could smell the vomit on my shirt. Otherwise, I was perfectly fine. Tip-top. No complaints. It struck me then that these are strangely defining moments. Something truly terrible could've happened tonight. But something terrible can happen on every night.

More than any one thing, I did not want to get into this ambulance. I did not want to go to the hospital. What I was thinking right then was that I did not need this. I had no insurance; I could not pay for it. And I told them all of this, too, but it was too late. The big cops turned unfriendly then, terse. Enough was enough, shut up or get arrested. And that was that. They drove away with my front tire sticking out of the trunk of the police car. I felt a tremendous sense of injustice watching them turn the corner and disappear. I had just lost my bike and I felt totally fucked.

The EMT stood there, looking tired, holding the back door of the ambulance. I frowned and finally did what I was told then, feeling like an asshole.

The truth was I had written a novel. This was the real reason I'd moved to New York. It started at my parents' house on Christmas Day and took over my entire senior year, all through the buildup to the Invasion of Iraq. It basically took over my life. I brought it back to school and kept going. It was important just to finish now, I thought.

Being in college couldn't possibly have felt any more irrelevant, so I just kept writing. I had no idea what I was doing, so I put every single thing I knew into this book. And yet I went to extraordinary lengths to detach myself from it completely. I wanted to make certain that no one could accuse me of writing about myself. I mean, the fucking novel was about *cows*! But it wasn't really about cows. It was called *A Cattle, a Crack-Up*, and I flattered myself with the idea that it might actually be an allegory about war.

Strictly speaking, it was a book about men, and weather, and the death of animals, and the idea that a tree could be an important character in a serious novel. It was about a dairy farmer named August Caffrey, whose cows were suddenly causing him to suffer a mysterious illness. This psychosomatic seizure that began with his body's rejection of milk and ended up in a kind of nervous collapse. It was a book about loneliness. It was a book about fear. It was a book about disappointment and loss. It was a book about paranoia and obsession and death. It was a book about one man's failure to carry his family name forward.

But it was all making me very strange, too. I had to stop telling people the things that I was doing. I carried around books from the library about the genuses of American elm trees. I kept scrupulous notes and wrote Latin names in the margins, knowing I would never return these books. I took the Metro out to the end of the Orange Line, and rode my bike twenty-five miles into Virginia, just to look at different cows and farms. I spent hours on the Internet learning the smallest differences between Holsteins and Jerseys. I was googling local dairies and cold-calling them, inquiring about nonexistent internships. I knew nothing, and I was totally obsessed.

I finished the novel in the spring, in a manic burst, only to discover that I'd tanked my GPA and would have to hustle just to graduate. I started bringing the full manuscript along to office hours, where stunned professors begged off the threat that I might actually ask them to read it. We worked out all kinds of creative solutions to make up the work that way.

I'd be lying if I said I hadn't come to New York under the illusion that I might meet somebody important. I wanted to believe that I was a writer. I was going to bowl them all over, of course. Sadly, I didn't even know how to get a single person to read the thing, let alone publish it. I spent two months working on a pathetically earnest query letter that ended up in the trash cans of prominent secretaries all over Manhattan. What connections did I have?

Sitting alone in the back of the ambulance was unnerving. The padded benches; the strange lights; the quiet equipment: all these important metals and plastics. The EMTs had not checked me out, or run tests, or done anything at all, really. They helped me into the back and closed the doors, and that was that. I was left there watching the city go by in a buzzy blur. They told me they were taking me to Bellevue. It was literally ten blocks: five minutes maybe, at this time of the morning. Still, I knew exactly how expensive it was going to be. They should have just called me a goddamn taxi.

And, all at once, I was struck by the feeling that I'd played it wrong. I should've let the cops arrest me. I should've called their bluff and gone with my bike. Jail, the drunk tank, whatever. I could've sobered up; dealt with the paperwork; paid the fine; and left on my bicycle. It made me nauseous to think about it this way now.

I lowered my head between my knees, and saw the note for the first time. Tucked into the front pocket of my shirt and folded in a square: *Mikey. You are in Manhattan. Your bike is at the 13th Precinct. Take the 4, 6 train to 23 & Lex. We'll hold onto it there.*

Well, *Je-sus Christ*, I just about cracked myself up. Relieved is one way to put it, but really I was touched. This unexpected kindness from my friends in law enforcement was too much. And after I had been such an asshole and everything. I almost wanted to cry. The big cop had written a great note. And funny, too.

When I looked up again, the ambulance was stopped. The back door opened and the EMT helped me down, taking me under the arm as we walked into the ER. The Bellevue emergency room at 5:00 a.m. is a sight to see if you ever find yourself living in New York City. Wall-to-wall hard-luck misfits, myself included. Junkies and old men and a Puerto Rican kid with a bone sticking out of his shin.

"Why isn't anyone helping that kid?" I said in a loud voice to no one as we passed him. I was staring back at his leg and it was making me dizzy.

I looked up to find that the EMT had left me at the desk with a stern lady nurse, who was already holding my driver's license and writing everything down. It cannot be stressed enough that this woman was not amused with me. Not at all. She handed the license back, barely willing to look at me. I smiled and played my only ace, producing the note from the big cop. I explained that I was expected urgently at the Number Thirteen Precinct, where there were pressing matters involving the retrieval of my bicycle. I told her thank you very much, but I would have to be going.

"No." The lady nurse scowled, pushing the note back unread. "You smell horrible like vomit, and I need you to sit down and stop talking until the doctor can see you. Do you understand me?"

Needless to say, her authority was absolute. I nodded meekly, feeling embarrassed for myself. The lady nurse left me in a chair looking out over the big open room: the swirling chaos of it all. As I folded my driver's license back inside the note, it hit me again: the cops; the ambulance; the doctors. I didn't have any insurance! How many times did I have to explain this tonight? I couldn't just sit here and wait for a doctor to come. What was a doctor going to do for me anyway?

As the lady nurse walked away to catalog the next catastrophe, I stood up. Trying to affect casualness, I walked across the length of the waiting room, past her empty desk. Past the Puerto Rican kid with the leg. Out the automatic doors. Gone.

Outside, the air had prickers in it. This last chill right before the sun comes shooting up. I was buoyed by my escape. I could feel how drunk I was, *even now*, as I passed into a kind of giddiness. I had no idea where I was going, just that I must keep moving away from the hospital doors. I was consumed by this childlike fear that the lady nurse could come rushing out onto the sidewalk at any moment, pointing: *Hey! There he is! Get him!*

It was a kindly old bum who finally told me where the stairs to the 6 train were. And from there it was pretty much clear sailing. Taking a seat and riding the empty train at the cusp of rush hour. I watched the car slowly fill as we trundled back downtown.

It was daylight when I came up out of the subway, and I shielded my eyes against it. I was thrilled to have pulled off this little trick: finding the Thirteenth Precinct on the Island of Manhattan. Never once did I consider that it might be a trap. Some kind of dirty civic tangle where they get you paying at the hospital and the jail, both. The fact of the matter was I was still sort of shitfaced at 6:00 a.m., stinking horribly, and walking into a police station of my own volition.

But inside all I found was another overtaxed waiting room. The smell of burnt coffee and the pulse of bureaucracy. It was not so far off from the OTB, save for the missing bay of televisions. I looked around warily for my friends the big cops, but I didn't see them anywhere. I walked up to the desk and passed over my handwritten instructions, like this counter was some sort of coat check.

The desk cop read my note with a blank face, seeming to miss the humor in it. He told me to have a seat as he passed it backward to a second cop, who also read it, before turning away and disappearing through a door. I busied myself watching the room, thinking it strange that I didn't see anything like the wheels of justice in motion here. Nobody looked particularly criminal, at least. No one seemed worried about much of anything.

And then, without further ado, a different door opened, and a third cop came wheeling out into the waiting room with my bike, calling, *LeMond*.

"LeMond? Guy LeMond?" They had written down the brand name off the side of the bicycle. "Ho, listen up, which one a youse is LeMond?"

I jumped up, waving at him. I couldn't believe my own stupid luck. "I'm LeMond. Me. Greg LeMond. It's *Greg* LeMond." I couldn't wipe the smile off my face as the cop handed back my bike, totally indifferent.

"All right, there ya go, Greg."

I hurried the bike up the stairs and out onto the street, and I suddenly felt incredible. My whole body was buzzing, almost vibrating. I wasn't even tired anymore. Gliding out into the morning traffic, weaving through the cars, some part of me just wanted to keep on riding. I thought about going straight in to work, just the way I was, but decided to sleep and quit instead. They liked me enough at the temp agency to find me something else.

I rode across the Brooklyn Bridge, taking this long route home. Past the joggers, and the dog-walkers, and the women pushing strollers. I was happy to be young, happy to be alive on this morning. Happy, even, to be living in New York City. I laughed out loud. There was no fucking way I was paying for that ambulance ride. Let them come after me now. I was set free.

YOKO

t all began with a robbery. This bizarro crime, executed in broad daylight, and reeking of junkie panic and ingenuity. This was the first time I met Lane Tworek. He knocked on my door to ask if I'd seen anyone breaking into his house. The way Lane described it, there was a thirty-foot ladder in his roommate's bedroom, while his own bed was out in the backyard.

"I'm sorry. What?" I tried to ask.

Lane figured some junkie had found the ladder lying out and carried it up the block, looking for an open window. After climbing into Lane's house, he pulled it up after him, so as not to draw undue suspicion. Then the guy just ransacked the place a little; taking CDs, and DVDs, and even Lane's PlayStation. All of which would've been a bummer on its own, except that he ended up finding the only thing in the whole house worth stealing: an envelope full of cash. This, Lane explained, was the rent money.

"You pay your rent in cash?" I asked incredulously.

"I pay everything in cash, dude."

Lane, I would come to learn, was more or less officially in arrears: barred from the world of credit cards and checking accounts. But the story wasn't done yet. Lane figured the junkie just about shit himself when he found the rent money. It's a wonder he even bothered taking the Butthole Surfers tapes, but the poor guy was probably in shock. It was time to get out of there, to go. Quick. Now.

Except that when he went downstairs he found out he was locked inside the house. We were all living in these beautiful, shambling rowhouses in a gentrifying Columbia Heights, where all the doors and windows had bars on them. Sure, he could've put the ladder back out the front window, but frankly, that would've been stupid. And, yeah, he could've dragged it to the back of the house and tried his luck there, but Lane figured all that money was making him light in the head. Either that or he'd lost his nerve for heights, which seemed unlikely given the fact of where Lane found his mattress in the backyard.

"You mean he threw your bed off the top porch and jumped?"

"That's exactly what he did. That motherfucker." Lane shook his head. "You really didn't see any of this?"

"Unh-uh." I smiled. "I wish."

———

Lane and I pulled back the fence between our yards, and I helped him carry his bed back up the stairs. We leaned over the balcony and marveled at the fact that a man with a thousand dollars in his pocket had jumped two stories, and no one even saw it.

"Should we try it?" I asked.

Lane nodded solemnly. "We have to."

We pulled the mattress back onto the porch and hucked it over the railing, watching it bounce and settle in the bare yard. I got excited then, right on the verge of losing my nerve. But Lane wasn't one to wait around and think about these things.

"Well . . ." He put his leg over the railing and threw himself off. Bang! Lane hit the mattress hard, right on his ass. He shot back into the air and nearly landed it, before crashing into the dirt. Lane got up wincing and smiling as he rubbed his tailbone.

"Case-fucking-closed, man!" he hollered up at me. "Go ahead."

Lane was shielding his eyes against the sun and grinning up at me expectantly. Obviously I didn't have a great feeling about this jump, but not jumping now was impossible. So I took a breath and I just did it. Windmilling my arms, I reached back underneath me and almost missed the thing. The impact of the mattress was jarring, and I smashed my arm into the ground underneath me as I sprang back up, nearly dropkicking Lane. We got up laughing too hard to speak, and I shook out my wrist, which was already throbbing and vibrating heat.

This was the way that Lane and I baptized our friendship in danger.

I had been going through a pretty good run of invincibility. For all I knew, I was indestructible. And besides, I was having real fun again. I was surprised how little my wrist actually bothered me. It puffed up and went back down, and eventually it was just a dull ache. If anything, it was a reason to go twice as hard.

Lane convinced me to take the next week off from work to help him build a nine-hole miniature golf course in his backyard. As Lane explained it, each hole would represent a different cataclysm of recent American history: 9/11; Waco; Oklahoma City; Exxon Valdez; the *Challenger* explosion; Ruby Ridge; Mount St. Helens; Columbine; and Super Bowl XXV (this last one was my own). Lane was enrolled in art school, and the whole thing was presented loosely as his thesis project. He'd even received a grant, which he promptly spent on Astroturf, lumber, and marijuana. Somehow he'd managed to get the rent paid out of this as well.

I was surprised to find that Lane was a competent builder. Not only that, but he ended up having all kinds of practical knowledge: carpentry; electricity; plumbing; cooking. I made a point of trying to soak up as much of this as I could, because it was all completely foreign to me. If something broke in my father's house, he called a guy to fix it. I'd always thought that was smart.

Each morning, Lane and I would drag the power tools out of the basement. We'd take our shirts off and smoke pot out of an apple, and go to work. Unfortunately, we only really managed to finish three holes before giving over to the greater desire to play the course. We were getting good, too, and began tossing around the idea of playing for money. But this was right when Lane's landlady found out what was going on, and threatened to have us arrested. She came roaring into the backyard one day, in her high heels and sunglasses, screaming at me about tearing the thing down. I didn't even know who she was. I was so high I could hardly keep myself from giggling. Covered in dirt and paint, I just stood there, holding my putter, letting her yell.

After that, Lane was stuck with a shit-ton of Astroturf. We laid as much as we could down for carpeting, and put the rest out to the curb.

There was a bar in the neighborhood that Lane and I liked to walk to most nights. We would show up with six beers in a backpack, and leave with three rolls of toilet paper lifted from the bathroom. We spent a lot of time in this bar thinking up new ideas for bands to start. Lane was convinced he could build us some contraption whereby we would pedal stationary bicycles attached to belts that controlled the speed and pitch of different record players and strobe lights. I would laugh because he was serious. He assured me he could get us a grant and everything. Lane would make the pretty bartender find him a pen so that he could sketch the whole thing out on a napkin.

"It looks like it's falling apart," she told him.

"That doesn't matter. We don't have any songs. It would

only have to hold together for five minutes," Lane said. "Besides, it's art."

Lane Tworek was exactly the bad influence I'd been searching for all along. He was a brutal kid, which was the thing I liked about him most. I had no idea what Lane could be thinking from one moment to the next, and I loved that about him.

He seemed to have no conception of himself as strange, either, which I found fascinating. I would catch him at things I couldn't even imagine. All these weird and compromised situations that Lane got into, just being himself. Everyone was using Craigslist by now—for jobs and apartments and bike parts—but Lane was already using it to look for sex. He would post ads with headings like: "Average Joe Seeks Blowjob From Hot-Model Type." *Hello!* the post would begin cheerily. *I will be walking home from the Raven Tavern at 2:30 a.m., and I would appreciate your company for some pre-slumber fellatio . . .*

I almost pissed myself when I saw these. I couldn't tell if this was real, or just another idea for his thesis. Lane could be very deadpan that way. But I couldn't get enough of it. I would wipe the tears from the corners of my eyes and make him post another one. "College Student Interested in Dating Your Sex Doll."

"Does anyone ever reply?" I finally asked.

"Oh, yeah." Lane smiled. "Always dudes."

"Really?" I could hear myself sounding disappointed.

"Yeah. It's great, though. They're all *very* confident in

their ability to convert me into a homosexual." Lane grinned. "I guess you never know, right?"

The truth, I found out, was that Lane had actually had a number of real sex encounters with older women through the Internet. I knew, for instance, that he'd been conducting a semi-regular affair with some friendly hausfrau out on Connecticut Avenue for over a year. The whole thing made me feel a little puritan by comparison.

Still, it took me a while to realize that Lane was actually making money on his computer. More often than not, this was where I'd find him. Up in his bedroom with his laptop open.

"What do you know about baseball gloves?" he would ask me with a blank face.

"Baseball gloves?" I'd ask back.

Lane would kick open a box filled with a dozen lightly used mitts. "Yeah, how much can I sell a baseball glove for, anyway?"

I picked one out of the box and tried it on. Punching my fist into the sweet spot. "Sell it how?"

"eBay, dude," he said with a laugh, like it couldn't be more obvious. We were eternally having some variation on this same conversation. Small electronics, jewelry, taxidermy, whatever. Lane was always coming home with a new box, and he always wanted to know how much I thought a thing was worth, for some reason.

"Dig around. I got some *Ozzie Smiths* in there. Pretty good, huh?" He was staring at me, waiting for me to put a number on it.

"Twenty bucks?"

Lane would always nod, pleased. Turning back to his computer and typing it in.

"Where do all these things come from, Lane?" I finally asked him one day.

"Hey . . ." he said, not answering my question. "Have I ever shown you all the pictures that Internet people have sent to me?"

I shook my head, and watched as Lane opened a file filled with thumbnails of men and women, in all shapes and sizes. This gross tapestry of flesh and hair and blurry naked parts. He smiled at me wickedly, and closed the laptop, as I tried to lean in.

Lane stood up and kicked the box of baseball gloves closed, too. It was more fun not knowing where this stuff came from anyway.

This was still at the very beginning of the Cicada Summer. Those dozy heat bugs had just begun emerging from their seventeen-year slumber to take over the city like a biblical plague. Thousands of nymphs crawling up out of the ground and taking flight. They served no purpose at all, buzzing and smashing into everything like little balsa-wood gliders with rubber-band propellers. The cicadas carried along the strange energy of a long hibernation come to an end. Singing into the night: sex and death.

Lane wouldn't stop telling me that cicadas were a delicacy in China, either. For days he had been urging me to eat a live one for his own personal entertainment. We were deep into a culture of dares at this point.

Finally I told him I would eat a cicada if he would eat a cockroach.

"Fine," Lane said, and we stood there, unsure how to proceed.

The cicadas were everywhere, and I plucked one out of the air without even trying. It buzzed and beat its wings against my fingertips as I held it out to Lane tauntingly. He was annoyed because there were no cockroaches out in the broad daylight. I was determined to eat my prehistoric bug before he could even find his.

And I did, too. Breaking the insect into death with my back teeth. Grinding it down to a sticky stillness. Its wings and legs scraped along my tongue as I fought my gag reflex. I swallowed it whole, in one terrible lump, grinning at Lane. Showing him my blackened tongue. It wasn't even that bad, really. I'd read in the newspaper that the only thing a cicada eats is leaves. Besides, it was over now.

"Mmm, done, finished. Delicious. What are you waiting for, Lane?"

Lane was down on his knees, under the front porch, getting frustrated. It took a minute, but he finally came out with a big black-brown cockroach. Holding it up for me.

"That thing looks repulsive," I told him, grinning wildly. "Cockroaches are not a delicacy *anywhere*. I just want you to be fully aware of that. A real friend would stop you now. He would report you to the Board of Health. For your own good."

"Watch and learn," Lane said.

He popped the roach into his mouth, and I could see right away that this was not good. Whatever unholy shit is on the inside of a cockroach, it had just come spilling out into Lane's mouth. His face went into a kind of contortion, and I was killing myself laughing. This was a truly beautiful thing. Lane kept chewing and chewing, but as he worked to swallow his body said no. He gagged loudly and retched the mashed bug out onto the sidewalk in a pulp.

"Ugghhh," I said, truly exhilarated. Lane looked green. I had never seen him this way before. "C'mon, pussy. Finish it!"

The insect's legs were still twitching inside the black slop. Lane showed me his teeth as he picked up the roach in his fingers again. Steely, he put it back into his mouth and swallowed it whole. Gone.

"There," he said, looking miserable. "Happy?"

"Verrrry happy," I said, with a shit-eating smile.

"I think I need something else," Lane said, examining the inside of his mouth with his tongue. Spitting black saliva onto the sidewalk. "I'm not sure. Malt liquor?"

"Okay," I said. "Let's go get you a Sparks, little guy." I put my arm around his shoulder and we walked down to the bodega.

I was really very happy with everything then. This can't be overstated: I was enormously, perfectly happy. In a lot of ways this was turning into the best summer of my life. So, of course, this was the exact moment when Lauren Pinkerton came back around looking for me. She wanted to be my friend again. She wanted to know where I'd gone, and why I seemed so happy now. She wanted in, all of a sudden, out of the blue!

"Well, ha-ha-ha," I said, from up on the porch.

"I'm serious. Why can't we be friends? I miss you, don't you miss me?"

"I was *ignoring* you, if you were paying any attention."

Lauren pouted, and I tilted my head toward her sentimentally, mockingly.

"What's wrong with your arm anyway?" she asked, pointing up at me from the sidewalk. I looked at my left wrist, which was still wrapped in duct tape from earlier in the afternoon, when Lane and I had been playing guitars in his basement.

"Nothing's wrong. I have two of them," I said, showing it for a fact. "Everything's hunky-dory." The truth was it had been nearly four weeks since I'd jumped off the upstairs porch with Lane, and I'd decided to stop asking those kinds of questions.

"I don't like the idea that you're not taking care of yourself."

"Yeah, well, anyway. I'm sort of busy around here . . ." I could hear a hoarse barking sound coming from inside of Lane's house, and I was desperate to go investigate. "See ya around, or whatever," I said, leaving Lauren out on the sidewalk. I resented her coming back like this. It pissed me off.

I let myself into Lane's house through the back door, and was confronted by the apparition of a big gray pit bull. Lane had hold of a thick, knotted rope, and he was playing tug-o-war with the animal. Laughing maniacally.

Lane's mousy roommate, Hannah Wasserman, stood watching in the doorway. Smiling uncertainly.

"What is that thing?" I asked, a little alarmed.

"He's a rescue dog," Hannah said brightly. "I just got him today."

This dog did not look right, not at all. And I was willing to bet he'd never known a bleeding heart like Hannah Wasserman in his entire life.

"He looks a little deranged," I said.

"He was abused. They were going to put him to sleep, but I saved him."

I nodded, taking a step back. Lane was still roughhousing with the fragile pit bull. Riling him up. Barking into the dog's face.

"You're a strong dog, yes-you-are. What's your name, strong dog?"

"His name is Lucky," Hannah offered cheerily. She was unnervingly passive about letting Lane wrestle with her new pet. I took another step away, spacing myself behind the couch. But Lane saw me do this, and he immediately tossed me the knotted rope. I caught it reflexively, as Lucky came launching over the couch behind it. I ducked and danced away as the big dog hit the parquet floor and went sliding into the hallway. Lane seemed to think this was hilarious.

"Hey, guys, don't . . ." Hannah said meekly.

"Dogs can smell fear!" Lane shouted. "Dogs can smell fear!"

Lucky turned and regrouped, barking loudly, and I slung the rope back across the room, trying to hit Lane in the head with it. But it thumped off the wall instead.

As Lane bent down to pick it up, the big dumb dog forgot what he was chasing and grabbed on to Lane's baggy T-shirt at the neck. As Lane tried to pull himself free, Lucky started to rip. It was everything Lane could do just to stay up on his feet then. The pit bull yanked and jerked, pulling the T-shirt right off of Lane's body in one long coil of fabric. He was literally spun out of his clothes like a cartoon character. This all happened in a blink—far too fast to be properly scared by it. Lane was just suddenly standing there in the middle of the room without a shirt on.

He looked at me with his mouth hanging open as we watched Lucky trot off into the kitchen with the T-shirt, like it was nothing at all.

"Oh, my god, *guys* . . ." Hannah said pitiably, looking traumatized.

"Ho-ly *shit*!" I shouted as Lane and I burst into hysterics. We laughed because we always laughed. This kind of stuff was bound to happen with Lane around.

Needless to say, poor Hannah Wasserman took old Lucky back to the pound for his dirt nap the next day. Rest in peace, puppy.

Lane and I kept kicking on. Raising hell. Cheating death. Riding bikes. Taking drugs. Breaking locks. Lighting fires. Trespassing in buildings. Jumping off of rooftops. Staying up all night. There were no rules. We were channeling danger and destruction, and making no apologies for ourselves, either. Ours was the kind of fun you just have to surrender yourself to.

Hannah Wasserman said that it was nice that Lane finally found somebody his own species. This was a love story, to be sure. But Lauren wouldn't stop coming around. She was curious about Lane now, and she was wary and jealous of my affection for him.

"I guess I don't get it. Is it like a *gay* thing?" she smirked. "No girls allowed?"

"Yeah, it's a gay thing."

Lauren crossed her arms critically. "Seriously, though. What do you guys do all day? Where do you go?"

"I dunno." I shrugged. "There's been a lot of good sports on TV."

"That's what you do? Watch *sports* on TV?"

"Yeah, I mean, there's all kinds of good stuff on *tee-vee* these days," I answered drolly. "We do other stuff, too. Like *laughing* and *having fun*. You wouldn't like it."

Lauren frowned and I smiled. I could feel her patience wearing down. We had been totally incommunicado for over a year, and suddenly she was back. If I was cruel and heavy-handed now, that was the point. This was all preemptive.

Lane and I started calling her Yoko. We thought this was hilarious, and the fact that Lauren hated it only made it funnier.

"I'm Yoko?" she said. "Why, because she broke up the

Beatles? Well, ha-ha-ha. I'm glad she broke up the Beatles. I wish she would've broken up the *Rolling Stones*, too."

Lane and I were speechless.

"I wish she would've broken up Led Zeppelin," Lane deadpanned.

"Or the fucking Who," I said, smiling. "Jesus Christ, how about *The Who*!"

And suddenly this was a game we were all playing. Van Halen, Lauren said gleefully. *Ae*rosmith, I shouted. AC/DC. Pearl Jam. U2. Yeah, *fuck* fucking U2.

"Yoko Ono," Lane said with real gravity, "should break up Bruce Springsteen already. No man should be allowed to put a goddamn saxophone on every single song for thirty years. It sucks."

And that was it. We were rolling around the porch, enormously pleased with ourselves for breaking up all these sad and tired bands.

"But not Peloton," I said solemnly.

"No. Peloton lives forever."

"What the hell is *Peloton*?" Lauren scowled, annoyed at always being one step behind. We laughed, and reveled in not telling her.

"Peloton is Peloton," I said.

"It's fucking *Peloton*!" Lane howled, and we laughed again.

Peloton was the band that Lane and I had started the week before. Lane played drums and wore a gas mask with a microphone in it, while I just tried to keep up on the guitar. That was it, really—it was every bit as crude and wonderful as it sounds. Lane hit the drums harder than any human boy I'd ever seen. There was a reason I was wrapping my wrist in duct tape. It hurt to play the guitar as fast as Lane wanted it played, and I loved every second of it. We wrote one song and declared ourselves ready to go.

Lane arranged for Peloton to play a single show, opening for Black Eyes at Fort Reno. We played for six blistering minutes to a field of confused friends and cringing strangers. It was assaultive. People actually put their hands up over their ears, and I could tell that Lane was feeding off of this. He screeched and yelped menacingly into his gas mask, as I repeated my few caustic chords in a whorl of pitch and distortion. I broke a string and pretty much forgot the whole song completely, but it didn't matter. We just kept playing and letting it all fly apart spectacularly, which Lane said made it great. We took a bow and cleared off the stage. People universally hated it, but Ian MacKaye came up to me afterward and said that he appreciated our restraint. He liked our six minutes and earnestly told me to keep playing.

But, of course, Peloton broke up immediately. We had to. That was the point. That was the whole fun of making a band in the first place. And yet, somehow, we still ended up on the *City Paper*'s "Summer Bands to Watch" list. And rightfully fucking so, we reveled in telling everyone.

In truth, it was Lauren who knew an editor there, which we thought was funny. Lauren had won Lane over, too, and I finally decided to stop fighting it. I kind of liked having them both around, together. I liked the way they played off each other. I liked the strange tensions it created. Plus there was a kind of peacemaking happening between Lauren and me now. Everything had a way of settling down. And, all at once, I began to acknowledge the possibility of a kind of second act: Friendship.

I liked seeing Lauren and knowing what she thought again. I liked telling her stories, and hearing her laugh. Lane, for all his charms, didn't care to talk about books or feelings or real life. It just didn't interest him. Lane liked violent and kinetic things. He lived with the earnest idea that the present moment would always extend forever.

It was harder to admit that I was still attracted to Lauren Pinkerton, though. All her sharp Tomboy features had rounded and softened, and I never really realized how long her hair was, or how much I liked it that way. My grandmother once told me that a woman's power was held in her hair. I always liked that.

I would catch myself letting my guard down in old ways, too. Lauren liked to push: asking inappropriate questions, saying pointed things. Somehow she knew that I'd started seeing a girl once I got back from New York. I could tell that she was amused and vaguely threatened by the idea. She hinted around it, entreating me to spill the beans already. But I was coy because my fling with that girl never amounted to much of anything. But I didn't want Lauren to know that.

I was surprised how easy it was just to talk like normal again. Lauren downplayed all the damage done, because that was just her way. There was something loose and beautiful happening now. Something that I worried I might need to protect myself against. Lane liked her, too, and I couldn't shake the feeling that she knew exactly what she was doing. Lauren was fun. She was funny and flirty and irreverent, and it all made me a little paranoid.

We were out at a bar one night when she put her arms around my neck sweetly. "I want you to kiss me," she said mischievously.

"Why?"

"See that guy over my shoulder, watching us? He comes into my coffee shop every morning and stalks me there for hours. He needs a bigger hint. I want him to see you kiss me."

I smiled at her and leaned away slightly. "No," I said.

Lauren laughed. Rebuffed. She squeezed my hand and danced away, into the crowd. She knew that I was watching her, terrified that she would go in search of Lane.

I couldn't blame Lane for wanting to sleep with Lauren, because I still wanted to sleep with her, too. But that wasn't healthy. We'd tried that for a while, before I left for New York, and there was no halfway. More than I wanted Lauren, I knew I didn't want anyone else to have her. Especially not Lane. Lane probably liked to suck on toes or have a finger up his butthole, for all I knew. How could I compete with that?

Or worse, what if they actually liked each other and I got spit out again? I'd spent every day of the last six weeks with Lane, and I hardly knew a real thing about him. I couldn't say that he wouldn't fuck me over, because I didn't know. It was obvious that Lane could feel this tension, too.

"Isn't this something?" he said to me at the bar. "You and me fighting over a woman."

He surprised me with this, and I didn't know what to say. Lane's eyes got big, and he laughed in a way I couldn't figure at all. That was it. I knew I had to tear the whole thing down again. Even though everything was good. Even though it seemed like Lauren and I had moved beyond all of this pettiness. It was still too painful for me.

So I went right back to frustrating her: turning off my phone; breaking a plan; arguing about details. I told her she'd only end up making out with Lane and ruining everything in the end. It was better just to save ourselves that unpleasantness, right? Needless to say, Lauren resented this deeply. But I didn't care. We had our blowout and she stopped coming around. And Lane and I went on our reckless, merry way.

This was right about the time the cicadas started dying off en masse. Their siren song was sung and the new eggs lay buried, silent underground. Structured birth and structured death. The cars brushed their husks to the edges of the road, where we crunched through them on our bicycles. And then one day they were gone completely.

Lane was just as happy to take or leave Lauren, in the end, which was another one of his virtues. I was the one who was stuck fixating. I was afraid to admit that I was still in love with Lauren Pinkerton, and now I'd gone and blown it all over again. It was right in the midst of all this self-pity that my wrist really started bothering me. Strangely, it was the fact that it *stopped* hurting that worried me most.

"I think I need to do something about my wrist," I said to Lane one day.

"I'm sort of perversely jealous of your wrist," he said cryptically.

"What are you talking about?"

"Once, when I was eleven, I fell out of a tree and tried to hide the fact that I'd broken my ankle," he said, lighting up. "But that's a tougher one because I was limping so bad. My mother figured me out in like an hour, and—"

"Jesus, who gives a shit about your eleven-year-old ankle, Lane? What am I going to do about my *wrist!*"

He just shrugged, seeming to have no opinion whatsoever.

Lane was getting weirder altogether, I thought. Or maybe it was just my patience that had slipped. Either way, I finally started to see how his current of nihilism ran deeper and more destructive than my own. We were pretty much hanging out by rote at this point. Drinking too much. Insulting each other. Destroying each other's property. We'd had two separate incidents in the last week where we each drew blood. Lane and I were getting sick of each other, plain and simple. This was a thing we found impossible to articulate. All the same shit, but only half the fun.

And then Lane went and started a brand-new band, called Tworek, without me. He had the brilliant idea of taking a player out of every band we liked to make a rotating lineup of ten kids. Forming an eponymous band was the sort of stunt that only Lane pulled off. The whole thing was made more amusing by the fact that Lane was not only *not the frontman* of Tworek, but he was hardly a blip in the sea of bodies up onstage. He just stood at the back, playing bass. Lane told me, with some pride, that he hadn't even made it to a practice yet.

But Tworek was actually getting some buzz going. They were the new hot-shit band you were supposed to go see live. The stage shows were these violent cataclysms of snarling guitar and convulsive drumming. Bodies jostled for space as the whole thing threatened to collapse under the weight of all its moving parts. There were three different drummers in the band (who couldn't hold a candle to Lane playing alone, I thought). But the whole thing was undeniably beautiful: everything rising up out of this wreckage, almost impossibly, into real songs.

Tworek was undoubtedly becoming the stuff of myth in these circles. Each next show was bigger than the last, amid swirling rumors (which I dutifully helped Lane circulate) that the band was breaking up. The truth was they were frantically trying to pull together enough songs to make a record for Dischord before the end of the summer. The whole thing hinged on the idea that they were going to be *fucking huge*, just so long as they didn't break up that very night.

I loved Tworek, the same as everybody else, which was the reason I resented everything about them and wished them unmitigated failure and misfortune. I had no idea why Lane didn't ask me to be in the band, and we never talked about it. It was his name and his idea, and I had to give him credit for that. But, yeah, I was sour. Tworek was fucking awesome, and I wasn't in it.

This tension built up to the morning that I woke up on the long, shared roof of our rowhouses. Lane and I had ended up there the night before, after the bars closed. We sat on the peak and stared out at the bleary lights of the city. Watching and not talking, as we finished the dregs of some awful bottle that Hannah Wasserman had hidden in a cupboard. I had this one perfect image of Lane standing up and throwing the bottle backward over his shoulder. It arced and disappeared, crashing down on the street between parked cars. Lane cackled, and I lay myself down against the cool metal roof, very careful. I had the spins.

The next thing I knew, I was waking up with the sun in my eyes, like a knifepoint. I was alone. I could feel the tin heating up underneath me and beginning to cook. And I realized, with a start, just how close I had drifted down toward the edge of the roof.

Sitting up, I was reminded for the one-thousandth time of the dull ache in my puffy wrist. This throb of recognition each morning before it went away. I scraped myself up from the unforgiving roof, feeling like I'd lost an entire year off my young life. I was light-headed, and dehydrated, and still a little drunk. I checked the hatch into my own attic, knowing it would be locked, and I climbed down into Lane's house instead.

I made my way down the stairs, toward the strange disembodied sound of a toddler crying somewhere out in the street. I found Lane there, in the living room, standing bare-chested with his back to me. He was holding the bars of the front door like an inmate, glowering out into the empty street.

"Jesus, will somebody shut that kid up! People are hung-over in here!"

Just like that the crying stopped. Lane turned around with a self-satisfied smile.

"Why did you leave me up on the roof?" I asked, accus-ing him.

"You were asleep." Lane shrugged.

"Did you sleep up there, too?"

"On the *roof*, no way. What am I, an animal? I slept in my bed."

"You asshole," I said, pushing past him toward the door.

"What?" Lane said incredulously.

"I almost rolled off the fucking roof!"

Lane couldn't help but laugh at this. A week earlier I could have stayed and laughed, too. But now I just wanted to get away from him.

"Pfft," Lane smirked. "What? Like you've never fallen off a roof?"

I grunted and pushed out the door, feeling stupid for being so angry with Lane. I couldn't shake this phantom feel-ing of nearly dropping off the house. It was running on an endless loop inside of my stomach, making me sick.

It was at one of these blistering Tworek breakup-shows a week later when I ran back into Lauren. She caught me leaning against the wall with a deep-set frown, and she stood there, mocking my crossed arms. This was when she noticed the cast.

"You fixed your wrist," she said, taking the whole thing into her hands. She turned the cast over, where Lane had written *Peloton Breaks Bones* in big rock-and-roll letters. He had wanted to write *Quitter*, but I told him no.

"What can I say? I guess it finally started to hurt."

The truth was I'd left Lane's after waking up on the roof and went home to call my parents. I told them some vague story about possibly, maybe having broken my wrist. They were sympathetic and urged me to go to the doctor. They offered to pay, and I begrudgingly accepted, even though it was the whole reason for calling.

It had been fifty-eight days since I'd jumped off the upstairs porch with Lane. I had broken the navicular bone in my left wrist, and a doctor had set it with a cast. He told me I was lucky he wasn't going to rebreak the bone, and strangely, I felt lucky then.

Lauren smiled and said that she was happy for me. I held my stare too long, and we turned away to face the stage, where the band was setting up.

"So what do you think of Tworek?" she asked expectantly.

"I dunno. They have good hair?"

"Oh, ha-ha. Why aren't you in the band, anyway?"

"Wasn't asked," I said, failing to mask this edge of hostility.

"Uh-oh, trouble in paradise?"

"I don't know," I said flatly.

"Well, maybe it's because you have a broken arm. You

know?" she offered kindly. "Besides, you were never exactly some sort of mind-blowing guitarist."

"Ha-ha-ha," I said. "That doesn't have anything to do with anything. Lane should've asked me to be in the band no matter what."

"Does Lane even make decisions in Tworek? I heard they were trying to kick him out."

"I wouldn't know," I said.

Lauren softened. "Don't you think you're being a little passive-aggressive?"

"I'll stop being passive-aggressive when Lane stops being nonconfrontational."

Lauren laughed. "Okay, then. Good."

I turned back to face her, feeling suddenly overwhelmed with how much I was missing her. Just having Lauren here, in front of me, at this moment, I was never going to push her away again.

"Do you want to get out of here?" I asked, wearing it all over my face. "Do you want to leave? We can go somewhere else, anywhere. It doesn't matter to me."

"Oh," Lauren said. "I should probably stay. I came here with Patrick." I looked up and saw Patrick Serf standing across the room. "Sorry."

"No, it's fine. I'll just go home, then, maybe. I can read a book or something. Lane discourages that type of behavior."

Lauren nodded and we turned to face the stage. As Tworek's drummers finally started the show, I looked around the room one more time, and I left.

————

Lane and I reconciled again a few days later, after a brief spell in which he actually *was* kicked out of Tworek. We both thought that was hilarious.

There ended up being only one more Tworek show that summer, though. It was at a house party on the Fourth of July, and it was a spectacular disaster. Lane got somebody to drive him out to Virginia, and he came back with a case of Sparks, a pocketful of pills, and a hundred dollars' worth of illegal fireworks. He was excited, to say the least.

It had already been such a strange day, all around. It was cool but somehow muggy still. The afternoon had been marred by a series of blowout thunderstorms that forced everyone off the streets. There was flash flooding in our backyard as the alley plugged and dumped a dirty torrent down the steps and into our basement. My roommates and I spent over an hour, barefoot and bare-chested, bailing water into hundred-pound garbage cans.

After the rain let up, I went over to see how Lane and Hannah had fared, but no one was around. I didn't see Lane again until I got to the party. By that time he had made it halfway through the Sparks and all the way through the pills, and it was clear that there would be no Tworek show this night. There were too many people at the party, besides. Bodies had begun to rub, and everyone was getting skittish. They really did want to see Tworek play, too. But Lane had been punched in the face by one of the band's drummers, and he was refusing to tell them where he'd hidden the keys to the van.

If that weren't enough, Lane was setting fireworks off inside the house. Nothing major, but enough to rile a crowd, and smoke out a room, and maybe even singe somebody if they weren't quick. The entire day seemed to coil up around this moment. Everyone was getting pissed off at Lane.

Finally, some punk girl with rings in her lips took matters into her own hands and tried to break a beer bottle over his head. But she missed and cracked our friend Tom instead. This was when shit went haywire. Derek caught Tom in a backpedal, before dropping him to the floor so that he could throw a punch at the girl. And suddenly everyone was swinging this way. Blood and beer were sloshing as people pushed back and forth across the room.

But it was Lane who found a skateboard on the floor and started swinging it through the crowd like a tomahawk, cracking some gutter punk in the head. I pushed forward in Lane's defense and bricked some poor asshole in the face with my cast. But this hurt, sending a stinger up my arm and into my shoulder.

The kid who lived there was standing on the kitchen table, screaming at the top of his lungs, freaking out. "Get the fuck out, get the fuck out!"

And as I looked around this madhouse, I put my cast up defensively and backed my way out of the kitchen. Past Tom, who was desperately trying to stanch his bleeding head with an American flag. Past George, who gave me a thumbs-up, as he held his ground and filmed the whole scary scene with his camera.

I made my way out onto the street, where the cop cars were already showing up to arrest people. Lauren was standing out there on the sidewalk with her arms crossed, looking worried. But she smiled when she saw me, and it calmed me down instantly. As the police started fanning out into the yard, Lauren reached down to take my hand, pulling me away. This small antidote to chaos.

It was still only nine thirty at night, and we could hear the fireworks starting in the distance. We climbed up a low fire escape, to the roof of an apartment building, where we could suddenly see everything. The big show down on the Mall, and the many satellite shows in the surrounding suburbs. Fireworks going off in every diminishing direction. I had never seen it happening this way before. We marveled at the fact that they staged these shows, all together, everywhere at once. It was a wonderful thing if you could see it from up on high.

Lauren turned to me suddenly. "I'm sorry if I broke up Peloton."

"No," I said, shaking my head. "Don't apologize for that. I like it when a great band breaks up. It means that it was worth it."

"Yeah, fuck the Rolling Stones already," Lauren shouted, and we laughed.

We lay back on the roof and stared up at the irradiated sky. And when the fireworks stopped, we were left only with the rippling quiet of night and the soft fugue of insect sounds. It was the stillness that made it easy to forgive ourselves. We could erase two years without another misplaced word. Up on this rooftop, where I kissed Lauren Pinkerton again. And everything started new.

SELF-PORTRAITS IN DISGUISE

Why are they together?" Lauren asked me.

We were sitting on a bench in Washington Square Park watching an older man kiss a younger woman lightly on the lips. They pulled apart and laughed airily.

"He's got money," I said.

"She has low self-esteem," Lauren answered.

This was a game we were playing. It had started in the back of the Chinatown Bus, on the ride up from Washington, D.C. And it carried over now, through the Lower East Side, to this bench in the park where we were waiting for Cokie.

"Why are they together?" I asked Lauren, pointing out a new couple. These bright young hipsters with their bleach-blond hair and their neon windbreakers. They were practically jamming their hands into each other's pants.

"She's got money," Lauren said, without affect.

"He has low self-esteem," I answered, the same.

We had arrived the day before on the Dragon Bus. This third-rate bus line that had been blowing tires and bursting into flames up and down I-95 for the past six months. Real deaths. Not just cheap thrills and excitements. Still, thirteen dollars got you all the way to New York City and back, *and* they showed you a bootlegged copy of *The Matrix 2*. It was a no-brainer for us.

"Why are they together?" Lauren asked me.

"He has an umbrella," I answered simply.

"Mm." She smiled. "Lucky girl."

Lauren had come with me to a downtown courthouse the day before, to deal with an outstanding legal issue, which I was happy to report was mercifully and speedily resolved. This was the reason for the trip. And now we were free to do whatever we wanted here. To go to the wax museum or the top of the Empire State Building. To eat lunch at Planet Hollywood or the Hard Rock Café. We could take a ferry to the Statue of Liberty or stand on line for tickets to *The Phantom of the Opera*. Or whatever else it was that real New Yorkers did for fun. But Lauren just wanted to see Cokie.

Cokie was in her first year of law school at NYU. We knew that she lived in a tiny studio around the corner from here, but we had no idea where. And Cokie wasn't answering her phone now, which was driving Lauren crazy. More to the point, she wasn't answering her texts. This was a concession to the fact that Cokie had apparently *stopped* talking on her cell phone. She would listen to your voice messages and text you back, but she would not pick up your call. Cokie had already broken off our plans for dinner the night before, and I had a feeling we weren't going to see her today, now, either.

"Why are they together?" I asked.

I was watching a young Hasid, in his stiff hat and his dark curls, as he whispered something into the ear of his woman. She tightened her lips and shook her head firmly, no. The man couldn't help but smile luridly then.

"Arranged marriage," Lauren said.

"True love," I answered.

We were staying in SoHo with Lauren's sister Rachel. We had other friends, other places we could go, of course, but this arrangement was nonnegotiable. It had something to do with the politics of sisters, a thing I could not fully comprehend. It had to do with old rivalries and new grudges. It had to do with sibling debts, which were to be paid out, over the course of a lifetime, in blood and tears.

Rachel Pinkerton didn't believe in the idea that she and Lauren should be allowed to grow apart gracefully. She nursed a fantasy of two sisters who were exactly alike. She was two years older than Lauren, and she always would be, of course. This gave her license to comment on the clothes that Lauren wore, or the way that she did her hair. She felt that it was her place to have opinions about the things that Lauren ate and the jokes that she told. Rachel couldn't help but give off this tension in everything she did. It emanated in the way that she narrowed her eyes and nodded at the things that Lauren said. It was a pressure and an expectation that she had been cultivating over the course of a lifetime. Rachel's was a well-traveled disappointment.

Worse, Rachel wanted credit. She wanted attention and affection. Buried under everything was a skin-deep plea for validation. She wanted Lauren to feel jealous of her somehow. This was why she'd been so insistent that we stay with her in the first place. We were there to meet her banker boyfriend, and sleep in her posh apartment, and pay witness to the life that she had made for herself here. The whole thing was a provocation.

But Lauren was nothing if not subdued in her reactions to all this pageantry. Answering questions blankly, as though she hadn't even known they were meant for her. She was coy, she was aloof, she was withholding. This was the thing that was most surprising to me, really. I knew Lauren, first and foremost, as a fighter. But in Rachel's presence she was suddenly deferential. She was vulnerable. She was noncombative.

But this was an act, too. Lauren had done this to herself, and there was no sense in making it worse by kicking and screaming. Even before we got there, Lauren admitted her mistake. She should've never told her sister we were coming to New York. Rachel would've never even known. But it was too late for that now.

For the last fifteen months I had been receiving weekly letters from the FDNY, compelling me to pay a $607 bill that I had no intention of ever paying. It was impossible to say what an ambulance ride was worth to any given person, of course, but it sure as shit wasn't worth a whole month's rent to me. I contacted my legal counselor (Cokie Braque), and we went to work crafting an increasingly elaborate appeals letter. Cokie was having a riot with this, generating byzantine sentences like: *Because I did not want, need, or request these services, I never explicitly or implicitly agreed to pay for them. In addition, the very fact of my being made to go to the hospital under such circumstances is coercive and unethical . . .*

Cokie finally texted me and told me to request an in-person appeal. She said that the city lacked the resources to pursue outstanding claims below a certain threshold. She figured there was a fifty-fifty chance that they would throw the whole thing out without even reading it. And if not, well, there was always another written appeal.

I had memorized the entire letter, ready to recite it on command before His Highness, the Honorable Judge. This included the closing remark: *Therefore, I respectfully request that you rectify this situation, with all speed, and reconcile your expenses, if need be, with the party that solicited these services in the first place.*

In other words, the NYPD. Har-har-har.

But there was no judge, in the end. There was no courtroom, either. I was directed to the basement office of a harried clerk with a stack of paperwork standing two feet tall on her desk. She asked for my driver's license and typed my name into a computer. When it came back clean she asked me to sign a piece of paper and told me I was free to go. The State now considered the matter resolved.

"That's it?" I asked.

"That's it," she said, waiting for me to leave.

It was only outside, on the steps of the courthouse, that I had the wherewithal to be ecstatic about this decision. I fought the law and the law gave up. But Cokie was nowhere to be found to share in my good fortune. And yet, we still had to pretend that we were hanging out with her for the benefit of Rachel, who was determined that Lauren and I should have dinner with her hedge-fund-manager boyfriend, Tad.

I had met Tad briefly on the first afternoon. The girls had disappeared into the bedroom, leaving us to talk vaguely about sports and the weather as we waited. We could hear the sound of their strained-but-even voices through the closed door. It was important not to rise to the level of shouting yet. Rachel simply wanted to make a point of saying that it was *fine* that Lauren had already broken their plans for dinner. And Lauren, in turn, just needed to say how much she *appreciated* that Rachel cared enough to try and plan the whole weekend to within an inch of its life.

I did my best just to nod in earnest as Tad listed off old friends who lived and worked in Washington, D.C.—congressional aides, and lobbyists, and policy lawyers—curious to see if I might know any of them.

"Maybe, yeah. Definitely sounds familiar," I said, trying to imagine a world in which I could possibly know a single one of Tad's friends.

I had woken up in the apartment, on Saturday morning, walking on tiptoes, with a desperate desire to keep the floorboards quiet. Lauren smiled at me, from the expensive pull-out couch, announcing at full volume, "Rachel's not here."

"She isn't?"

"No. She spent the night at Tad's."

"Oh." I straightened to my full height again. "Why aren't we sleeping in her room, then?"

Lauren just shook her head.

"C'mon. I wanna do it in Rachel's bed."

"Gross, no. Absolutely not."

"At least let me roll around naked." I was wriggling out of my boxers.

"No!" Lauren laughed, as she leaped up off the couch and caught me at the door. Blocking me with her hips. The whole thing made me a little hard, and I pressed myself into her. But Lauren's body lost its tension immediately. She was looking past me toward the door. It was never going to happen here.

"I'm supposed to go hang out with her this afternoon," she confessed.

"That's okay."

"Yeah, for you, maybe."

"Why are they together?" We were sitting on a bench in the Canal Street station.

"I don't know," Lauren answered seriously. "Because he has money and she has low self-esteem, I guess."

We were talking about Tad and Rachel. I was trying to figure out what it was that Lauren's sister did here in the city, to live the way that she was living. Rachel told me she was working as a "brand consultant," a title she seemed to be inordinately proud and haughty about. It was a thing that sounded made-up to me, or at least highly dubious. But Lauren told me it was real. Rachel had been trying to rebrand her tomboy little sister all weekend.

"How much does she pay to rent that place?" I asked.

"No idea," Lauren answered, not at all convincingly. I smiled at her as she glanced away from me, before turning back, annoyed. "Fine, I'll tell you, but you can't tell anyone else. Rachel is sort of embarrassed about it."

"I swear," I said, putting my hand to my heart.

"Twenty-four-hundred dollars."

"Oh. My. God. *Lauren!*"

"Yeah."

"A *month?*"

"Yeah. It's like all the money she makes."

"Your sister's lost her fucking mind."

Lauren laughed. "I'm serious. Don't tell her I told you."

"God," I said, leaning back against the wall. There was something staggering about this number. It was like being punched in the stomach. It felt invigorating to me.

"Tad basically pays for everything else. That's how she justifies it, at least. I'm pretty sure she's just biding her time until she moves in with him."

"Right, well . . ." I said, with nothing more to say about it.

"Why are they together?" Lauren asked me, after a pause. We were watching two middle-aged lesbians strike a pose of laughter and affection across the tracks.

"They just haven't met the right man yet," I said drolly.

We stood up as the lights of the uptown train appeared along the tile wall, with a whinge of metal and a whoosh of hot air. Lauren was going to the Upper West Side to meet up with her sister. I kissed her goodbye and watched the doors close, as she pressed her palms to the glass like a captive. And then she was gone.

I went up the stairs to cross the tracks to the Brooklyn-bound side, and ended up going all the way to street-level instead. I decided I would rather walk now. I didn't have much of a plan in mind, anyway. Just some friends across the river. I figured I would point myself in the direction of the bridge and see where it took me.

It was admittedly kind of fun to be back here, after so long. New York wasn't like other cities. There was a kind of dirty magic about the place. There were things to see here: celebratory things and things in dispute. New Yorkers liked to make a fuss. They needed a commotion. They reveled in a scene. The thin air was buffeted with the sustained blast of car horns. Horns all day; horns for no reason, it seemed. These were just the general complaints of a nervous city.

There were fire trucks and garbage trucks and men up on lifts. There were cranes that floated over the skyline on invisible swinging pivots. There were Jersey barriers and metal scaffolding, which appeared in the nighttime, and never really went away. There were cavernous holes in the ground; holes being dug at all hours of the night and day. Roads were ripped up, razed, diverted. Traffic was slowed down, shut down, rerouted. Things could change irrevocably in an instant here. Hence the reason for the horns.

The hot garbage smell of summer was gone now, too, replaced with the bowels-y stench of ginkgo trees in bloom.

The air felt cool as it funneled in off the East River. I walked across the Williamsburg Bridge, happy just to watch the people. There were beautiful women everywhere: honest-to-god supermodels with legs running up to your throat, and just the everyday kind, too. There were famous actors walking around, riding the trains like nobodies. And then there were the ones who looked famous—who should've been famous—who weren't famous, and never would be.

The plan was to meet up with Lauren and Cokie at a bar in Williamsburg. I got there first and waited with my beer, watching *Wheel of Fortune* on mute, above the bar. Lauren came in suddenly, flying through the door, alone, and in a state.

"Where's Cokie?" I asked.

"She's not coming."

"I thought you said you were meeting her?"

"I don't wanna talk about it," Lauren said, as she dropped her bag on top of the bar and exhaled loudly.

"What happened?" I asked anyway.

"We got into a fight."

"You and Cokie?"

"No!" Lauren snapped, like I wasn't listening. "Me and Rachel."

"Right. Okay."

"And she said this really fucked-up thing to me."

"What?"

Lauren hesitated and looked away. Looking for the bartender, looking for the stool standing right there in front of her. "Do you have any money? I need a drink."

"Yeah, of course. Sit down." I pulled out the stool and she climbed up on top of it. The bartender brought her a whiskey, and she slowly started to breathe.

"It's so stupid," she said. "It's like she walks around with no cash in her purse, all day, right? And she keeps asking me to pay for things."

"What things?"

"Everything! And she's not even asking. She's just like, *Hey, can you get this?* like it's this expectation. Money for coffee; money for cigarettes. She loses her MetroCard and she makes me swipe her through. And it's not like *I* have any money, either, you know."

"Right," I said, stopping again. "So that was the fight?"

"No. I didn't even wanna *have* that fight. I didn't even really give a shit, you know? But then she started spending all this money on *me*. In this stupid way; charging things and showing off. And, out of nowhere, she tells me that she's gonna take me to some bourgie fucking salon in SoHo so that I can get my hair cut."

"Really?"

"Yeah. And I was like, wow, okay, thanks, but no, I can't. You know? And it's insane. This is like a hundred-and-fifty-dollar haircut."

"You didn't want it?"

"That's not the point. I was already late. And she was

pulling this shit on me on purpose. It's this fucked-up control thing she has. And, seriously, like a hundred other reasons why not. We're right there on the verge of killing each other. I wasn't gonna sit in some salon with her for two more hours."

"Right." I nodded.

"And Rachel says, 'Oh, well, it's easy for you because you don't care about being a woman.'" Lauren's face filled with rage. Trying not to cry.

"She said that to you?"

"Yeah. I mean, like, what the fuck? And I just *went off* on her. Right there on the street, in front of everyone."

"Wow."

"Yeah." Lauren stopped again, taking a breath. "And the worst part of everything is that I really wanted that haircut."

I couldn't help but laugh.

"I'm serious. When am I ever gonna pay a *hundred and fifty dollars* for a haircut? And at this insanely fancy salon. I mean, it's disgusting. And I *really* wanted it." Lauren allowed herself a smile, finally.

"I just needed to talk to Cokie. You know? That's what pissed me off the most. Rachel can't help herself, fine. But Cokie's not allowed to do this to me."

"What is her problem?"

"No idea," Lauren said blankly. She turned to me and put her hand on my leg. "Anyway. That's it. I didn't mean to dump all of this on you, really." She glanced around the bar absently. "Where are your friends?"

I shrugged. "They're at somebody's house in Gowanus, wherever that is."

"Sounds far," Lauren said. "Should we go?"

"No. I don't care. I'm happy just to sit here with you."

Lauren leaned in sweetly and kissed me.

We were on the train again, going over the bridge. Lauren had her head down, smiling as she read a text message. I could see her rushing to reply before we plunged back into the tunnel and out of service.

"Is it Cokie?"

"No . . . Rachel. She's staying at Tad's again tonight."

"Oh," I said. "Good, then, I guess."

If I didn't know Rachel Pinkerton, it was because Lauren didn't want me to know her. And that was fine, too. It didn't matter to me who was right or wrong. All of my sympathy was reserved for Lauren this weekend.

"I think she's feeling bad about this afternoon," Lauren said, looking up at me. "She wants us to meet them for brunch in the morning."

"Brunch?"

"Stop."

"Do we have to call it brunch, though?"

"Call it whatever you want. Tad's paying."

"Oh. Free brunch."

"Exactly." Lauren closed her phone and stuffed it back into her bag. She pressed her head to my shoulder as we trundled off the bridge and down into the tunnel.

———————

"Where is Cokie?"

This was the first thing Rachel asked when we sat down at our table the next day.

"I don't know," Lauren answered, keeping her head down, as she tried to read the menu. But Rachel was insistent.

"Well, is she coming or not?"

"No."

"I told you to invite her."

"She's not returning my calls," Lauren snapped. "Okay?"

"Yeah," Rachel said, in a softer voice then, backing off.

Tad and Rachel pored over their menus, prattling on about carbs. This was a thing that they were suddenly dogmatic about. Lauren had warned me about this. She'd told me how her sister had been shaming her away from carbohydrates the entire weekend. It was the reason that Lauren made a point of asking the waiter about the buckwheat pancakes. She was baiting him into a recommendation.

"Mmm, that sounds delicious. I'll have that," Lauren said, snapping her menu shut.

We sat back with our Bloody Marys and did our best to honor this minor institution called brunch. Brunch was all about the surface of things. Sitting together; eating together; seeing and being seen. Even the name itself was a surface: *brunch*.

I was made to understand that conversation was more or less determined in advance. Poor Tad was doing his best just to keep things moving along this path.

"So did you fly up or take the train?"

"Neither. We took the Dragon Bus," Lauren answered simply. It turned out the cocktails here were stronger than expected.

"Don't say that." Rachel glared at her.

"Why not?"

"Is *Dragon* the name of the bus company?"

"*Dragon* is a slur, Tad."

"No, it's not," Lauren scoffed. "It goes from Chinatown to Chinatown. What else would you call it?"

"The *Chinatown Bus*. Not that that's any better, really." Rachel turned to her boyfriend with a scowl. "It's some kind of illegal bus line."

"It's not illegal," Lauren laughed.

"It's just not really regulated," I said.

"*Oh*, okay. These are the buses that keep catching fire on I-95."

"Right. Exactly."

"I don't understand why anyone would take that bus in the first place," Rachel said, clearly disappointed at the depths to which we had dragged her brunch.

"It's practically free," Lauren said.

"And they show you terrible movies," I added.

"But why do they keep crashing?"

"*Tad*," Rachel said.

"Well, I mean, they're old buses," Lauren conceded.

"And the drivers keep falling asleep at the wheel."

"Right." Lauren nodded. "I read in the newspaper that some of these guys drive back and forth five, six, seven times in a row."

"Jesus," Tad said.

"And they're all wired up on Benzedrine and diet pills, too," I said. "By the middle of the night these dudes are tripping their balls off. I guess it is kind of scary, when you think about it like that."

Lauren laughed. "And they drive *fast*, too. Like, way too fast."

"Can we please talk about something else?" Rachel asked. Tad nodded and cleared his throat, trying to rescue us with another mild non sequitur.

"So what brought you up to New York, then?"

"I had to go to court," I answered simply, fishing the olive out of my drink. Lauren tried to stifle her laugh.

"*Court?*" Rachel asked pointedly.

"Yeah, but not really. I mean, I'd been hoping for something that looked like *Law & Order*, you know? But it was really just some clerk's office in the basement of the building."

"I'm sorry, did I miss something? Why did you have to come to New York City to go to court?"

"Well, it's a long story, but basically I was refusing payment on an outstanding bill for an ambulance ride."

"What was the ambulance for?"

"I mean, that's the long story, Tad. But the point is I've been contesting it with the city for over a year." They looked at me without comprehension.

"Another *Bloody*," Lauren said, catching the waiter's attention.

"Two," I said, raising my hand.

"Why wouldn't you pay for your ambulance?" Rachel

asked critically. "You took it, didn't you? I mean, imagine if we all stopped paying."

"I'd be in favor of that," I said with a shrug. "And, anyway, they threw the whole thing out. The lady ripped it up. I won."

"Oh. Uh, congratulations," Tad said.

"Thanks, Tad," I said, lifting up my empty drink in salute. I clinked his glass as Rachel Pinkerton scowled.

An hour later we were walking up Prince Street, following through on a brand-new plan with Cokie. I steered Lauren around the sidewalk traffic as she held her head down, punching out a text.

"Cokie says to stop at the next block," Lauren said, raising her head to find it. "They're gonna pick us up in a white van."

"A white van?" I asked. "Is that a joke?"

"I dunno. Apparently we're going to somebody's house."

"And Cokie's driving a *white van*?"

"I don't know who's driving it! I'm just telling you where we have to go," Lauren said, betraying her own impatience.

But as we got to the corner, we saw the van pulling off to the curb, right where it was supposed to be. The door opened and we climbed inside. Cokie leaned over the backseat to kiss our cheeks and wrap her arms around us ecstatically. As she sat down again we saw that there was a guy with his arm across her seat-back. He looked uncannily like one of the Strokes. It was the drummer, or the guitar player, or one of the other ones. I was sure of it.

Cokie introduced us to the people in the van, but the names went right past me. We shook her boyfriend's hand,

and pretended not to know who he was. And, all at once, I wanted to start laughing. I was ready to give Cokie a pass for the whole weekend. She was blowing us off in order to make out with a Stroke. How does that even happen? I exchanged a glance with Lauren, but she wouldn't smile back. It was clear she felt that Cokie was still avoiding her somehow. Lauren went silent for the rest of the ride, which was a thing that Cokie couldn't help noticing. Lauren was not relieved to find out she was less important than The Strokes, and she was hiding it very poorly now.

"Where are we going, Cokie?" I asked.

"Uptown," she said. "To Harlem, I guess. Right?"

"Right." This was about as much as our rock-and-roll friend said.

"Yeah. It's just a day party. Somebody's house or something."

"Right," he said again. "Sean's house."

We parked on a leafy street, lined on both sides with ancient brownstones. Lauren and I followed behind the kids from the van, up the steps, and through the unlocked door of a townhouse. *Sean*, it turned out, was Sean Lennon. Lauren laughed and grabbed my arm. Where the fuck were we? We wandered through the rooms in a kind of daze. Outside the house, I had felt some loose allegiance with the people in the van, but they'd all since scattered. And Cokie, too, seemed to keep disappearing on us, flashing in and out of rooms, as we searched for the liquor.

"Why are they together?" I asked Lauren as I handed her a drink.

"How do I know?" she said with a blank face. It was clear she didn't want to play this game anymore. "Do you think we're underdressed?" she asked seriously.

"Not me. I was going to wear this anyway."

Lauren smiled and reached out absently for my hand. Clinging to me in this room full of strangers. "What are we doing here?"

"We were invited."

"Right," Lauren said as she watched Cokie drift through the room one more time. The tension between them was making this whole thing feel that much weirder.

"I'm gonna go find her," she said.

"Okay."

"I just need to talk to her."

"It's fine," I said. "You should go." And she did then.

Ending up at a party like this is supposed to be thrilling, of course. It's supposed to be wild and indelible. But, in reality, it was still daylight outside, and the majority of the guests were remarkably well behaved. More than anything, this house became the setting for Lauren and Cokie to work through this rift in their best-friendship. A quarrel that was never fully articulated to me in the first place. But if I knew nothing else, I knew enough to get out of the way of a thing I didn't understand.

Boredom always follows expectation at a party like this. It's like any other party, really. I walked through the house, taking books off of shelves and entering into vague conversations with strangers. I was doing my best not to stand out, or get kicked out, or otherwise draw attention to myself unnecessarily. No one really cared, though.

I was determined to stall now for as long as I could. I was eager to give Lauren and Cokie the wide berth that they needed. In the end, though, my hand was forced. I walked around a corner and found three long-haired kids blowing coke off the white piano from "Imagine." They looked up at me with their blank and buzzing faces, and I froze.

"Oh," I said, as though I'd just found someone sitting on the toilet and knew I'd have to turn around. "I didn't realize anyone was in here." I couldn't stop myself from cracking up as I hurried away. I was already retelling this story in my head. It just wasn't possible for me to wait any longer now—I had to go and find the girls.

I was relieved to find Lauren and Cokie laughing and passing a cigarette in the backyard. They were sitting out on the garden patio, conspiring like old times. Whatever tension there had been between them was suddenly and mercifully gone.

"Sean Lennon just told me it was good to see me again," I announced with a smile. "What the hell is going on, Cokie?"

"Don't ask me." She shrugged. "The dude I'm making out with is in *The Strokes*. You know that, right?"

"Duh, Cokie," I said pityingly.

"Why didn't you just tell us that?" Lauren asked.

"I don't know . . . It just sort of happened. I didn't even know who he was for like a week." Cokie laughed, clearly enjoying herself. "All I know now is that it's gonna have to stop soon. They're gonna kick me out of school.

"Speaking of which . . ." Cokie beamed at me. "Lauren says you won your court case." I took a small bow and the girls began to clap.

"We should celebrate," Lauren said as she picked up the champagne bottle that was resting at her feet. I dumped my drink into the grass and sat down beside them. Lauren filled our glasses, and we raised them in a toast.

"To law school."

"And the FDNY."

"And the Tomboys," I said simply. Lauren and Cokie smiled then, looking almost touched. We clinked our glasses together and drank.

It was a relief to find the apartment empty when we got back to Rachel's. We were in and out and back down on the street in ten minutes. Hurrying through the sketchy beating heart of Chinatown at eleven thirty at night. We searched for our bus under the eerie sodium glow of streetlights, laughing as we clasped hands and hurried down the damp streets. We sped up instinctively as we passed the silent men standing in the doorways smoking cigarettes. Past the mysterious store-fronts, with their graffitied metal shutters pulled down to shoulder height.

We stowed our bags under the bus and found our seats in

the back, with the engine warming up. The cool smell of diesel clung to the static air. I pulled an ugly-looking can of beer out of the brown paper bag that I'd been carrying for the last half hour. It had a picture of the Chinese zodiac and an unreadable name. The stone-faced old man who sold it to me actually smiled as he pushed it across the counter, which was strangely thrilling.

"Wait," Lauren said, as I scratched my nail under the tab. "I have some pills."

"What pills?"

"I found them in Rachel's medicine cabinet." She smiled wickedly. "I stole them."

"You *stole* them?" I laughed. "What are they?"

"I dunno. I think it's probably MDMA."

"MDMA? Like *ecstasy*?"

Lauren nodded, pulling them out of her pocket to show me. "I just figure maybe we shouldn't drink anymore if we're going to take them."

"I've never done it," I said, feeling strangely prudish.

"Oh, good. I can be your first, then."

I nodded, and we both began to laugh. Growing giddy with the promise of strange drugs. The doors were closing, and I felt the pneumatics under the bus lift. I watched as the television screens flashed on above our heads.

Lauren tapped a small green pill into my open hand. "It's funny that Rachel has these," I said. It was too perfect, really. This image of Lauren's prim older sister squirreling away club drugs in her bathroom tickled me.

"I bet you they're Tad's," Lauren said. "Patrick Serf told

me that Wall Street dudes eat MDMA on the weekends like it's candy."

"Seriously?"

"Yeah. Which hopefully means that it's good."

"I'm not sure I'll know the difference," I said, as I pinched the pill between my fingers, studying it. "You're sure that this is safe, right?"

"As safe as this bus." Lauren handed me her water bottle, and I put the pill onto my tongue. Smiling as I swallowed it.

We held each other's hands as the Dragon Bus crossed through Lower Manhattan, and the city lights, into the semi-darkness of the Holland Tunnel. Lauren laid her head against mine as we watched the twelve-inch screen hanging down from the ceiling. It took me a second to realize what was happening.

"Oh, no," I said. "It's the same movie." They were replaying *The Matrix 2*, this terrible, off-brand copy of the mediocre original.

"No," Lauren said, pointing at the screen. "This is the next one."

"What do you mean? There's a sequel to the sequel?"

"Yeah. This is *The Matrix 3*!"

We couldn't stop laughing over this. It was like a joke being told for our benefit alone. As though the whole reason to keep making these hundred-million-dollar movies was to entertain us on these bus rides. It felt like flares shooting across the screen. It was impossible to watch, almost. Nonnarrative. Nonsensical. And distracting as hell. It had something to do with kung fu and space insects and the FBI, I thought.

"These are the post-9/11 movies we deserve," I said, shaking my head.

"I don't even know what that means," Lauren said with a laugh.

"Just tell me what's going on."

"I don't know. I can't follow it."

"Follow *what*, though? It looks like a screensaver."

"What are you looking at?"

"I'm not even sure. It's like one of those magic eye tricks. I'm mostly trying to concentrate on Neo's face. But it like *doesn't move* when he talks."

"Yeah. I've noticed that, too," Lauren said. "It's awesome."

We stared up at the screen with our eyes doing pinwheels as the drugs coursed through us. The tunnel swallowed up the skyline, leaving us with a ceiling above a ceiling, and a movie that couldn't be stopped. The light got brighter, and the colors bled apart. Our fingers intertwined in the dark as the serotonin dripped. A chemical approximation of love was commingling with the real thing now. The walls and the ceiling of the bus seemed to open up as we were shot out the other side of the Holland Tunnel and into the night.

"Why are they together?" Lauren asked as she stared into the screen.

"Who?"

"Trinity and Neo," she said.

"Because he's *The One*," I answered simply.

Lauren smiled at me with a liquid feeling of empathy. There was contentment with the world and with each other.

Love was a feeling floating just outside our bodies. Lauren's face began to glow as I kissed her in the dark. We smiled into each other's mouths and laughed into each other's eyes as the whole bus disappeared. The gravity released us, and we were suddenly weightless. Somewhere high above New Jersey.

LIFE DURING WARTIME, PART I

We went out looking for the lights and the noise and the crowds. Something, anything, we didn't really know. It was New Year's Eve and we had no idea where to go still. We laughed at ourselves for this, for walking down to the Eiffel Tower, but it was all we had. We knew something would happen at midnight, at least.

We were happy for the crowds: the people waiting and howling up into the night. There were a half-dozen languages floating on this rabble. But after a garbled countdown at midnight . . . nothing. The crowd laughed and jeered and resettled again, before, bang! The Tower was set off in a flash of twinkling LEDs. This rippling, epileptic glimmering set against the murky violet sky. We felt a thrum of human heat rising up off this gathered mass. Strangers cheered and lovers kissed as the Dame de Fer shook and danced for one long minute. And then it stopped.

The sky went dark and starless, and the show was over. People laughed and cursed as they held their ground with nowhere else to go. They called out for some inanimate body to run the Tower again: to let it play, to keep it all running now. No one was ready to go home yet, and the lack of a real planned performance here was making the people restless.

Small fireworks hissed and banged across the infield, under the Tower, as people *oohh*ed and *ahhh*ed halfheartedly. Young men threw bottles into the wrought-iron arches, where they popped and rained down shards of glass. Somebody put a lamp out with a rock this way, and we all cheered lustily. People shouted and scowled as they pushed back and ceded the middle ground to these violent young men, turning the infield into a kind of bullring. Different bands took up the charge, taking turns, showing off and fighting, to the delight of the crowd. Flashing lights and honking sirens followed, and we loved this, too. A phalanx of French policemen, carrying sticks and shields, pushed a path into the bullring as we jeered them. They fanned out, shoulder-to-shoulder, in a wall of black riot gear, determined to break up this loitering now.

But the young men lingered, smirking at the police, unsure what their action was supposed to be. They cursed and taunted *les poulets*, pelting them with rocks and bottles, which were all deflected easily. We watched as the cops began to link their arms in preparation for a bull-run on the middle ground. And with a nod of the head and a puff of air, the hooded policemen came charging forward, swinging their batons at the bare-chested drunks. Thwack! We watched some poor kid get brained with a stick and go scrambling off on hands and knees. But strangers rushed out and dragged him into the crowd before the police could grab hold. And our merry little riot carried on.

The gendarmes pushed and shouted but convinced no one here to leave. There were angry screams and cackled French reproofs, and I was glad to be buried deep inside the crowd with Lauren. Staring out at the restless young men, looking so surreal and romantic in their smokescreens. We passed a bottle of syrupy champagne, and it made the lights and the violence feel buzzy and bright. I clung to Lauren inside this crowd, and I did not want what the bands of young men wanted tonight.

We had been in Paris five days: not sleeping, not eating much. We bought cheap alcohol and expensive desserts. We could have stayed for free at my cousin's apartment in the Latin Quarter. She was back in Buffalo on a school break, and the French woman she lived with said it would be fine. But Lauren didn't want to stay with the older woman, and I didn't want to fight about it. So we went to a hostel instead, where we slept in narrow bunk beds with noisy backpackers. But Lauren didn't like these kids, either. She didn't want to share their wine, or play their card games, or tell them any secrets of any kind.

So we struck out on our own, insulating ourselves this

way. We rode the Métro to its edges and made long treks back through the arrondissements. We crisscrossed the Seine and climbed the old stone staircases. We set out looking for churches and gravestones and museums, just because. The drizzling rain was a constant, and we sloshed around through tremendous puddles in the old city. We drank hot coffee and ate buttery crepes with chocolate in them. This was when Lauren seemed most happy to be in Paris: just walking around the streets, just the two of us.

We would joke about finding jobs, and learning French, and staying on here long-term. I told Lauren I would write something new. Something trashy and obvious that would sell like crazy and make us ugly little piles of money. I liked to get her daydreaming on this fantasy of being rich with me. I told her we could leave Europe and go to Russia or China or Chile, wherever. I told her we could move to Nepal and live on the side of a mountain, if that was what she wanted.

But Lauren would laugh and tell me I was playing the game all wrong. She said it was important to live like the nouveau riche that we were and spend our money with contempt. She wanted to go to Oslo and Tokyo and Rio. She wanted to shop compulsively and get her hair done when she felt a little blue. She wanted to put on costumes and go to operas and polo matches where she could talk shit like a real lady of standing. She said we needed to hire gurus and yogis and tennis pros, and fire them unconditionally. Lauren wanted to live in posh hotels, and pay for expensive cars, and eat small, endangered animals at fancy restaurants.

She was kidding, of course, but I still found it a little startling how much thought she'd already put into this. Sure, I would say: spend it all; whatever you want.

But Lauren still wasn't happy, and I didn't know what to do about it. She'd grown tired of my pap, romantic daydreams, and had begun cursing Paris instead. She was sullen and sour and suddenly worrying about money for real. We had tickets to leave in four days, but Lauren was ready now. She argued that paying to change our flight would cost us less than spending four more days in *this city*.

It was true that there was a kind of forced anti-American strain running through Europe then. Ostensibly it had to do with making a monkey of our president, who had just won reelection. But why wouldn't he win reelection? It was boom times back in the States. The wars were over. George Bush, Jr., had caught Bin Laden and found the WMDs. He'd liberated the proud democratic people of Iraq, and addressed their General Assembly in pitch-perfect Arabic, proclaiming, *Ich bin ein Iraqi!*

Sure, John Kerry probably shouldn't have given him the Skull and Bones handshake on national TV, but Bush was the Decider. He was making things right between the USA and Jesus Christ again. And he was actively upholding his number one campaign promise to investigate steroid use in Major League Baseball, which sent his poll numbers through the roof. Somehow he even found the time to finish reading *My Pet Goat* to those schoolkids down in Florida. So what if he went back on vacation immediately after? There was brush to be cleared at the ranch. We didn't understand what the rest of the world was so uptight about.

That was our grim running joke, at least. But Lauren lost interest in it, and she suddenly seemed to take the whole thing personally. She'd started scowling back at the French people, saying they were brutes and pointy-headed boors. I would laugh and try to pacify her, but the truth was I had no idea what was going on now. She would hit me with these silences that were deafening. Right in the middle of everything, when I was sure that we were having fun. The more insistent I became that she enjoy herself, the more short-tempered she got.

We kept to the outskirts of the Tower and watched the game of cat-and-mouse begin to escalate. The young men were laughing and frothing as we spurred them on. We had no idea what we were watching, really. It was violence without context for us. We rooted for the kids against the cops, but it hardly mattered when the cops won. We were here for the spectacle.

After a while the young men decided on something inspired. Taking a page from the police, they linked themselves together in a human chain. Rival bands made one, out on the infield. And after a crazed beat, somebody shouted go, and they took off running at the cops this way. Screaming their war cries as they crashed into the barricade. A second line followed, launching projectiles, hitting and felling several policemen. The cops took a startled step back before slamming forward and absorbing this rush. The young men were knocked down and caught in space then, as the police surged. They cracked their batons and beat back a manic retreat. Wild-eyed teenagers running backward as they hiked up their blue jeans. But others were not so lucky. Young men were being pinned down everywhere, with a knee or a club, so that their wrists and ankles could be bound up with zip ties. The spectators laughed and booed as these casualties were carried offstage. The battlefield cleared once again.

I don't know why it took so long for the police to fire tear gas into the bullring, but it missed the young men completely. The wind took hold of it invisibly, casting it out into the crowd of onlookers. We could taste the awful tang in our eyes and noses, even out where we were standing. People turned and pushed against us, and the circle broke apart for real then. There was a feeling that the scene could change and darken very quickly in this rush. Everything could topple as we all retreated at once, and there was something sickly thrilling about that.

All day long I'd been walking around with a dirty dream in my head. I'd woken up in the hostel that morning stuck to the sheet. This had not happened to me in ten years, and it paralyzed me. Worse than that, I liked it. This was a dream rendered so real that it jerked me up out of a dead sleep, right at the moment of consummation. It was just a dream, and yet I had ejaculated all over my underwear. I marveled at the strangeness of this as I tried to imagine what a body could look like in that moment of release. It all felt perfectly right, and yet it was humiliating. What had been so warm had turned so cold against my thighs so quickly. I was alone in a narrow bed, in a dark room, in a foreign country, surrounded by strangers. This must be the world's saddest sex scene.

I never told Lauren, either. I didn't think that I could. It all felt squalid and cheap in the daylight, somehow. She and I had not had sex in weeks, because of travel, because of stress. I didn't know why. I was afraid that she would ridicule me now and make me suffer this thing that I'd enjoyed. This simple palpitation of the body that had felt so mysterious and wonderful to me. This warm dream of sex that had made itself into sex. It was something verging on extraordinary, if you let yourself think about it that way.

Of the dream itself, I remembered almost nothing. I had no sense of time or place, or where my body started and the other stopped. As I watched myself in the dream, I kept closing my eyes to watch something else. And yet somewhere I retained this one perfect afterglow of Lauren. Standing up before me with a beautiful tumescent belly. Everything growing from our sex in a kind of hypergestation. Her breasts swollen with milk in a full silhouette of smoldering heat. I remembered the elegant way that she lifted and carried her new body, as it changed underneath her. A perfect grace of posture: healthy and strong. This was the most beautiful thing I had ever seen. I had never been more in love with Lauren Pinkerton, or more afraid.

I stood up out of bed, at a loss for what was real. What if Lauren really carried this child now? What would I be asked to carry? But Lauren was asleep in the bunk above me, looking tired and thin as I stood this close. I could hear the soft wheeze of her breath. I could see her quiet stomach rise and fall, and I reached out to place my hand against her belly. Hardly even touching her, as her eyes flickered and her head turned over on the pillow. I smiled at her, knowing that she wouldn't remember this in the morning. And it all made sense as what it was then: just a wet dream.

I rifled my bag for another pair of boxers, and I changed them right there in the middle of the dark room. And then I got back into bed. Alone.

There was a small girl, about twenty, with dark eyes and dark eyebrows, who found Lauren and me in the rush to clear out from under the Eiffel Tower. She grabbed on to my forearm absently, without looking up.

"Are you all right?" I asked her.

"No. I don't know. I lost my friends," she said in a perfect, mannered English that was impossible to place.

"Where are you from?" I asked, staring into her big doe eyes.

"Israel," she said, pulling her hands up near her neck, as though something might fly out of the periphery and strike her. "I don't know where they went now. I'm sorry. Can I stand here with you? I don't like this."

She huddled in closer as people brushed by.

"Yes, of course," I said. But when I looked up at Lauren she was making a face I couldn't decipher.

"Why don't you just go back to your hotel?" Lauren asked

her, not unfriendly. "Wait for them there. Your friends will show back up."

"I don't know where it is. We haven't checked in. We said to all meet here first."

"What is your name?" I asked, but the girl didn't hear me.

"I'm sorry. I'm scared."

I nodded absently. She was thin and vulnerable, and really very pretty. She had a kind face, and I was drawn to this idea that we could help protect her.

Out on the infield, the cops were losing their sense of humor, and people were getting hurt. More police were arriving, along with ambulances, and even the heartiest stragglers were beginning to turn away. A police van pulled up onto the sidewalk where we stood, and I dropped my champagne bottle to the ground, reflexively. I looked around for the Israeli girl and saw her wading back into the sea of bodies. Lauren took my hand and pulled me out toward the street.

"What about the girl?" I asked.

"Who cares about her," Lauren said. "Let her go."

I nodded blankly, but this wasn't what I wanted. I looked back again, wanting the girl to stay with us. She could come to our hostel, I thought. She could use our computers, or our phones, at least. I still wanted to help her find her friends.

"She'll be fine. She's an adult," Lauren said sourly. "Besides, I don't even know if I believe her."

"What? What does that mean?"

"I mean, for all we know, she was trying to scam us. I would check for your wallet, if I was you. And your passport. I watched her grab your arm."

"*Jesus*, Lauren," I said, pulling my hand away, and we separated in the street.

"What? Is that really so crazy? Why are we even fighting about this? You should have just gone with her, if that's what you wanted."

I stopped walking then, pissed off. Lauren kept going and didn't stop for ten more feet. Finally turning with a deep sigh. "Why are we even here?"

"I don't know. Because we wanted to come! Remember? We planned it out; we bought our tickets; we spent all our fucking money! Shit, Lauren. I'm doing the best I can!"

Lauren suddenly started to cry. All at once, without a buildup, or a warning shot, or anything. This wasn't a thing she did, and it confused me. It seized me up and made me feel awful. And underneath it all I couldn't stop being angry.

"Stop," I said. "Why are you crying?"

"I don't know. I'm sorry," she said, blubbering.

"No, don't be sorry; *I'm sorry.* Just cry, it's fine." But this only made her cry harder, and I pleaded for her to stop all over again. Just for the night, just so we could go to sleep now.

"Please. I'm an asshole, fine. I'll let you yell at me in the morning, all you want, I swear to god." I was begging her for a smile, but she wouldn't. "I just need to go to bed now. I'm just tired. I'm sorry."

For some reason Lauren started to laugh, which only made

her cry harder again. These teary jags that made her whole body shake, and I felt sick.

"What? What did I do?" I asked, exasperated. "Tell me what it is and I'll stop. Tell me and I'll change everything."

"No, nothing, I'm sorry. I don't even know why I'm crying. I'm not even really upset. I just can't stop. I just . . . gimme a second."

This was stress, I knew. You could only hold it down so long before it popped on you. It's just too hard to walk around feeling all shut down. I could feel my whole face begin to open in a smile, a victim of my own stress. I felt so strange and powerless, standing on this drippy Paris street corner, waiting for Lauren to stop crying.

"You should learn how to treat a lady, mate."

I looked up out of my smirk and found this Australian backpacker wearing a short-sleeved soccer jersey with a scarf. He was watching Lauren cry.

"What?" I said in disbelief.

"This gal's in tears here and that's funny to you, eh? Does it make you feel like you're a tough man?"

"Fuuuuuuck you!" I said, laughing in his face.

"What did you say t'me?" he said, puffing up.

"I said, I'll make you cry, you little baby bitch." It felt good to yell. I wanted to wind him up and make him angry. Who the fuck was he? Let him take a swing, if that's where this was going. I couldn't care less.

"Unbelievable, unbelievable," he said to himself, nodding and exhaling, trying to work himself back down. He pointed at me suddenly. "You'll watch your mouth, mate."

"Eat a dick, mate." I was mimicking now, of course.

"You okay, sweetheart? Heh? You know this guy?"

"Will you fuck off already? *Please!* Jesus Christ," Lauren screamed, startling the Aussie. I couldn't help my smile again. I'd never been so proud.

The guy finally quit then, throwing up his hands and cursing us under his breath. "Fucking cunts . . ."

"You're the cunt," Lauren shouted back. "You cunty, cunting, cunter!"

Well, shit. I was in tears, I was laughing so hard. Doubling over, with my hands on my knees. And this dude looked like he was about to explode. Turning back with his jaw in a vise. Balling his fists to let me know that this was real. He would knock me down and teach me a lesson. This would be his pleasure.

But Lauren and I were laughing too hard. We were laughing at him, and laughing at nothing. It was a tired kind of laughter that can't be slowed down or turned off.

"Fucking American assholes! Go home!"

And we roared as he said this to us, laughing. Tears in our eyes, we were laughing so hard. We held each other up in the street, just laughing. Everything would be all right if I could just keep Lauren laughing, I thought. That was all I wanted.

LIFE DURING WARTIME, PART II

"Hey, fuck you!"

Someone yells this at me, or I am yelling it back. It doesn't matter. A man gets out of his car and challenges me to a fight. This has happened. More than you might think, actually. Who are all these men who no one really knows? One thing is certain, the quicker they get out of the car, the less they have to lose. All around. This is what makes these guys so dangerous in the first place. You would have to kill this fucking dude to make him back away from a fight. *Put your hands up, faggot*, you have suddenly become a concubine for this man's violence.

So you fight. Or you don't. Those are your only real choices. It depends on many unnamed complexities in the great natural order of men. Just like the cavemen must've done it. There is the night itself. And probably there is alcohol.

We are fighting with our girlfriends. We hate our jobs and our coworkers. We have grudges with our parents and our siblings. We have friends who have disappointed and abandoned us. And now we have both been out in the city tonight, and this street is not big enough for the two of us. I don't know this guy and he doesn't know me, but we are about to get intimate.

And now, oh, boy, look, his trashy bitch girlfriend is out of the car. Talking with her hands and screeching something awful. This is bad. She is pissed off at him, or at me, I can't tell. She is talking too much, too fast; she doesn't know how to shut the fuck up. And this is getting sort of good now because she has him off his game.

"Get back in the car!" She is saying this to him, or he is saying it to her. And I'm just standing there, smiling that big shit-eating smile that I do. Making that one face.

"Shut the fuck up, bitch!" I am yelling this at her now, or he is yelling it at me. "Shut. The. Fuck. Up. Mother. Fucker." Everyone is yelling, yelling, yelling.

And then there is nothing to be done for it. We have exhausted all good street diplomacy, and there are consequences to be paid out. So, okay, sure: let's fight. It's easy for me to imagine this man closing his eyes and uncoiling his body into a single punch. Smashing me in the face. This flash of white light in his hard, closed hand. I can feel the slap my body will make when it hits the cold concrete ground.

But as he roars forward like this, it's me—I'm the one who inflicts the first blow. The *only* blow. Fighting dirty, because fuck him. Hitting him hard and breaking our every unspoken code, right off the bat. I pull the U-lock from my back pocket and I swing it around wildly, like I'm trying to bury a hammer in his head. Hitting the bone. Connecting with his skull and felling him like a fucking oak tree. I see a spark suspended in the dark, static air where I've hit him. The delayed sound of it: CRACK! I think I've just broken my bike lock. I've never hit *anything* this way before, and it makes me feel a thousand feet tall.

I stare at him, rolling on the ground, holding himself so strangely, and I can't figure out what just happened. How did he end up like that? How did his body get so small? I surprise myself with a laugh that comes rushing out like a tremendous expiration of breath. Confusion. Exaltation. Release.

But now his girlfriend is *screaming*. Really going nuts, with that face that she painted up for a night out on the town, running and melting all over the place. I take a step backward, stunned. Waiting for what comes next. Waiting for her to give me mine now. And when she doesn't, when she just bursts into tears and shrinks down onto her knees, I can't even look at her anymore.

I pick up my bike and I ride it away as fast as I can. I am standing up on the pedals, pumping like crazy. Taking off. Fleeing. Flying through the thin air. But I'm smiling again, too, and I can't even help it. Unscarred; unscathed; untouched. It makes me turn away down a street that I don't know. And then again, down another. And I end up taking this long circuitous route home through the neighborhoods. Because I have to now. Because it's necessary. Because I'm so fucking smart. Because I am scared.

It would be impossible to count up all the times and ways that it has almost come to this. The simmering violence of traffic. There are days when it feels like every single car is about to pull out in front of you. Charging you at a stoplight and leaning on the horn. Accelerating through an intersection and brushing you in a blur. Sometimes traffic sharpens up and closes you into corners. Sometimes it slows down and makes a threat through the window. Laughing it or screaming it. All these angry people pointing their cars and trucks in new and threatening ways. Taking something out on you. There will always be somebody around to pay for everything.

People like to watch you flinch and stop. They like to see your foot come down off the pedal. You are expected to yield or they will show you just how close the whole thing can come. It pisses them off if you don't. It pisses them off if you hold your line and just keep going. And it really pisses them off if you do something strange, like lean into their mirror as you pass them. Because no one is expecting real contact, no one wants to see any real violence—that will be your idea. Unwinding your fist into their door so that it dents, so that it hurts. That can get expensive fast. And now you're the one who is looking back for a reaction. You want to make sure they've seen you shrug it off and ride away smiling. Because this is *your* neighborhood, and there is no way for them to find you here. These traffic circles and one-ways are like a forest to you. No, they don't like your violence, either, which is what has made tonight so inevitable.

————

A car actually hit Lane that winter, which put everyone on edge. Lane, it's worth noting, collected a tidy little sum for his troubles. The settlement paid his medical bills and allowed him to quit working for a year. He was ecstatic, even with the hard new limp. Lauren was convinced that Lane had let the car hit him on purpose, but I didn't want to think about a thing like that.

Believe it or not, I used to get *really* angry. I used to want to fight with people. I used to want to provoke and harass them, the way that I felt harassed. I used to court violence just to see where it would go. But I'd been trying to stop all of that. It just wasn't tenable; it takes too much out of you. It was a zero-sum game that you were never going to win. And how long could this angry-young-man phase go on for, anyway?

Lauren and I would ride our bikes together, and I would watch her suffer something else. Catcalls and drive-bys with different laughs completely. My instinct in these situations was to pull us back. I didn't like for Lauren to escalate a con-frontation with these men. The world is a sick and dangerous place, I would tell her. Be safe, play aloof; don't give them the satisfaction. But Lauren would laugh and tell me I was a hypo-crite. Everyone needs to push back against aggression. There are spaces around our bodies that we need to protect. A car would cut Lauren off at a light and she would fly her middle finger through its open window. Arresting somebody with a scowl. Calling people cunts and cocksuckers, just to see their faces blanch. She would freeze these drivers and take the last word as she rode away through the red light.

These were survival techniques. It didn't matter if someone wanted to laugh and pretend they weren't affected.
Everyone is affected.

But even Lauren couldn't just walk through the world saying
fuck you to everyone. You have to read these situations carefully. You have to give some ground, too. There was an incident, recently, in which she had been driven home in the
front seat of a police car. Coming into the house, after midnight, looking frantic. Lauren woke me out of a dead sleep
to tell me how this cop had harassed her. This disgusting
goateed animal, with fat shoulders and matted hair. He had
turned off the engine in front of the house and insisted on
taking her phone number. One last piece of business before
Lauren was allowed to leave. Sitting there, in the dark of the
police car, under the guise that this was all just standard oper-
ating procedure. After all, this was the man who had stopped
her from getting arrested.

"Arrested for what?" I asked, sitting up in the bed. "I
don't understand what you're saying."

I had left Lauren at a bar, in Northeast D.C., and come
home early. After the bands played, and the room cleared out,
Lauren found herself walking the streets with Tom and Derek.
The same street names, the same architecture, and yet it all
felt completely different here. We almost never came to the
Northeast for anything.

They eventually found themselves circling a derelict theater with boards on the windows. Its crumbling marquee
shooting high above the street. They just wanted to see it,

they said, as they squeezed through a hole in the fence. Stalking around the edges in the dark. Tom went up to one of the doors and pulled the handle, stepping back as it swung open and banged against the wall on the other side. To their astonishment, every light in the building was on and burning brightly. The shock of this alone almost turned them back for good. But the whole space breathed a kind of emptiness that pulled them forward. Holding their breath as they entered each next room. Derek finally broke this tension with a scream meant to announce their arrival completely. And when nothing came back they were ecstatic. Set free to go romping through the ancient hallways at their leisure. Upstairs and downstairs. In and out of offices and dressing rooms. Everything was totally and utterly wrecked; gutted and left in a magical state of disrepair. There weren't even any seats on the main floor of the theater.

But there was, in fact, a stage. And Lauren couldn't help herself from climbing up on it. Leaping and pirhouetting, as she performed to the empty house. Tom and Derek scaled a ladder hidden behind the curtain, and all at once they were standing over top of her. Bounding across a narrow iron catwalk. They called out, with their voices ringing off the ceiling, entreating Lauren to follow.

But as she put her hand up to shield against the glare of the lights, she thought better of this. Sitting down on the stage, she told them she would wait where she was. There was an echo of footfalls, and the whoosh of a metal door, before the room went silent. Lauren looked up at the ceiling again, noticing the frescoes in the arches for the first time. And, in this moment, she thought of me, thinking how excited she would be to bring me back here.

This was the exact moment when the lights cut out.

Lauren froze in the vibrating darkness, listening for something, anything, before calling out for Tom and Derek. Getting no response, she hurried up the seatless aisle, under the dim light of her cell phone. Down a hallway and past a concessions stand. Into the lobby and out the front doors. Lauren suddenly found herself standing below the once-grand marquee, staring at an empty police car. As she gathered herself to run, a second cruiser came barreling in on top of her. She froze as the goateed cop jumped out, demanding to know if she had come from inside the theater. Lauren looked at him blankly and answered no. The man paused before pushing past her and rattling the heavy door himself. Finding it locked, he turned back to Lauren.

"This was the cop who drove you home?" I asked.

"Yes."

"What did he do?"

"Nothing. I don't know. He was actually trying to help me," she said. "It was the other cops who were assholes. They dragged Tom and Derek out of the building and made them lie facedown in the street."

This was criminal mischief in the age of the Patriot Act. This was misdemeanor trespassing in our proud National Seat. Because misdemeanors weren't misdemeanors; they were felonies. And felonies weren't felonies, either; they were veiled acts of terrorism. But all of this was just bluster, too. Intimidation was an instrument of control. And Lauren's cop told her this as he moved her back, away from the scene, urging her to stop cursing the other police.

Technically, Lauren was free to go at this point. But she made the decision to follow Tom and Derek to the police station, to see if she could help. It was there that she found the goateed cop suddenly doting on her. Offering his assistance in any way he could. And, quite frankly, Lauren was in no position to reject a friend. This good-natured authority figure doing everything in his power to get a decision made on bail. But it was no use. Tom and Derek were spending this night in jail.

"Why didn't you call me?" I asked.

"Because you were asleep. It wasn't like I was being arrested. You couldn't have done anything anyway."

I couldn't help but bristle at this. I didn't like hearing these kinds of things after the fact. I wanted to do something *now*. I was ready to hold somebody accountable.

"Why would you get in his car?"

"Because he was a cop. And he'd been there the whole time. I thought he was trying to help me. What did you want me to do, *walk* from Northeast?"

"No," I said. "I'm not saying that."

The Metro stopped running at midnight, and Lauren didn't have the money for a taxi. The cop knew this, and he offered her a ride instead. But something changed. This man who had seemed so anxious and anodyne in the hallways of the police station suddenly took on a kind of looming authority in the front seat of the cruiser. Lauren felt naïve for having flirted with him so unthinkingly. It surprised her the way that he picked up this ball and started running with it. Turning almost brazen as he put his arm behind her on the seat-back. Every gesture seemed to magnify the smallness of this space now. Lauren and the cop were alone in the moving car.

"What happened?" I couldn't seem to stop asking this.

"Nothing happened. He just kept asking questions."

"What questions?"

"It doesn't matter. Everything I told him was a lie. The first thing I said to him, coming out of the theater, was a lie. I was only trying to keep Tom and Derek out of jail. I was just trying to get everybody home."

"But I don't understand. Did he do something to you or not?"

"No. I don't know. It was just the way that he was looking at me. The way that he was talking." She stopped. "He wanted me to keep driving around with him."

"What does that mean?"

"He said his shift was ending and he wanted me to keep him company." I could feel the blood boiling in my head. "He just kept smiling and saying it. Telling me how I could take a shower and change my clothes first, if I wanted. He said that he would come back and pick me up."

"*Fuck*," I said. "Why did you give him your phone number?"

"I didn't do it on purpose. He asked me, and I said it. I don't know . . ."

I could feel my jaw tighten as I tried to slow myself down. "You need to file charges," I said flatly.

"Charges of what?"

"Harassment! Sexual harassment."

Lauren practically laughed in my face. "And who am I supposed to file them with? The police? He *is* the police!"

"That doesn't matter. He can't just do whatever he wants. He needs to be punished," I said. "Tell me his name."

"No."

"Yes!"

"It's not worth it," she said in a hollow voice. "Nothing even happened to me."

"That's not the point."

"Of course it's the point!" she shouted. "I'm not gonna file charges against a cop. I mean, give me a fucking break! Charges of *what*? The fact that he didn't arrest me? Or that he stuck up for Tom and Derek? Or that he offered me a ride home when the subways stopped running? What? Tell me!"

I could feel my face growing hot with shame. I had no idea what I was supposed to say to her. All of my questions came out sounding wrong. Worse, it seemed like Lauren didn't even trust me. "I just want to help," I offered meekly.

"It's fine," she said, softening again. "It's over now anyway." She got up off the bed and walked toward the closet.

"What are you doing?"

"I don't know," she said, sounding empty. "I just want to take a shower and go to bed."

I stood up and wrapped my arms around her. Stopping her and holding her there. I could smell the sweat under her arms. The stress and adrenaline that had been purged tonight. I felt her body tense, before releasing into me. Finally letting go.

———

Most of these men were harmless, most of the time, Lauren said. Everyone can't be a murderer or a monster or a rapist. They just want a reaction from a pretty girl on the street. They just want to steal a smile if they can get away with it. Getting a woman to stop and turn her head, in traffic, is just another cheap thrill. The violence is a good wet laugh.

But I knew these men wanted something else from me. Cops and civilians alike. Everyone was daring me to react. Begging me to flash my anger back at them, in all situations. Because the truth is some people actually walk around looking for a fight, or at least the pretense for one. Knowing this, understanding it, I would always take a step back. Smiling at them with my teeth and riding away, furious.

I didn't strike the man on the street with my U-lock. I never bashed his head open, or left him for dead. All I did was cut him off with my bicycle as he tried to run me over with his car. With the both of us flying into a rage then. Cursing and spitting and puffing ourselves up. "Fuck you, shut up, bitch, motherfucker, fuck you!" I didn't know this man, and he didn't know me, but we were about to get violent.

But as he roared forward like this, it was his girlfriend who caught his arm and pulled him back. Interrupting our moment of brutality before it could begin. She pushed him away and held me off with her curses. And, in this moment, I suddenly stopped. I picked my bike up off the ground and I left them there. Standing up on the pedals and pumping like crazy. Unscarred; unscathed; untouched.

So why did I feel so bad about it now? At home, inside the dark house, I was sweaty with panic. I was thinking of my own inaction on the street. Replaying it in my head, over and over. It made me angry that I had not cracked this man's skull and sent him reeling to the ground. I was holding the U-lock in my hand. I felt like I might need to sit down, or vomit, even. I made a vow to stop drinking, starting right then, forever. Starting tomorrow, maybe. For a whole month, or maybe just a week. And yet I couldn't stop feeling justified in my own instinct for violence. He was the one who'd stopped his car, right? He was the one who had threatened me. This man had it coming.

I paced the kitchen, in the dark, and I went into the bedroom, finally. I woke Lauren up, and I startled her because I was suddenly crying there on the edge of the bed. She put her hands up against my face and neck. *What is it? What's wrong?* she asked me, looking scared. But I just shook my head. I had no idea what was wrong.

CANNIBALS IN LOVE

auren announced that she was chopping off her hair. I laughed and told her she wasn't allowed. Lauren laughed back and then we fought. Everything was a reason to fight these days. We would keep the doors open when we pissed just to keep a fight going. We were like depraved virtuosos this way. This was art.

We'd been living together for almost a year, breathing each other's fumes. Madly in love and madly in hate. It was the claustrophobia that we refused to surrender. Lauren and I always had to be funnier. Smarter. Meaner. We needed a winner and a loser at all times, always. We knew that someone should leave the room; someone should just back down and quit; but no one ever did. I had come to understand that Lauren would eventually kill me in the way that many coupling insects go.

Lauren cut her hair off the next day, too, like I knew she would, and it gave us a reason to fight all over again. Then somewhere, in the lull of insults, I admitted I might actually like her new hair a little. She smiled and nodded, pleased. Letting me kiss her then. Letting us laugh all over again. This was the dance we did. The truth was I was devastated by how beautiful Lauren Pinkerton was with her bratty new haircut.

But the thing we were fighting about now was money. It could always come back to money. Money was this beautiful occult invention that allowed human beings to argue at heroic lengths. Money was loaded with deception and accusation and hurt feelings. It could be personal and emotional and irrational. It was really just too easy, almost.

I was writing and not working again. I told Lauren I had abandoned the idea of ever making any real money, years ago. This drove her crazy and she accused me of lying. She accused me of ego and ambition and sloth. Lauren was constantly worried about money. It was one of the few things she was genuinely neurotic about. She mismanaged her bills and debts. She accumulated late fees and penalties. She hedged credit cards against each other and overdrafted. And she despised me for cobbling together work from friends, and living hand-to-mouth the way I did. Something was always falling into my lap. I never missed a bill, ever.

But I couldn't help smiling now, because I'd just asked to borrow five dollars.

"What do you want it for?" she asked, sitting up.

"What does it matter what it's for? I just want it."

"Unh-uh, no. Sorry."

"Okay, I want a beer from the bodega. Is that all right with you?"

"Gosh, I don't think I'm interested in making an investment in that sort of thing," Lauren said, enjoying this.

"Hey. If you give me a little smile, sweetie pie, maybe I'll even come back with a chocolate bar for you."

"Oh, yeah? You're gonna buy me a treat with my own money? You promise?"

"Yeah, sure thing. I just need the cash first." I held my palm out to her.

"Your drinking's getting a little out of hand lately, don't you think? I mean, what time is it right now?"

"Don't try to domesticate me, woman," I said, shifting characters. "I'm a man, and a man drinks ice-cold beer. I'm not asking for your permission."

"Ho-oh, but you don't have any money. So you *must* be asking for permission."

I sat down in the armchair with a heavy sigh, losing interest in this. "Maybe I'm just stressed out and I want a beer," I said without affect.

Lauren laughed. "What stress do you have? You don't even work!" She was glowing now, taunting me. I'd put her into this position, of course; I'd done it to myself.

"You know what, never mind. I don't want your money if you're going to be such a bitch about it." This amused Lauren.

"Aw, c'mon. Can't I beg you to take it from me? Please."

I just sat there, not looking at her. This is the point where a normal person gives up and cuts his losses. It's not worth going on and on this way about trivial things. It's not healthy. It doesn't do anyone any good. But I didn't care about any of that.

"You know what? You're going to make some man a great ex-wife someday," I said, hardly able to suppress my delight.

"Yeah, someone with some fucking *money*!" she shot back, but I knew I'd already stung her. It was very much on purpose. More than I wanted her five dollars, more than I wanted a beer, I wanted Lauren to pay attention to me. And I had her up on her feet now.

"And fuck you for saying that, also. You think you understand certain things, but you don't know anything about anything." Lauren was the product of divorce, and this was another rare sensitivity. And now we were really fighting, too, which was good.

"Why are you even asking me for money anyway? Can't you just go into your trust fund, you little bed-wetter?"

"Ha! My trust fund! Oh, right," I said, starting to have fun. "I wish."

"Don't deny it. You're not fooling anyone. Nobody can live as poor as you live. I'm not even entirely sure how you take care of yourself."

"Well, I'm either secretly rich or egregiously poor. Make up your mind."

"You're both," she said dismissively. We held our faces straight, like a staring contest. To laugh first was to lose. This was the game. We were always returning to this sick, shared laughter.

"I could keep a job, if all I wanted was to keep a job," I told her maddeningly.

"Liar."

"What I want," I went on, smiling, "is for somebody to pay me for being *clever*."

Lauren didn't even have to say anything. The scorn was written all over her face.

"A job like that would suit me just fine, I think."

"Just admit that there's a secret trust fund right now, and I won't ever ask you anything about it again. I swear to god."

"You're paranoid. I'm just better with money than you are."

"You know what?" Lauren said, with a new smile coming over her. "Never mind. I think I just figured out your secret. You're a fucking spy!"

"A *spy*!" I guffawed. "Oh, man. Oh, man." This was really good. I couldn't believe she'd found a way to say that to me with a straight face. Lauren was trying desperately not to laugh, too. It was important to stay angry. She was still pissed at me for calling her an ex-wife.

"Admit it," she said. "What are you doing in Washington, D.C., anyway? Who comes here to study *literature*? It's not even a good cover."

"Okay," I said. "You caught me. Which side do you think I'm on? Hmm? What's my agency?"

"Shut up," she said, breaking down a little.

"It's the CIA, all right? This is serious, though, Lauren," I said with gravity. "You need to listen to me very carefully now because someday you might need this information. It might just save your life . . ."

"Shut up!"

"*The red rooster crows at dawn.* Remember that phrase, okay? I'm serious. *The Indian never crosses the same stream twice.*" I was almost in tears, cracking myself up with this. "Are you listening? Don't be crazy! Write this down!"

"Shut up! Just stop! Shut! Up!" Lauren was screaming to drown me out.

But as I lay there, rolling on the floor, I could see that she was laughing, too. She couldn't help herself then, letting it all go. Lauren sat down on the floor with me and we laughed, and the laughter was a reset. This was what we did for fun.

But after a while, she went back to the couch and started flipping through her magazines again, making a show of ignoring me.

"Well . . ." I said.

"I'm getting tired of talking to you now. Can we just have some quiet?"

"Oh, right, I'm sorry," I said. "Would you rather have us talk about celebrity gossip or the way that jeans fit?"

Lauren looked up mischievously. "Yes. Could we?"

"No, we can't," I said with crossed arms.

Lauren shrugged and dropped back into her glossy pages. Lately she had become a prodigious reader of these celebrity tabloid shitrags. I knew that she was smarter than me, too, which was why it galled me so much that this was the only reading that she did anymore. Lauren refused to confirm the fact that she had a photographic memory, but I knew that it was true. I envied her for this, and felt like she was wasting it working as a secretary. I told her she was depressed, but really I was talking about the both of us.

Lauren flipped the pages sullenly, and I could feel her losing interest in fighting with me.

"Why don't you love me?" I asked her out of nowhere.

These were always our most tedious conversations. I knew at my worst that I was needy. Lauren told me this. That was why it was necessary to be cruel sometimes. It was about trust. It all came down to some unbearable need to be loved. I was terrified of the idea that Lauren could not or would not love me back. Worse yet, she liked to say that she didn't even believe in romantic love. She said that she couldn't.

"I want to know," I said. "It's a real question."

I was calm and earnest, which was just another way to push her buttons. We needed to shock and undermine each other, always. We needed the tension and the drama of it, because in a sick way it worked. Part of the charm of our relationship was the fact that we engaged these parts of each other's personalities that no one wanted to touch. The ugly parts. The mean, unhappy, quarrelsome parts. The parts that are small and petty and drive normal people away. They were important to us.

Lauren stood up suddenly and put the magazine down. "Do you think you're losing your hair?" she asked with her blankest face.

"What?" Every nerve in my scalp tightened reflexively.

"It's not a big deal to me. I just think we should be able to talk about it like adults, if you are." She was trying not to smile.

"I'm not," I couldn't help myself from saying. And I wasn't. But it was too late then, I had already taken the hook. Lauren would do this sometimes. Asking me about my weight or my drinking or my libido. Asking me if I thought the ways in which I behaved were somehow irregular or abnormal, maybe.

"I'm just saying that you've been acting different," she said.

"Different?"

"Yeah. Ever since your hair started falling out, you've been acting weird."

"Ha-ha-ha," I said. "That's very funny."

"Hey, don't get defensive. Either you're losing your hair or you're not. It's not a big deal to me." Long pause. "But if you *are*, I just think you should be able to talk about it with me. Your girlfriend."

Lauren didn't even bother masking her smirk then. I glared at her, hating her.

"Don't look at me," she said with feigned innocence. "Look in a mirror."

"Why won't you marry me?" I asked suddenly.

"You're crazy."

"Not now. Marry me in ten years."

"Oh. I think I'm busy then."

"Marry me in ten years when you're fat and unhappy, and your youth and your looks are all used up," I went on, smiling. "Say that you'll marry me then."

"I think I'm washing my hair that night," Lauren deadpanned.

I stood there, waiting for her to crack. I was so pathetic and vulnerable. This, too, was part of the game. I would ask her to look at me, to love me, to stop all of this now and let me love her back. I smiled because I knew how uncomfortable this could make her. She found the whole act sentimental and sappy in all the worst ways. She said it was moronic to talk about our lives as a kind of love story. She said it bored the shit out of her. And yet we were both laughing again, too.

"You're killing me, Zelda," I said.

"You deserve it, though. You're so boring. God. How can anyone who calls himself a writer be so bo-ring?"

"No. I guess we should all become secretaries."

"Oh, you'd never make it as a secretary. It's a lot of hard work. You have to show up *every* day."

"Yeah, you're a fucking working-class hero," I said. But I was suddenly thinking about my hairline again. Involuntarily. I wanted to go look in the mirror. Just quick, just to see. Was it possible that I'd missed the fact that I was going bald?

"Hey," Lauren said, putting up her hands. "All I'm saying is that you should have a plan for when this *writing thing* doesn't work out. Is that so crazy? Are we not allowed to talk about that?" She was just barely smiling, but not. We were right on the verge of some eruption here.

"You're an elitist, you know that?" I said coolly.

"You are."

I laughed with contempt, wanting not to be vulnerable anymore. But all at once I felt unbearably sad. Sad about us. Something had changed. We were fighting too much these days; everything was too raw. These fights used to be shorter. Cleaner. Funnier.

"What's going on now? Are you going to cry?" she asked,

beaming at me. Lauren was the only girl who had ever made me cry. And despite the fact that I'd made her cry a half-dozen times at least, she held it over me, bringing it up on these occasions.

"Maybe." I sighed. "I don't know."

Lauren's face changed. "Come sit down next to me," she said, pushing her magazines onto the floor. "You know I don't mean it. It would kill me if you started crying right now."

I could almost believe her, too. But I was tired. I just stood there, refusing to sit, refusing to cry. "Will you just give me the five fucking dollars already so I can buy myself a beer? *Please?* You know I have a check coming on Monday."

"When I was a girl," Lauren began cryptically, "I always imagined I would have a boyfriend who was a doctor or an architect. And he would bring me flowers, and take me out on dates to fancy restaurants."

"Yeah," I said unkindly. "And I feel sad for you for everything you'll have to do to earn your money, honey."

"Exactly. I need a man with a big cock that eats big, bloody steaks."

"I hope you choke on it."

Lauren laughed with her angry face crumbling. "Choke on what?"

"All of it," I said, and we were both laughing again, in spite of ourselves. But this was exhausting. This was not really fun.

"Aw," she said, looking sincere. "Why are you always doing this to yourself? Working yourself up like this. You wouldn't be able to take care of me anyway. You can hardly take care of yourself."

"And who's going to take care of you when you're not so pretty, huh? When you have big matronly arms and dry, brittle hair. Who's gonna love you then, huh?"

"You will," she said simply.

"Goddamn right I will."

The only thing I wanted in the whole world was to believe in that, to agree with Lauren now. But I resented my own flailing desperation. I couldn't be sure that I believed in any of this romantic pap any more than Lauren did. Maybe she was right about love. Maybe we really were all doomed.

Just looking at each other was enough to bring on another sick smile, though.

"Come down to the store with me," I said. "I'll let you pick everything out. I'll let you make a big show of paying for it and emasculating me in front of the old guy who works there."

Lauren looked at me strangely, not saying anything, and I felt myself sigh. I didn't even care about the beer anymore.

"What if I let you slap me in the face for five dollars?"

"What?" she said, slightly startled.

"You heard me."

"Hard?"

"Yeah, as hard as you want," I said, suddenly impatient. "As hard as a *girl* can do it, anyway." These were fighting words, and I could tell that she really wanted to slug me. "Yes or no? It's a onetime offer."

With that, Lauren was up on her feet, ready to smack me.

"Whoa, whoa, whoa. Pay up," I said, taking a step back.

Lauren stopped and crossed the room, looking for her

purse, as I followed behind her, taunting. Rushing her. I was making her angry all over again.

"Jesus. Shut up," she said in a small fluster. But when she was done digging out balled-up dollar bills she was one short. "Shit, shit!"

And then I really laughed. This was as good as any outcome I could have wanted.

"Look," she said seriously. "I can write you a check for ten bucks, right now."

"Don't insult me," I said. "The price is five. Cash money. One time only." I was gloating and claiming victory now. I was getting pedantic.

"This one scenario is a microcosm of all your larger problems with money, Lauren." I laughed, growing giddy. "You see some shiny thing that you just have to have, and then—"

WHACK!

Lauren spun around and slapped me good. Uninvited and off guard, and pretty fucking hard. It stunned me a little, and I turned away defensively.

"Oww, Jesus. *What the fuck*, Lauren?" I said sourly.

I stretched my jaw and touched my hand to my cheek where it stung. Lauren's mouth was hanging open like a guilty little kid.

"Oh. God. I'm sorry," she said in a small fit of laughter. "I don't know what came over me. That felt incredible. Let me see your face."

"No," I said, turning away again, annoyed. "What a dirty cheap shot that was."

"Aw," she said, finally feeling bad. "I didn't mean it."

Lauren's face turned genuinely sweet then, and I let her come a little closer. I dropped my hand and measured this. She touched my cheek softly and shook her head. "Look what you made me do."

"Shut up," I said, not wanting to give her the satisfaction of a laugh.

"You just make me so *mad* sometimes," she said, growing fond of this voice. "I only hit you because I love you, baby. You know that."

"Shut up," I said, grabbing her arms. We laughed with our faces coming closer, and I couldn't stay mad because this was all too much like sex. And Lauren could feel it, too, as I pressed my hard-on into her hip and she cooed something soft in my ear. She was sweet and careful with me. She kissed my cheek and told me how sorry she was. And all the barriers fell away then. We kissed each other, slow and tender, before our mouths began to open. Lauren grabbed on to my belt and I pulled at her sweater. And when I picked her up to carry her into the bedroom, she squealed happily.

This was how it always ended when we set off fighting to kill. We were tearing off our clothes and fucking loudly on the bed now. Lovers. Lauren would let the sound build out of her. Unh-unh-unh. This thing that she couldn't stop, erupting into orgasm. Unh-unh-unh! Her body generating a kind of scorching radiant heat under mine. We came alive in this way that made me feel insane. We lost our bodies in the bed. There was no self, and there was no other. We fell into the space between, letting it close and disappear around us.

Good sex was always very primal. This tingle across the back, climbing the base of the spine, as we started to sweat and stink. The smell of us mixing together violently. The richest, most pungent, skunky smells of sex. The squish of our bodies catching and slipping together. I could feel all the blood moving in me at once. My legs were taut like electric lines. My toes curled. Nerves fired and muscles flexed, everything on loan from the brain. You could shoot me in the head in this moment and I wouldn't die. We had become one giant, physical beating heart. Overfilled with a dangerous, vibrating energy.

Sex was galvanizing after a fight. It was indestructible. Incorruptible. In this moment it was impossible for us to destroy each other any more. I pressed my forehead into Lauren's as I rocked between her legs, and I begged her to forgive me. I asked her to love me forever. She caught her breath and told me yes. I couldn't help but make her say it again. Yes, yes, yes.

"Don't ever leave me," I said as I buried my face into her body.

"No," she said. "Never, never, never."

THE WEDDING

The streets were filled with teenagers and other sociopaths. I was staring out the window, astonished by this. The mall was boarded up. The movie theater was shut down. The bookstore and the record store were both gone, too. I had been back in Lockport for less than twenty-four hours, and I had begun to catalog the things I was seeing. Everything was exactly the same, only completely different.

"I used to have a girlfriend who pierced ears in that mall," I said wistfully.

"What?" my brother asked.

"Where did everything go? What are you supposed to do if you live here?"

"There was never anything to do to begin with."

"Yeah. But now it's so much worse."

My brother, Peter, and I were driving down Transit, having just picked up our tuxedos for Kerry's wedding. We were on our way to Cullen's house, so that I could get a haircut. Kerry had warned me to deal with this before I got there, and she was less than pleased to see that I hadn't. But the haircut was nothing. The thing she was furious about was the fact that I'd had the audacity to show up in Lockport without my date. Kerry all but accused me of trying to sabotage the wedding.

Lauren was supposed to come with me, of course. This was never not the plan. I had wanted her to come; she was excited to be here. She bought a dress and a necklace and a plane ticket. And then, all at once, everything went to shit again. I don't really know how this happens. I told her not to come, or she was refusing to go. It didn't really matter. The story ends the same both ways.

Peter was dateless, too, of course, which wasn't helping anyone. The seating arrangements were wrecked. The symmetry was gone. Two dateless brothers meant that everything was fucked. There was no arguing with Kerry on this point. There was no sense in explaining how two dateless brothers had its own kind of symmetry. Peter and I had agreed to be in the wedding months ago, though we were never really given a choice. Our new brother-in-law, Greg, didn't have much say in the matter, either. This was about what Kerry wanted. This was about the pictures and the cake. This weekend was her weekend, and everyone knew better than to cross her.

"Where is Lauren?"

People had been asking me this question for days. The

truth was I didn't really know. Lauren and I had a fight. It was several fights, really. She got angry and left the apartment. It was only after that that she told me she wasn't coming. Or maybe I had already told her I didn't want her there. Who could remember if it happened one way and not the other? It was just one more fight.

"Where is Lauren?"

They all kept asking this. It was not a thing I cared to discuss with them, frankly. I had thought I was making myself reasonably clear on this, but they all kept asking anyway. So I started telling them things, making it up. Dissembling on Lauren's behalf. I was amused to find myself presenting her to the world as some kind of do-gooder.

"She's building relief housing," I offered soberly.

"Relief housing for what?" they'd ask.

"The hurricane," I'd say blankly.

"Oh, wow. In New Orleans. Wow."

But I exploited other tragedies, as well. I was just as happy to mention the tsunami. Or the earthquake. Or the typhoon. I spoke vaguely of famines and droughts and civil wars. There was always something terrible happening somewhere. A whole wide world of generalized misery. People were left stranded, and abandoned, and in need of intervention, all across the globe. In my version it was Lauren who was there to help them. She was the one who comforted and protected all these good people. She was the person who was easing their pain. She was the *only* one.

This was hilarious to me, of course. But how could anyone here possibly get my joke? It didn't matter anyway. I was sure that most of them weren't even listening. Lauren's was just another name—like Greg's—that they'd memorized in preparation for this happy event. I could count on two hands the number of people, in any given room, who had actually met Lauren Pinkerton or had any idea what she looked like.

"Where is Lauren?" they all asked eagerly.

"She's around here somewhere," I told them with a smile.

"Oh, good. I feel like I'm the last one to meet her."

I was sitting bare-chested, in a wooden kitchen chair at Cullen's house, as he stood over me with his clippers. "Thanks for doing this," I said.

"Of course," he answered, as he tilted my head to the side. There was a lit cigarette dangling off his lip. "I barely even use these things anymore."

"Uh-huh."

"I mostly basically use them for one thing."

"Right," I said.

"To get rid of excess hair."

"Uh-huh," I said, not flinching.

"To clean things up downstairs."

I nodded.

"To shave my balls," Cullen said, grinning flatly.

"Yeah, I know. I get it. Thanks, Cullen."

"You're very welcome."

Cullen flicked the switch and the clippers went blurry in his hand. My head tingled as he touched the razor to my scalp and started carving out swaths. The hair came off in peels, fluttering down over my shoulders and onto the floor.

My brother was sitting silently in the corner, petting a fuzzy orange calico. This was Cullen's cat. We were in Cullen's kitchen. Cullen owned this whole house, actually. A three-bedroom foursquare, down by Outwater Park. "Sixty-eight grand," he told me proudly, as we took the tour of the stark and empty domicile. Cullen had been working for the last three years as a certified public accountant, making a decent amount of money, clearly. *Dullsville, USA*, Louis called it.

Louis had his own job working as a straight-up repo man. *Collections*, he insisted on calling it. I was tickled by the idea of Louis driving around the city, knocking on doors, repossessing property. Gas grills and Sub-Zero refrigerators and flat-screen TVs. Anything could be put up for collateral if both parties agreed on its value. Once a debtor went into default, it was Louis's job to get their attention. After a period of civility, there was a period of threat. And then there's just a knock at the door. By that time, your brand-new boat has been hitched to the back of a truck. True repossession comes without warning, in the end.

The whole thing fascinated me and I pressed Louis for details. I wanted him to tell me stories. I was looking for something I could write about, something I could steal. This was the stuff of fiction, I was sure of it. But Louis failed to see the beauty in how he spent his days. It was just a job to him. If you couldn't pay for your shit, it had to be taken away. Besides, Cullen was the one who told me that Louis spent most days sitting at a desk, talking on a telephone. He wasn't wrong about the absence of drama.

No one in Lockport, it seemed to me, had anything at all to say about the thing they did for a living. It was just work. It never really changed, because, how could it? I mean, can you actually imagine if Cullen went through the blow-by-blow of being a certified public accountant for you? Hour-by-tedious-hour. Day-by-drudging-day. Who could even tell the weeks apart after the first one? And why would you ever need to?

Peter and I went straight from Cullen's house to the rehearsal dinner at the Lockport Town & Country Club. Someone handed me a drink and I found myself walking a gauntlet of aunts, and great-aunts, and second cousins. These plump and smiling women, with their tinted hair, and lipstick on their teeth. They beamed at me as they stood there and stirred their martinis with polished fingers.

"What about law school?" my aunt asked me, apropos of nothing.

"Excuse me?"

"Have you ever thought about going to law school?"

"Oh. Sure," I lied.

"Good," she said, seeming relieved.

"You're next, then, right?" another one chimed in.

"Next what?"

"To marry!" she cried.

"I'm only twenty-five years old," I said, stricken by the thought. They all laughed at this, as though I'd just told a joke.

I caught my reflection in the window, looking down over the eighteenth green. I was surprised to find myself looking like a stranger. I ran my hands over my shaved head, feeling it prickle. Why had I done this to myself? I wondered. It felt like it was supposed to matter, but it didn't. Hardly anyone seemed to notice, as they repeated the mantra of the weekend.

"Where is Lauren?"

"She's around here somewhere," I kept on saying now.

"Oh, good," they all said. "We can't wait to meet her."

But as the previous day's stories of Lauren Pinkerton's relief work—in New Orleans and around the globe—began to circulate, I found people grabbing on to my elbow to repeat them back to me in earnest. This little game of telephone had taken on a life of its own. They were suddenly asking me to account for Lauren's work in places I'd never heard of. Disasters I hadn't thought to invent.

"She must be helping children, then, right?"

"Sometimes, yes," I said, as I took a carrot off a silver tray. "She mostly deals with lepers, though. That's her specialty."

I was not trying to be an asshole, I swear. This was an act of self-preservation for me. What other choice did I have? I didn't know the answer to the question they were asking me. *Where is Lauren Pinkerton?* It simply was not possible for me to open up this vein on this weekend. What was to stop me from bleeding out all over the floor? I wouldn't know how to stop talking if I let myself start now.

Not that anyone wanted to have that conversation with me anyway. This was a party, and we were here to celebrate. All they needed was a story. So I propped Lauren up for them. I made her go down easy with a spoonful of sugar. And then

I changed the subject. No one was listening anyway, I thought. We were all just making conversation.

"Where is Lauren?" they asked again.

"She didn't want to come," I said finally.

"Oh," they said, letting it hang there.

"Yeah."

The mall and the movie theater were closed. The bookstore was boarded up. The record store was shut down. But the bowling alley was alive and well. Peter and I slipped out early to go meet Louis and Cullen there.

We waited for fifteen minutes at the rental counter before wandering in and spotting them, at the scorer's table, smoking cigarettes. Forget the fact that New York State had had a smoking ban in place for almost two and a half years. It simply was not enforced here. Worse than that, though, was the fact that my friends had brought their own balls and shoes. There was no punch line to all of this. Louis and Cullen were not being ironic. They were really here to bowl.

I wasn't sure how to feel about any of this until Louis stepped up and rolled the first ball of the night. A dead-center smash. "Steeeeee-rike one!" Louis announced, with his arm cocked maniacally like a baseball umpire.

"Good, great, terrific," Cullen said indifferently. And, all at once, I was happy I was here. Watching Louis and Cullen perform bowling-as-psychodrama was about as good as it got for a Friday night in Lockport. I knew enough to know that none of this was for my benefit, either. This was really just the way they acted.

Bowling itself had almost everything to do with drinking for me. I spent the first pitcher of beer just trying to work out the kinks. It was hard enough to find a ball where your fingers felt natural in the holes. Then there was the question of weight. Each next turn saw me picking out a new board on the floor to aim at. Every shot was its own surprise. The rhythm, however, was familiar. I was calling up ancient muscle memories of birthday parties, and Cub Scout meets, and snowbound Saturdays gone by. And, when all else failed, I was just whipping the damn thing as hard as I could.

Everyone's game seemed to peak around the second pitcher of beer. This was the golden rule of bowling. The nerves had settled out and we were filled with the strange sensation that we knew what we were doing here. I forgot all about the mechanics and just started grooving the ball. When it was right, it was a thing you could feel in your fingertips. I knew each next strike the moment it left my hand. Crrrrrrrsssssshhh!

By the third game, Peter and I were done, though. We were useless. I was leaving pins all over the floor in inconceivable combinations. I would smile and slide the ball into the gutter, so that I could sit back down. "Mark it zero," I'd announce blithely.

But Louis and Cullen were a different breed completely. Athletes. The alcohol didn't seem to faze them. They were up there bending shots left and right, on command, well into their third pitcher of beer. I marveled, as the ball seemed to stop—spinning on its axis for a beat—before snapping forward into the pins like a rubber band. Bang! This was the stuff of magic tricks.

If anything, the beer just made them mouthier. Bowling was a game of intimidation the way that my friends played it. It was a head game; it was a war game. But there was a limit to how much they could actually talk about bowling. There was a threshold, even, in their energy for going after each other. And soon enough they started in on me. Or, more to the point, they wanted to talk about Kerry. They were baffled by the fact that they had not been invited to my sister's wedding. They kept bringing it up throughout the night, playing scorned.

I just laughed and told them I had nothing to do with it. I told them I didn't particularly want to go myself, but they didn't care. Their feelings were hurt, they said. It didn't matter that Kerry hated their guts, and had never liked them, going all the way back to grade school. Even now, as an adult, she seemed to go out of her way to be rude and unwelcoming toward them. They loved this about her, of course. Louis and Cullen felt like part of the family. They honestly thought that they deserved to be there.

But this was just another crude end-around for them to keep talking about Kerry. Objectifying my poor sister. They wanted to know why we had not thought to bring Kerry out with us on her "last night of freedom." This is what they kept calling it.

Peter glowered as he split the uprights on his spare. My brother had lost all interest in keeping the company of Louis and Cullen, and his bowling was suffering.

"Skip the rest of my turns," Peter said flatly, as he gathered up our pitchers and disappeared into the bar. *Perfect*, I thought, *there goes my designated driver*.

Cullen was in the middle of a confession now, anyway. This secret that he and Kerry had kept for the better part of a decade.

"Bullshit!" Louis said loudly.

"I swear to god," Cullen answered. "When I was sixteen."

"You fucked her?"

"I didn't say I fucked her. I said she gave me a blow job."

"Where?"

"On my dick." Cullen gestured down to his crotch.

"Where on the *earth*, retard?"

"In the attic of Mikey's house." Cullen shrugged and took his turn.

"Bullshit," Louis said again, though he was grinning wildly now. I was pretty sure that he was telling us the truth.

Cullen turned around to face me, looking suddenly concerned. "She's not wearing white, is she?"

Louis practically fell off his chair, he was laughing so hard. "Fuck off," I said, trying not to smile, as I sent another gutter ball hobbling off the dance floor.

Cullen had recently begun to let go of some of these secrets. He had a lot of them, too. For years Cullen didn't have to tell us anything. He didn't need to brag or make things up. There was nothing to be gained in that—he was getting laid like crazy. Cullen knew better than anyone not to go around spoiling young girls' reputations. All that could come of that was drama. Besides, it's a lot harder to fuck two best friends, at the same time, if they find out you've been talking about it. Or sisters, even. Sisters don't want to have sex with the same guy. Although some do, of course. And Cullen was just as happy to keep those secrets as well.

Sadly, the time in Cullen's life for coyness had already passed. At twenty-five years old, he was entering, irrefutably, into a period of physical decline. Frankly, I found the whole thing startling. Cullen had always been our golden boy. At sixteen he was prettier than the girls. That's what made it so strange to see his skin go sallow and his hair fall out. He was paunchy and blotchy in ways I'd never noticed before. Cullen's youth and vitality were fleeing him now. Unfortunately, you don't get to skate on your reputation as a high school lady-killer when it comes to adult fucking.

Ironically, it was Louis who seemed to be coming into his own at the exact same moment. He was having more sex now than he'd ever had in his entire life. It made him jubilant to find himself coming up at the very moment that Cullen was falling down.

"Shut up and bowl," Cullen said, trying to head him off.

But Louis found it very hard to just shut up. Unlike Cullen, he was ready to talk about his exploits at the drop of a hat. He was telling us now about some girl who had given him mono.

"It's because of the way she kisses," Louis said.

"How does she kiss?" I asked innocently.

"Like a whore, I'm guessing," Cullen said, losing patience.

"Well, I mean, she's got this really long tongue, right?" Cullen made an audible sound of disgust. "And as soon as she sticks it in my mouth, it's practically down my throat. It's like she can't even help herself."

Louis leered at Cullen as he licked his lips and wiped the sweat off his brow, before finally taking his turn. Another dead-center strike.

Cullen stood up hastily and rushed his own shot. A terrible-looking ball that was lucky to clip two pins. He whipped back around on Louis. "That's not how you get mono, either, you know. *Kissing?* That's just an old wives' tale."

"It's called the *kissing disease,* Cullen," Louis said pedantically. "I'm surprised you didn't know that."

"You don't have mono!"

"How do you know?"

"Because you're too old."

"Says who?"

"Says facts. Mono is for fourteen-year-old girls."

Louis smiled. "She might actually *be* a teenager, now that—"

"Be serious!"

"Adults get mono all the time. Tell him, Mike." Louis turned to me, wanting me to settle this.

"I dunno. It would be sort of unusual, I think."

"Great. So you're both fucking doctors now." Louis frowned. "Fantastic."

"You're just out of shape, dude," Cullen said, patting him on the shoulder. "You're lazy. You have poor moral character. You don't need a doctor to tell you that."

"Shut up and bowl," Louis said.

Cullen smiled and cleaned up his spare, which had been sitting there yawning at us. He turned back around, slapping his hands clean. "Spic-and-span," he said.

We were at the end of our final game now. Long after Peter had returned with the extra pitchers of Genny. Cullen had a comfortable lead, and he wanted Louis to appreciate this. Louis would need three strikes in the tenth frame to win.

"Uh-oh," Cullen said, working through the math. "Looks like you need a clean sweep, little guy."

"Yeah, yeah, yeah," Louis said, as he stepped up and rolled the first one without hesitation. A stone-cold strike. Louis stood there with his hand dangling over the air dryer, as he stared at Cullen, waiting for his ball to pop back up. And Cullen stared right back. My two oldest friends; these grown men who hated each other's guts. I hadn't had this much fun in weeks.

Louis's second strike was a real wobbler, which he seemed to topple over with a thrust of his hips alone. This lurid gesticulation that sent the pins scattering. Louis allowed himself a cackle then, but Cullen stayed stone-faced. Staring up at the scoreboard, and double-checking his math. Always the professional accountant.

"This is only going to make it that much better when you miss the next one, Repo Man." Cullen smiled.

Louis said nothing as he tucked the ball into his chest and made the sign of the cross, a florid gesture that was for Cullen's benefit alone. And, with that, Louis turned on his heel and crouched down into his approach. Rearing back and letting it rip. Before the ball was even halfway down the alley, Louis turned his back to the pins. He stared at us and raised his arms over his head in a vee. Waiting for the unmistakable sound of it: Crrrrrrrssssssshhh! A dead-center strike.

I was in tears, I was laughing so hard. But Cullen was pissed off. Only then did Louis allow himself the hint of a smile. He wanted to shake hands, of course, but Cullen was already walking away. I stood up and shook Louis's hand instead.

"Bad teams lose these games," he said with a shrug.

It was only as we got away from the clatter of pins that I recognized the music coming from the back. Not *live music*, exactly, but something else. Something damaged and in-between-sounding. As we got closer I realized that the bowling alley bar had transformed itself into an after-hours karaoke club. The stage was hung with paper lanterns now. A mirror ball floated across the ceiling.

My brother took me by the elbow as I began to walk into the room. It was obvious enough that we were too drunk to drive the car home. I told him not to worry about that; I told him I would figure something out. Peter nodded dimly and disappeared.

I couldn't take my eyes off the stage. There was a tremendously fat young woman, in a billowing polka-dot dress, singing "November Rain" with the voice of an angel. I was not expecting this at all. We stood there at the back of the room, feeling helpless. Completely transfixed by this zaftig blonde and her beautiful singing voice.

Louis leaned in and whispered, almost reverently, "God's

a real sonovabitch for giving fat girls such beautiful voices." I turned to him with a smile and saw that he was serious. Shaking his head in astonishment. "It must be like a goddamn concert hall inside that body."

As the song ended, Louis left us and approached the stage.

"A hundred bucks says he tells that little fatty that she's *right up his alley*," Cullen said with a sneer. And as we watched the girl lean down, we could practically read Louis's lips. "Ugh, what an idiot," Cullen said, leaving me there at the back of the bar.

I watched him walk past the tables strewn with blue plastic binders, to the DJ booth, where he wrote down a call number on a slip of paper, from memory. There was something perfect about this image of Cullen singing the same song, week after week. What choice did I have now but to stick around and find out what it was?

And, all at once, I was happy I was here. It felt good to be out with my friends again, *my real friends*. No matter how much energy I spent fighting it, I knew we were the same. And besides, I was starting to have fun here. Fuck it, I thought. There'd be plenty of time to sober up before the wedding. The only thing in the world I wanted right then was to sing a song in this ugly little room.

But before I could get my hands on the songbook, a girl reached out and grabbed my wrist. This pretty face that I was sure I'd never seen before in my life.

"Hey," she said.

"Hey," I answered, cluelessly.

"I'm about to sing 'Let's Hear It for the Boy' for you."

"For me?" I asked, almost laughing. The absurdity of this pickup line had me swooning. She must say this every single week.

The girl nodded, smiling right back like she got the joke. So, okay, sure, let's go with this. We were two drunk strangers, encountering each other beyond the point of inhibition. It was all pretty simple, really. Clearly we were biding our time before we slipped into a back booth, or a bathroom stall, and started making out sloppily.

"That's so funny," I said, grinning stupidly. "Because I was just about to go sing 'Fat Bottomed Girls' for you."

"Oh, wow," she said, laughing. "What a coincidence." And for the first time all week I didn't miss Lauren Pinkerton at all. I was glad she hadn't come with me.

"Can I ask you a question?"

"Anything," she answered.

"What are you doing tomorrow?"

"What's going on tomorrow?"

"I need a date for a wedding."

"Oh, yeah?" she smirked. "Who's getting married? You and me?"

"No. My sister," I said simply.

"Oh, good. I was hoping I would get to meet your family soon."

"Perfect, then. It's settled." We were both laughing now, having fun with this game. We wanted to see who would blink first.

"There's one condition, though."

"Tell me," she said.

"You have to pretend that your name is Lauren."

"My name is Lauren? At the wedding?"

"Yes. Tomorrow your name is Lauren Pinkerton."

"Okay." She nodded, taking it all in stride. This girl didn't seem to know how to flinch. And for the first time since I met her five minutes before, I understood that she was really going to come with me to my sister's wedding.

"But you can't break character."

"I'm Lauren Pinkerton," she said, seeming to enjoy the name.

"Not under any circumstances," I said, trying to convey my seriousness.

"Right," she answered, and I could tell that she was serious, too. She was calling my bluff now. This was a bet we were making, and it was clear that she intended to win.

"It's really important, Lauren."

"I understand completely."

"You don't have to worry, though. It's just a bunch of aunts and uncles who are going to be asking for you. I already know for a fact that they're going to love you. And besides, they're all going to be drunk tomorrow anyway."

"Good," she said. "I'm going to be drunk, too."

"Honestly, you can say whatever you want. Tell them stories. Make things up. Just make sure that you're charming."

"I can do that," she said.

"You have to be sweet to my grandmother, though. That's the second rule."

"Oh, yeah? Grandma's gonna be there?"

"Yeah, but it's no joke. You have to be nice to her. You have to make her love you."

"I understand completely," Lauren said, clearly understanding nothing.

"She's eighty-five years old. She's not gonna get many more of these things. Okay? You can't fuck this up for her."

"I love old people," Lauren said, laughing blithely.

"If you do anything to upset her I'll have to kill you," I said, laughing without her.

"What?" she asked, not sure that she'd heard me.

"I said, if you upset my grandmother at the wedding I'll have to murder you." I was leaning in to be heard over the din of the karaoke. "Just so you know. It's that important to me."

I watched her face go slack. I could practically hear the record skipping in her brain. I knew I'd gone and spoiled the whole thing.

"What did you just say?" she asked unkindly.

"Which part?" I said stupidly. I was holding on to my smile. I'd meant it all as a joke, of course. Or did I? As I watched her face darken now, I wondered where I'd ended up. I wasn't really going to take this stranger to my sister's wedding. Or, at least, I didn't think I was. This girl was a sure thing. I just wanted us to sing our songs and go back home to her place.

"I just called Mom," my brother said, appearing at my side.

"Okay," I answered, not understanding this.

"She's on her way," he said blankly. "She's coming to pick us up."

I turned to Lauren as I answered him. "I don't think I'm coming home."

"Yes, you are," she said with a scowl. And with that she walked away, leaving Peter and me standing in the dark. My brother didn't say a word, staring down at the thin red carpet. There was a kindness in his silence now, I knew. I could hear Louis's voice coming through the speakers as he took the microphone off the stand. And, all at once, I knew that it was time for me to go. There was no sense in even saying goodbye.

As we left the bowling alley I chastised Peter for waking up our mother. "Why would you do that?"

"She told me to. She doesn't want us driving drunk."

"Nobody's *drunk*," I said, stumbling through the doors and out into the parking lot. We sat down on a warped metal bike rack and waited in silence. We stopped speaking entirely then, as we stared out into the distance. I knew that Peter was not going to mention the ugly incident with the girl inside the bar, and I loved him for that.

We eased ourselves up off the rack as my mother's minivan came into view. But, as it pulled into the parking lot, it was Kerry who was sitting there behind the wheel. We stood on the sidewalk, frozen, as she circled the island of parked cars to pick us up.

"I thought you said you called Mom," I whispered harshly.

"I did."

"Jesus. Fine. Just try not to sound drunk."

"I'm not even going to speak," he said solemnly.

I nodded as the minivan slowed to a stop in front of us. Peter slid into the backseat silently, leaving me to sit up front with Kerry.

"Hey," I said, cautiously.

"Hey," she answered.

"Sorry to make you pick us up."

"It's fine. I wanted to come," Kerry said. "I had to get out of the house anyway. Mom won't stop circling me. She keeps thinking of *one more thing* we need to do."

I nodded. Even Kerry, it seemed, had a threshold for the ritual of marriage. All these ancient sacraments, passed down through the glossy pages of bridal magazines. In the end, she found herself locked up in my parents' house on the night before her wedding, like some strange courtesan.

"I'm just ready to be done with it now, you know? I'm just ready to be married and living in my own house with Greg."

"Right," I said.

Kerry looked at me with a sideways glance that was impossible to read. I had been watching these gears turn my entire life. Kerry's gaze had always possessed the uncanny combination of the *mean* and the *well-meaning*, and I braced myself for impact.

"It's not really what I had in mind, you know. Your hair," she said, smirking.

"Right," I said, touching my head reflexively. I'd almost forgotten I'd done this.

"This is because of Lauren, isn't it?"

"What?" I said, taken aback.

"This dramatic *gesture*," she said, smiling. "All I ever asked was that you cut the hair out of your eyes. You didn't have to go all *Full Metal Jacket* on us."

"I didn't," I said defiantly.

Kerry sighed and shook her head. "Your problem is that you take it all so hard."

"I don't know what you're talking about."

"You've always been this way. You've always been the girl in every relationship. Even when you were in high school. You can't help it."

I frowned and looked away. Kerry never knew when to shut up about anything. I didn't know who she thought she was describing, but it wasn't me. Or, at least, it didn't sound like me. Then again, I could barely even recognize myself in a mirror.

"I like Lauren, you know. I'm just not sure that she's right for you."

"Well, I don't know what to tell you. I think that you're wrong."

"I know you do," Kerry said sadly.

I was staring out the window, feeling trapped inside this conversation. I resented her imposition. Who the fuck asked Kerry anyway? Where did she *always* get the nerve? I wanted to turn on her now. I wanted to tell her all the disgusting things that Greg had said and done, among his frat-brother groomsmen. But Greg was every bit the choirboy that Kerry knew. He was peace-loving to a fault. And my sister already had his balls in a vise, besides.

"The two of you broke up?" she asked, continuing to press.

"We don't believe in putting labels on it," I offered snidely. Where did Kerry come up with this? Who had told her these things anyway? I was desperate just to slow her down now, to make her stop. But Kerry could go on this way forever.

"I'm sorry," she said softly, disarming me again. I wanted to open the door and roll out into the street, or at least curl up on the floor. I'd been sitting on these feelings like land mines for weeks. And now was no time to abandon my post.

As we pulled into the driveway, Kerry reached out and touched my head. She pulled me close and kissed the soft bristles. Reaching into the backseat, she forced Peter to take her hand. And, for a moment, she was there: our older sister; our protector.

"Get some sleep," she said. "Both of you. No one's allowed to be hungover tomorrow." And with that we opened our doors and fled the car in three different directions.

The next night I broke down and called Lauren's phone. It was always me who blinked first. Pulling open my shirt and offering my chest to her bayonet. And it was Lauren who never failed to show mercy in these moments. I could hear it in her voice then. She was feeling every bit as ripped apart as I was.

We laughed at the way that these fights could pick us up

and drop us down so far outside of our selves. It was hard to even know what had happened. There was no great flash point. It was not possible to say for certain who had decided that she was not coming with me. This was a gun we had been pointing at each other's heads for weeks.

"It must be awful," she said, sounding guilty.

"It's not that bad," I lied.

"I never should've left you all alone."

It was strange. Now that I had her on the phone, I found I couldn't speak. As I listened to her breathing I could feel her head pressed to mine for the first time in weeks. And yet, there was this static on the line between us that refused to lift. I didn't want to feel this way anymore, and neither did Lauren. We had a hole in our guts that was the shape of the other person. It was hard for us to exist with the knowledge of that hole. We didn't know how to live. We were reaching out to pull each other in. We were desperate just to crash back into each other and live off the heat from the wreckage. In endless reconciliation there is infinite hope.

"I've made a mistake," she said finally.

"It's not your fault."

"I want to fix it, though."

"What do you mean?" I could hear the urgency in her voice.

"I'm going to buy a plane ticket. I want to come to the wedding now. I can be there in the morning."

"The wedding is over," I said simply.

"What?"

"It was this afternoon."

"Oh." We both started to laugh. "How was it?" she asked.

"I dunno. It was fine. It was a wedding."

"Right."

"We got drunk. We danced. I got lonely. I called you."

"Aw," she said, and I could feel this little tremor through the line.

"Are you at home?" I asked her finally, knowing that she wasn't.

"No. I'm in New York. I'm staying at Cokie's."

"Are you going to be at home when I get there?"

Lauren sighed and answered without malice, "I don't know. I hope so." It hung there between us like a death.

"I hope so, too," I said.

"Maybe we shouldn't go home, though."

"What do you mean?"

"I mean, maybe we should find a new home."

"Yes," I said. "We need to get out of D.C."

"It's poisoned. It's wrecked. We can't just keep living there forever."

"No, exactly. You're right. We could go anywhere we wanted to."

"You could come here to New York," she said hopefully.

"Or we could just go west."

"Mm," she said quietly, saying everything she needed to say. "Let's not talk about it tonight, maybe."

"Right," I said, stopping.

It was impossible not to search out a change we could make that could save us from our fate. But it just didn't matter. The point was to keep breathing into the phone now. To listen and to laugh for each other. To make the other feel less alone.

"Are you still there?" I asked over the silent static.

"I'm here," she said.

"Good," I said. "Good."

MENTOR, TORMENTOR

had broken up with Lauren for the last time and was suffering a new compulsion to live like a monk. I wanted to be like the Old Man who put his possessions into a rowboat, paddled it out to the middle of the lake, and sank it. I gave away everything I could and abandoned the rest. I returned my library books and I left town. I wanted to make a change: to give up dairy and drinking and masturbation; to keep a journal and a garden and a job. But real change can be hard to navigate.

I'd been sleeping on a couch in Portland, Oregon, for months: going out too much, drinking too much, screwing unhappily. I let my hair grow long, just because. Stress, depression, self-doubt, I was a fucking riot, man. I was losing weight, too, and I worried seriously that I might have a parasite or a cancer or worse. Or maybe it was just the Indian cart where I'd eaten lunch every day for the last month. It didn't really matter. I had a thousand dollars left in the bank, which I thought I might try to live off of forever.

And then, amazingly, improbably, I was hired as a baby-sitter.

This nice rich couple wanted me to pick up their thirteen-year-old son outside his private school each afternoon. That was it: ride the city buses; hang out for an hour; same time tomorrow, easy as pie. It baffled me at first. Avi seemed perfectly capable of navigating the public transit on his own, just like all his friends. Except that Avi didn't really have friends. He was a pathological liar and an inconsiderate shit-head. He made things up and talked shit on people, and then he laughed about it to their faces.

Dick and Virginia, so concerned with doling out the gold stars and self-esteem, were clueless. They didn't expect enough, didn't enforce enough, weren't strict enough by half, to even get on this kid's radar.

Still, I knew we had it pretty easy. I was no great moral-izer. I had no interest in going heavy on Avi. I wasn't a snitch or a bully. I didn't give a shit if he swore. I didn't even par-ticularly care if he did his homework. God knows I was no authority figure, and I could never stomach a paper tiger be-sides. I was just trying to level with the kid and teach him how to get through the day a little easier. It was simple: I didn't want a job any more than Avi wanted a babysitter.

The worst of it, though, was that Dick actually made me think I had a shot at getting through at all. He downplayed the lying and the failing grades and the friendlessness as some kind of run-of-the-mill growing pains. I tried to remember, too, that Avi was just a kid. A certain amount of pathology is par for the course, I thought. But Avi bucked and resisted everything I did. He didn't respect my overtures of friendship and fraternity and peace. His game was to try and steamroll me to figure out how much abuse I would actually take. He felt entitled to it because his parents had bought me for him. I was Richard Pryor in *The Toy*.

The last time I'd seen Avi had been fairly typical. It was some sort of bogus teacher conference day, which meant he had the whole day off. Virginia asked me to come over to the house around nine, and I showed up fully expecting to find myself locked out. Avi understood that I had a key, but he couldn't help taking some sick pride in making me use it. To my surprise, though, the door was open. I came inside and leaned my bike up in the front hallway.

"Hey!" I called up the stairs. "Wake up, fatty. We're going running today."

"Run my dick," Avi squealed nonsensically. I could hear gunshots and explosions upstairs, and I understood that Dick and Virginia had given him his video games back.

I took my raincoat off and looked inside the refrigerator for some orange juice. As I poured from the carton, I stared blankly at Avi's report card, a sad collage of C-pluses, tacked up on the fridge. I was struck by how overwhelming it must be to have to worry about your children. All these constant little disappointments.

I heard a crash upstairs that might've been anything. I

rinsed my juice glass and set it in the dishwasher. I looked inside the freezer to see if there were waffles or bagels, or something else. And then, when I couldn't think of any more delays, I finally went upstairs to find Avi.

"What are those retarded glasses on your face?" he sniggered as I ducked my head into his bedroom. I'd ripped my last contact lens that morning: a three-month pair that I'd been wearing for over a year.

"These are my glasses."

"Well, they make you look fat and ugly."

"Okay," I said. "Thank you for your honesty."

Avi laughed and unpaused his video game again. A barrage of military caterwaul and confusion, turned up like a jet engine. I watched the killing field blankly for a beat.

"I thought Dick and Virginia took away your hard drive?" I asked rhetorically.

Avi just laughed airily. I knew he knew all his parents' hiding spots. As hiding spots go—in the closet, under the bed—they were truly uninspired. This was the problem really, all these half measures. *I* was a fucking half measure!

"You're a disgrace to the honor system," I said flatly. "You know that?"

"What the cocksucking hell is the honor system?" Avi asked over his shoulder.

My phone started ringing in my pocket and Avi paused the game again. He spun around in his chair to face me. "Who is it?" He asked this every time my phone rang. More than anything, he wanted to know if girls were calling me. He wanted to know how many female names there were inside my cell phone. Avi had a lot of earnest questions about how and where an adult man meets adult women. The idea seemed to titillate and stress him all out of proportion.

"It's your mother," I said.

"It's *your* mother," Avi mimicked reflexively. I answered the phone and walked back into the hall.

"Hello, hi. You've arrived?" Virginia asked. "Oh, good. Did you see my note?"

"Your note," I said, looking back at Avi. "Where was it?"

"Right on the front door," Virginia said blankly. I watched Avi put the note into his mouth and chew it into a wet pulp. He looked incredibly pleased with himself.

"Oh, right, I see it now. Avi brought it inside for me."

Avi fell off his chair, making a comic show of choking on the paper. He laughed and coughed the wet note onto the floor like a dog. I knew Virginia was just going to go over everything on the phone with me now anyway. She would read me a list of things that had been taken away from Avi that week, like the computer. A list of restaurants that we could and could not visit. Movies that were and were not acceptable, etc., etc. None of this meant anything unless I could actually get Avi out of the house.

I hung up the phone and he looked at me expectantly. "Do you want me to tell you to get off the computer?" I asked him.

"Yeah," he said.

"Too bad. I don't give a shit. Do whatever you want. I'm on the clock."

"What do you mean?" Avi asked suspiciously. But I was

already walking back into the hallway, where I'd seen a *New Yorker* on the table. I was more than happy to let him play his video games and wear himself out. I would read, and we'd both be happy.

But as I sat back down in his beanbag chair, he looked at me with something like contempt. As soon as you gave Avi permission to do anything, it lost all its magic. He had no interest in playing video games anymore; he was pissed.

"You can't read," he said. "I'll tell my parents."

"Go ahead. I'm not afraid of your parents," I said, cracking the magazine. Avi was never sure what to say in these moments. He liked to hold the threat of termination over my head, but I knew he didn't really want to get rid of me, either.

This was when Avi smiled sickly. I followed his eyes across the room to a big dent in the drywall. "Jesus," I said, remembering the crash I'd heard downstairs. "Did you put that fucking hole in the wall?"

"No," he said, matter-of-fact. "I threw the chair. The *chair* put the hole in the wall."

I looked at him in disbelief. He wasn't even smiling. What do you say to a person like that? "Well, let's not be stupid. Help me move the dresser in front of it."

"You move it," Avi snorted. I reached out and grabbed him by the back of the neck then. I was losing my sense of humor.

"Okay, okay, okay," he said, and I let him go. We pushed the dresser over three feet. The last thing in the world I wanted to do was have a conversation about this with Dick and Virginia. This was not my problem.

I was actually annoyed that Avi wouldn't just sit still and play his fucking computer games like a bad little boy. We both knew that's what he wanted, and it was my experience that a little video-game violence had a pacifying effect on the kid. Two hours of unbroken mayhem and slaughter was like a little shot of laughing gas for him. It would make our whole day together a little more pleasant. Avi would get giggly and tired, and we would move on to something else.

There was, of course, a whole other period in which Dick and Virginia tried to swap out Avi's war games for educational fare, like *Flight Simulator*. But they eventually saw what I saw, which was Avi crashing the plane on purpose over and over. He was aiming at the buildings, like it was some sort of pimply jihadi training game. Avi loved that this could inspire a more genuine outrage than simply blowing the heads off of alien zombie Nazis or whatever.

I told him to stop crashing the flight simulator and he refused, so I yanked the plug right out of the wall. Oh, man. You should've seen the little guy freak out then, telling me about RAM and ROM and memory space, while I tried my hardest not to laugh.

"Fine," he said now, after we'd moved the dresser. "Let's just go eat, then. I need some mo-fucking French toast."

And that's what we did. The whole day went by like this, the way our days always went. We made plans, then argued and stonewalled each other. I would resist or give in, and then Avi would get bored. All these endless little battles in a zero-sum game.

Somehow I never could seem to explain it to him, either.

We were on easy street here. We had carte blanche. Dick and Virginia had given me a credit card that we could use to go eat lunch, and watch PG-13 movies, and play arcade games, whatever. But Avi refused. He was deeply suspicious of every idea that wasn't his own. He acted as if I were trying to trick him. I told him to come up with something else, then, anything. I didn't care what we did, as long as we did something. But he refused. Avi took great pleasure in refusing me. Grinning with the word no.

We would end up walking around endlessly, riding the city buses in circles, doing nothing. We would make a plan, get all the way there, and Avi would call it off. I would try to force him to follow through, to strong-arm him. I would get mad, but it was no use. It seemed like this was the thing he'd wanted all along: to get a rise out of me.

I would try to relax and remember I was on the clock, and it didn't matter what we did because I was going to get paid either way. But the time just *crawled* this way. We were wallowing in a thirteen-year-old boy's infinite boredom.

The strangeness of the job was not lost on me, either. My friends thought the whole situation was hilarious. They would beg me to recount days spent babysitting for their own amusement. They were charmed by this little boy's prankishness and off-color cuss words. They wanted me to bring Avi out to the bars and make him do parlor tricks. "We'll give Little Bro a handful of quarters for the pinball machine," they would say. "And then you can set Daddy's credit card up on the bar." Har-har-har, everybody wins.

But I never did bring Avi around, which was too bad, really. He would have loved these stupid dudes. They were living out a teenage boy's wet dream of adulthood: drinking and smoking and watching skateboard videos all day. If they wanted to look at porno on the computer, or eat pizza and ice cream for dinner, they just fucking did it! There were no adults to say no to us. We were the adults!

It would be unfair to say I didn't take the job seriously, though. I tried to look out for Avi without pandering or kissing his ass. I was brutally honest with him in a way that I wasn't sure anyone else could be. He was a good kid deep down, I knew. He was lucid and funny and spontaneous around me. We had our inside jokes and little routines. We were capable of having honest-to-god real fun together.

In the end, though, I had no idea how to help this kid. The only great wisdom I had to impart was to stop being a shithead. I told him this over and over, waiting for it to sink in. This is the reason you have no friends, I would say to him in earnest. You lie and then you laugh about it. You talk shit on people for no reason, and that is a terrible, terrible plan. But I never really got anywhere this way. Avi loved my little pep talks. He would squeal with delight whenever I tried to play the adult.

If anything I am understating the lying. You could hardly have a real conversation with the kid. It was like a reflex that he wasn't in control of. Lies about everything, constantly. Lies about the lies. Lies right to his parents' faces that they didn't bother calling him on. Dick and Virginia never stopped it, that's for sure. There was an air of frazzled obliviousness about their house. Dick told me about a therapist they'd taken Avi to the previous winter, but the kid knew exactly what she wanted to hear him say. He had a whole act of contrition he was able to perform at will. He could be very smart that way.

So the lies carried on, unchecked. Lies about bands I didn't listen to and movies I didn't watch and celebrities I didn't know. Lies about parties and tests and sports scores that never happened. Lies about the plots of television shows and summaries of book reports that Avi claimed to be writing. Lies about the crimes he had committed and the girlfriends he had unceremoniously dumped. All these endless exploits with a revolving cast of imaginary friends. They were eternally skipping school and drinking beer and smoking cigarettes together. They were destroying public property and finger-banging ninth-graders. This endless litany of dangerous things that Avi claimed to have seen and done. The thing that killed me was that most of his lies weren't even in service of anything. He wasn't lying to avoid punishment or gain tangible things; he was just lying.

At first I found it amusing, and sort of refreshing, that Avi was still so sheltered about the world that he had to invent danger this way. I would play the game with him, peppering him with follow-up questions to see how far he could stretch the lie. I would call bullshit on him endlessly, until he finally admitted that what he was saying was impossible. I would hector him into giving up.

But Avi would just laugh because it didn't mean anything. It didn't stick to him. He saw no consequences; there was no remorse. Every empty contradiction was a chance to reset the lie. It was incredible. I never *really* got him to cop to anything.

Our relationship had soured lately, though. I was locked into the hard routine of it: the bike ride, the bus routes, the school schedule. Sadly, I needed the money. I was every bit the paper tiger I'd despised: the adult *in loco parentis*. I knew that Avi could tell I was getting tired of his bullshit, too, and it only made him press harder, almost unbearably.

As I rode my bike into the West Hills toward the Jewish day school, I tried to put him out of my head entirely. What I was thinking about then was an email that had come to me, out of the blue, from a New York literary agent named Bettina Kleins. She'd read a short story I'd published in a small magazine about fighting with Lauren Pinkerton. She wanted to know where I was, and what I was doing, and what else I had written. Bettina was excited and I was easily flattered. Having smoke blown up my ass was a brand-new experience, and I was surprised to find how much I enjoyed its gross effects.

In a fit of vanity I sent Bettina Kleins four hundred pages of *A Cattle, a Crack-Up*, my convoluted novel about a dairy farmer on the verge of mental and physical collapse. And almost before I could regret it, Bettina got back to me, saying that she loved the book and felt certain she could find a publisher, as long as I was willing to do a rewrite.

"You just have to rewrite it a little," Bettina assured me.

"It'll be great. There's a wide-open market for this Middle America hipster ennui stuff right now . . ."

This embarrassed me a little. "Is that what I wrote?"

"Well, no, not the book. You!"

"Oh," I said, feeling queasy. I had no idea what this meant, but I already doubted my ability to pull it off.

Bettina and I exchanged three more emails, and another rushed phone call, about what exactly *rewrite* meant to Bettina. Rewrite how? In what way? To what end? What exactly was I supposed to keep intact in the rewrite process? Bettina seemed to think it all pretty much self-evident, imparting her confidence in the repetition of the word *rewrite*. This was the proverbial punch in the arm. *Go get 'em, tiger,* she might as well have said to me.

Bettina was exceedingly kind, but I wasn't sure I trusted her taste in my book. Or any books, frankly. I had reread *A Cattle* again and lost my nerve completely. I was clearly punching above my weight, and I couldn't imagine having the thing published at all now. It was a fucking mess. Who writes an Iraq War allegory about a dairy farm in the midwestern United States? And was that stuff even in the book anymore? Hadn't the country moved on? I wasn't sure how to stand out in front of any of it. I mean, Jesus Christ.

The prospect of rewriting anything in this book was daunting, to say the least. I could barely remember having written it to begin with, and now I had no way of getting back into that space. *A Cattle, a Crack-Up* became an albatross that I carried around my neck like so much dead weight.

The book hung in purgatory: not published, not rejected. Everything hinged on the simple idea that I could just *rewrite* it.

Bettina invited me to come talk to her about it in New York (at my own expense, of course). I found the whole thing intoxicating and disappointing all at once. New York City was the last place I wanted to go, which hardly mattered, since I had no money anyway.

"Portland!" Bettina bellowed. "You can't get out much farther than that, huh?" Needless to say, I did not mention the babysitting.

At three thirty the school doors flew open and Avi came out, desperately untucking himself and smirking like a criminal. "Let's go to Starbucks. I need a mo-fucking coffee."

"You're not allowed to drink coffee, dum-dum. We go over this every day," I said patiently.

"Nuh-uh, no. My mom changed her mind."

"Stop lying."

"It's true. She saw some study on *60 Minutes* about how coffee improves your test scores."

"Uh-huh, right, I saw that study."

"You did?" he asked with a new kind of smirk.

"Yeah, it said that coffee makes your wiener shrink, too."

"Shuuut up."

"It's the truth," I said, trying to stay humorless.

"Fine, then your wiener is shrinking like crazy. You drink coffee all the time."

"Dude, did you even *watch* the show?" I asked, with my

own smirk now. "That's the *opposite* of what it said! They talked *specifically* about middle schoolers. *You*, buddy." I tried to offer this with great gravity.

"Yeah, yeah, well, whatever . . ." Avi said, losing interest completely.

Every day was like this now. I had started taking the last word, just because I could. Because it was easy and it shut him up for a second. It was pathetic, but I was pathetic, too. Believe me, I had no illusions of being a good babysitter, or a role model, or even a good person. But I was competent and I was safe. I wasn't going to let this kid torture any animals or burn anything down on my watch. Of course it would have been nice to help Avi in some perfect world, but I was pretty much phoning it in at this point. I was unabashed about going through the motions. I told Avi he had gotten very boring to me. I told him outright that the only reason I kept showing up was for the money. Dick and Virginia had raised a shitty kid who didn't have any clue how to treat other people. Liberal parenting, I told him, was an exploded myth!

But Avi would just laugh at me. He thought my complaining was hilarious. He barely even listened when I spoke anymore. I was just some furniture to beat up on. More than anything, Avi needed attention. Friendlessness had starved him this way. He needed to show off in my presence, to abuse me. Any calm I could engender, he felt duty-bound to shatter. It was like a little bell going off in the back of his brain. Avi wasn't happy unless he was getting some sort of rise out of me. Finally, I realized that he did think of me as a friend. His only friend. And that just made the whole thing sadder.

Strictly speaking, there was one kid, named Josh, who tolerated Avi pretty well. Josh waited for the #44 bus with us after school, and I understood that he kept coming around for the spectacle as much as anything. Sniggering as Avi sing-songed in swear words: *fuck, fuck, fuck, fuck, fuck*. Lobbing them at me, the adult. They would laugh and titter as I'd confirm that, yes, I was a gay retard, so what?

But today, Josh was up in my face with his mucus-y braces. I could see that he was reveling with something to say. "I told my mother you hang around with Avi after school."

"So what?" I said, stepping out into the street to look for our bus.

"So, she says she doesn't trust you. And that I should be careful when I'm around you."

Avi and Josh burst into a churlish laughter. I turned away, trying not to care. But today was really just the wrong day for this shit.

"Yeah, well, your mom sounds like a real bitch," I said.

Poor Josh's face dropped. He had no idea what to say to this. Avi was squealing like a pig, pointing at him, as he turned red. No, this did not make me feel any better, but what did I do? I didn't even *know* this lady, and I wasn't gonna take any more of little Joshy's bullshit today. Getting called a pervert? Fuck that.

Unfortunately there was some precedent for this. Avi and I used to walk to the park after school, which sounds perfectly wholesome and good. Except that this park was at the back of an elementary school, and it was swarming with eight-year-olds. Avi would drag us down there just to sit and watch.

I'd try to get him to kick the soccer ball with me, but he wouldn't. He was fixated on the hierarchies of the children. I had no idea what to make of this until one day he actually worked his way into their games. I'd never seen Avi this way before, coming alive as he shouted out instructions and remade the rules. He was funny and charming and domineering. These kids treated him like he was some sort of fucking god!

Anyway, I had to tell Avi no way, after that. Mothers were looking at me and starting to whisper. And I couldn't disagree! The whole thing was totally inappropriate. A thirteen-year-old boy and a twenty-five-year-old man cannot sit on a picnic bench watching eight-year-olds play four square. We looked like some kind of professional team of pederasts! Unh-uh. I was sorry for him, but I had to pull the plug on the park.

In some way, I knew I wanted Josh to tell his mother what I'd said, too. She could call Virginia and complain. Nice and easy, tidy, done. Getting fired would be a relief, I thought. Let somebody else take this abuse. But I knew Josh could never say that word in front of his mother. And, by now, I was sorry I had said it; I had no beef with Josh. I actually wished it *were* his mother paying me thirteen dollars an hour to ride the city buses through downtown Portland with him. But Josh didn't need that kind of supervision.

The thing was, I actually showed a lot of restraint around these kids. I wasn't particularly interested in corrupting them in any way. I wasn't there to show off or give anyone a hard time. I just wanted the whole thing to be low-key and un-eventful. But the #44 bus was taking forever today. Josh ended up leaving on the #64. Mondays were soccer practice or Tae Kwon Do, or something else. I think it goes without saying that Avi had no sports or activities. Avi had me. And there we were, alone again, waiting for our bus.

I walked out into the street and turned back to find Avi breaking off a tree branch. I watched him slap it against the sidewalk brainlessly, before, BANG, he smacked my bike with it. He was beaming and begging me to react, but I didn't say anything. Avi stabbed the stick through the spokes of my wheel and started rattling them hard. I reached out for him and he flinched, backing away, laughing.

"Cut the shit," I warned him. "I'm not in the mood today."

Avi giggled and jabbed me in my side with his stick, hard enough to feel it. I turned and backed him off again. Suddenly this was a game we were playing.

"You touch me with that fucking stick one more time and I'm gonna rip your liver out and eat it, little boy."

Avi snickered happily. "I thought you were a *vegetarian*?"

"I'm a fucking cannibal," I said, showing him my teeth.

Avi tittered and backed away again as I looked for our goddamn bus. All of a sudden, WHACK! That little fucker slashed me across the back of the legs. He looked at me with a wolfish grin on his face, like he could hardly believe his own gall. I almost lost it, backing him up and ripping the stick out of his hands, as he begged for mercy.

"I'm sorry, I'm sorry, I'm sorry."

I cocked the whip back, ready to slash him in two. Avi

flinched, and I launched the stick over his head into the woods.

"There. Now fucking stop it. Just stand still and don't touch anything. I'm not kidding."

Avi loved it when I got surly. He knew that he was winning and he'd start giggling uncontrollably. I glowered at him as he drifted back to the tree.

"Don't even think about it. I'll leave you here in a heartbeat."

Avi's eyes got big and he begged for me to go. *"Please . . ."*

"No," I said. "As long as it's making you miserable, I'll stay." Avi smiled, and I smiled back, watching him pull down the next branch. "Don't do it, dum-dum. Use your brain."

But Avi did it, and the new stick was longer, too. He was dizzy with its power. Jabbing it at me theatrically, like a fencer. I stood my ground and made a show of not flinching. I was cold and unimpressed.

Boom! He jabbed it right past my head, just missing. I batted at the stick wildly, looking like a fool. And suddenly I was furious all over again. Avi loved it, shuffling backward. I stared daggers into him as he giggled at me. This was the closest I had ever come to hopping on my bike and just abandoning him.

Avi wasn't stopping, either. There was a kind of crazed chortle in his throat as he danced around. And before I even realized it, he lunged and stabbed me in the face! I pulled my hand up to my cheek reflexively, checking for blood. We looked at each other then, stunned. I didn't even think, I just took two giant steps forward and kicked my thirteen-year-old ward in his bony ass as hard as I could. A kick that was four months in the making if it was a day! And it felt fucking great.

Avi went flying, but he didn't fall. He looked back at me with his mouth hanging open, stupefied. I turned away angrily, embarrassed. I could barely process how enraged this whole situation had made me.

I watched as Avi threw away the stick and turned to me, unsure.

"Did that hurt?" I asked him.

"No," he said uncertainly, and we didn't say anything after that.

We waited for the #44 bus in silence. I saw Avi touch the back of his leg and I was ashamed of myself. What kind of monster does a thing like this? Right here in front of the school and everyone? It was probably caught on camera, for all I knew. And what if it left a bruise? What if Avi showed it to Dick and Virginia and those rich, liberal fucks called the police on me? I could already see my picture in the newspaper: "Babysitter Kicks Kid." How do you live a thing like that down?

And yet, I still wasn't ready to apologize to Avi for anything. And now the #44 was finally coming, too. I put my bike onto the front rack and paid our fares, and we sat down together like always. I tried to think of something placating to say. Something that could save me and reset everything. But before I could think of anything, Avi turned to me with his mischievous smile intact.

"You know what I think?"

"What?" I asked, nervous about where he was going with this.

"I think we should get out at the Starbucks. I think we need some coffees."

"Coffees?"

"Yeah, a bunch of coffees," he said. "Shit-tons of coffees."

"All right." I nodded uncertainly, wishing I would've thought to buy him off all along. "I don't care. It's your parents' money."

"Damn straight it is," he said. This kind of irreverence was like scratching a dog's belly for Avi. He was beaming at me again. "No, no, no. Let's get pizza instead. I just changed my mind."

"You're too fat for pizza," I said blankly.

"Ha! Look at *you*! You're like ten times fatter than me."

"No, I'm not. I'm a vegetarian, remember? That means I'm skinny."

"You're the fattest vegetarian I ever saw!"

"Your mother's a fat vegetarian."

"*Your* mother's a fat vegetarian," he said incredulously.

"Good one." I nodded, and Avi erupted into squeals again. "Aw, shit, there goes the Starbucks!" I said, pointing over his shoulder. Avi gasped as he turned.

"Sike! C'mon. You're not even trying."

"Your mother's not even trying!" Avi bellowed, laughing again. The #44 shot down through the bus mall and wheeled around a corner. Avi pulled on the cord like he wanted to snap it off. The bell dinged and the bus decelerated toward the curb.

"Wait for me while I lock my bike up," I ordered him.

"No way," he shouted, as he pushed out the side doors.

Avi skittered blindly into the street, between parked cars, desperately trying to join the crowd of walkers. He was pretending he was on his own out here. Pretending he was set loose in the city. Pretending he was free.

AIDS

bundance is the mother of neurosis. I would repeat this to myself to prove that I was fine, that I was not crazy. I was young and fully alive. But it was no use. On some level I knew that I was dying, and that there was nothing I could do to stop it or slow it down. It was already happening. It was done. This was a fact.

The door was locked, that was the first surprise. I was looking up into an eyeball camera, not sure what I was supposed to do.

"Appointment or walk-in?" the camera said.

"I'm sorry, what?"

"Appointment or walk-in?" the woman's voice asked patiently.

"Walk-in, I guess," I said, louder than I wanted to. The door buzzed, and I pushed it open into a small waiting room.

It was then that I realized how they could've kept me out there indefinitely. This nice lady asking open-ended questions while she called the cops, on the other line, to come check out this jittery character trying to gain access to the Planned Parenthood. Abundance is the mother of neurosis, I told myself again.

The friendly voice inside the machine put her hand up and smiled at me. I crossed the room, looking only at her. It struck me for the first time that I might see someone here I knew. What then? Was the protocol to talk or to ignore each other?

I told the woman my name in a soft voice. She nodded and ripped off a comically small square of paper, sliding it across the counter.

"If you like, you can write down the reason you've come in today. If you're more comfortable that way."

I looked at this piece of paper and almost laughed. How could I write anything down on this? How could I explain how the last five years had led me here to now? I picked up the pen and scrawled *AIDS* on the paper, sliding it back. The woman looked at this, and then up at me.

"I'd just like a test, I guess, I mean," I said meekly.

She smiled in this beautiful, selfless way again, and I wondered if someone had taught her how to do that. "Okay," she said, handing me a clipboard. "Have a seat. We should be able to fit you in this morning."

I shook the water off my raincoat and took a chair. This was still my first real winter here and I was continually trying to adjust. The short days and the low ceiling and the endless columns of gray light. The clouds did not thunder here, they dripped. Weather could happen very quickly, too. The sky gathering itself in speed and direction as the dull sun ducked in and out of cloud walls. These mountainous cloudscapes that obscured the actual mountains and made everything feel low and tight around you. The rivers and the bridges and the evergreens, all lost in a scrim of fuzzy mist. I had a vague feeling of the landscape going in and out of focus sometimes, and an illusion that the sea was much closer than it actually was. I had not seen Mount Hood in months, to the point of forgetting it was still right there. Eventually you were left with only the bone-soaking cold and a pissing rain. Your shoes could fill up and stay wet for days if you were not careful. It had rained twenty-eight of the last twenty-nine days, and I actually sort of loved it.

It was only then, sitting in my chair, that I had the guts to look around the room at the other faces. Nearly everyone was a teenage girl, or practically, it seemed. They were young and tough. Black and Latina. They didn't seem nervous or scared. They were bored as they gossiped and played with their cell phones. I had no idea why they were all here this morning. I wanted to believe that these girls were looking at me and asking themselves the same questions, but they weren't. I took some comfort in the fact that I was invisible to them. It re-laxed me.

There was only one other male in the room with us. Younger than me and pizza-faced. Expressionless. He sat beside his girlfriend, I thought. They were here for a pregnancy test, maybe. Or an abortion. Did they do that here?

I was still thinking about leaving. I was thinking about standing up and fleeing now. I would look at the woman behind the counter and make some mumbled excuse. Nodding, nodding, and getting out of the Planned Parenthood. I was thinking about my house. Recently I'd been struck by the unabating feeling that I'd left the stove on, or that the door must be unlocked. Maybe both. Abundance is the mother of neurosis, I said without saying. Everything was fine; I was fine. I should just go back home now. It was still early. I could sleep for another hour, maybe.

I had a brand-new job, working from home, actually. I was writing spam emails for money. It didn't make much sense to me, either, but there it was. I was finally getting paid to write.

It started off as a joke, obviously. I answered an ad on Craigslist, never expecting a reply. I attached a résumé and a writing sample, and I forgot all about it. But an hour later a man named Roman Holliday called me from a blocked telephone number. He spoke to me for two hours about spam, and the First Amendment, and himself. This, I realized afterward, had been my job interview.

Spam, like much of the Internet, is shrouded in a cloak of secrecy. And Roman Holliday was no different. He spoke frenetically with the distinct and voluble whine of a man who had spent some portion of the morning snorting Adderall. He told me he was an anarchist and a capitalist, and, above all, an Internet purist. The muddled contradictions seemed intentional, I thought. I had spoken to Libertarians before.

"The thing that they don't want you to understand is that

people *want* to give you their money. They're dying to give it away, you know? They don't even know what to do with it all. It makes them sweaty just thinking about it. *Help me,* they say. So all I'm saying is: *Sure. Hey. How about this?* You know?"

"Uh-huh," I said, though I didn't know anything about this.

It did not seem strange to me that *this* should be the man who was in charge of an enterprise like spam. Roman Holliday was eternally banging the drum for free speech. He could talk endlessly about the "open exchange of ideas." Every email we sent was couched as a defense of the First Amendment. Roman was not shy about presenting himself as a freedom fighter, either. He delighted in this positioning as the only civilized man among the savages on the Internet.

"I'm offering you the chance to become a foot soldier in a movement that is larger than yourself."

"Uh-huh," I said, worried that this dude was never going to pay me in a million fucking years. I could feel Roman Holliday—with his florid con man's name—fluttering a handkerchief before my eyes. I was watching him slip his hand inside my vest. There was nothing I could do to stop it.

I worked the whole first week with every expectation of getting stiffed. And when I didn't—when the first check came, exactly as promised—I nearly fell on the floor laughing. Never mind the fact that this check was issued from a bank I'd never heard of, signed by someone called Rolf Federlein. It cashed. And, suddenly, I was making money again.

So I just kept going. Producing numb and meaningless content. Throwing pennies into the void. The Internet demanded it: this filler that showed up in waves, in people's in-boxes, all across the country. Around the world, really. Actresses in Malibu. Politicians in The Hague. Soldiers in Iraq. There is no such thing as immunity from spam. Even the astronauts in outer space were receiving my communiqués now. I had an audience of millions!

Still, people could not seem to wrap their heads around what it was that I was actually doing for a living. It was hard for them to accept the idea that spam could be a real person's job. It was easier, I knew, to imagine these uncanny missives born of unthinking, unfeeling computers. Or, at the very least, they must be coming from India or Africa, right? People had an image in their minds of an overcrowded Internet café where swarthy-looking men, with heavy mustaches, came in to buy international phone cards. Where else could these sentences possibly come from, if not from the hand of someone using English as their fourth or fifth language? How else were we meant to account for such strange and unsettling syntax?

But it was really just me. Sitting there in my boxer shorts, hungover: me. Sleep-deprived, and sex-obsessed: me. Young, white, American, middle-class: me. I had a college degree and an unpublishable novel, for fuck's sake. And the worst part of all was that I was getting really good at this. I could make almost two hundred dollars a day writing spam, if I really put my mind to it. All of which threw a thin mask over the fact that I was just one more cold-blooded mercenary hiding among the multitudes.

————

My whole life had begun to feel like a blur of aging young people. Girls who smoked cigarettes and drank whiskey. Boys who took pills and drove drunk. We were all drinking too much, fighting too much, starting unnecessary trouble. The casual sex and self-destructive behavior; the phobic incidences and fear of dying. "What the hell's so great about living to a hundred, anyway?" I could remember Lauren saying as she laughed at me. We carry around these memories that cling to us for years. Not the big, specific errors that put a fork in the road, but just a general guilt and depression over all the little ways we find ourselves living. Everything replaying itself endlessly in our heads. What is it supposed to mean, and what is it asking of us? Or is this just some glitch in the brain's grand and ancient architecture?

There was a girl who spoke to me in baby talk. It made me feel agitated and expendable. Worse, she talked to her dog like he was a sentient, intelligent being. She would ask him questions and take his opinions, and explain her own complicated belief systems to him. I was made to feel in competition here. Clearly it was incumbent upon me to distinguish myself from the dog. It made me want to strangulate that fucking thing.

There was a girl who lived in an anarcho-collective where they brewed their own beer and raised farm animals in the side yard. She would go out at night and spray-paint George Bush's name with a swastika onto stop signs. She was prone to strange acts of whimsy in the kitchen, like putting squash in our nachos and pumpkin seeds in our spaghetti sauce. I would protest, and we would actually fight about these things.

Eventually she told me that she found it hard to take me seriously. That made me laugh.

There was a girl who was a Christian and a virgin, who was into kissing and heavy petting. She would describe herself to me, in earnest, like a horoscope: optimistic; enthusiastic; generous; independent. She said that she wanted me to take her virginity and I told her that I couldn't. She seemed grateful to me for this, and I didn't know how to feel about it then. Everywhere we went she held my hand. I eventually decided I was wasting her time—I mean, she barely even drank.

There was a girl I only saw after midnight. She had begun to seem like a weird nonperson to me. She'd started eating the things that I was eating. She was reading every book that I had read. I found this strangely disconcerting and claustrophobic. And yet it wasn't enough to stop me from going home with her because she really seemed to want me to. Plus she was like a fucking mental patient in bed.

Even now, I fixated on these faces. I tried to make them whole in my memory, but I couldn't. They were all the same Tomboys in a different city. And I didn't want that anymore. They were too tough, too sharp, too young for me now. I wanted a fat happy woman with some hips and an ass and a little skin under her ribs where I could hang on to her. I dreamed of soft arms and big breasts. I wanted to know a real female body with some stillness about it. Something calm and confident. I was ready to fuck and feel happy again.

But I was perpetually ending up naked in these strangers' beds. I was not a hero and these were not conquests. We were the children of privilege: insulated; overeducated; under-employed. Eternally running away from home and playing at being adults. I had started having unprotected sex, too, for reasons I couldn't comprehend. I would feel a tremendous guilt about this and vow to stop. But I wouldn't, and I didn't. I would wake up next to these nice, middle-class girls with a sad memory of coming too quickly and not caring. What is sex without the connection between two bodies but a sad act of ego. We were just two people flailing and not hitting, not really giving ourselves over to anything.

Last night, there was a tiny blond girl at the bar. She was a German exchange student with red, red lipstick who had been touching my head strangely all night.

"I think you have too much bangs," she kept saying, laughing.

We kissed a little in the bar, and I begged her to take me home. My body felt empty and numbly undrunk. I flatted my bike somewhere and we walked it in the cold to her apartment. I listened to her laughing, and I asked her to speak to me in German, because I didn't want to understand anything about this night. I knew that I'd stopped talking somewhere, too. I was almost sleepwalking when I realized we were inside of the house, already in her bedroom, all at once. She had a huge lofted bed with a ladder.

"I will be back in a meanwhile," she said with a laugh.

As soon as the bathroom door clicked shut, I took my clothes off and climbed into the loft, where I curled myself up in her down comforter and promptly fell asleep.

I woke there this morning, buck-naked, beside this funny

German girl who was nothing if not a total stranger. I asked her awkwardly to tell me if we'd done anything. She laughed and seemed amused by the whole idea. She wanted us to go get breakfast, but I told her I had somewhere else to be. That's when I came here to the Planned Parenthood.

I could still smell this girl on myself, or maybe it was my imagination. I suddenly wished that I had taken a shower. A long, hot shower with scalding water that hurt. I had been wearing these same clothes now for days. Over and over and over again. I tucked my thumb and forefinger behind the waistband of my jeans, and I felt at my crotch surreptitiously, pretending to adjust my belt. I pulled my hand back out and secretly smelled it. I couldn't be sure at all. I was confused, except that I knew I liked the smell.

"Are You Tired Of Being Alone?"

These were the subject lines I wrote. "Want To Meet A Beautiful Woman Near You?" They had ceased to mean anything to me. "Are You Depressed?" "Find Local Sluts!" "Want To Add Three More Inches?" "Make Money Fast!"

It was all a matter of pornography in the end. Sexual, spiritual, or financial. Spam was an offer to fill an unfillable void. This was the "product." This was the reason that everything had to be phrased as a question or an exclamation. It was preying on your greatest fears and desires. "Want To Lose Weight Fast?" "Make Money From Home!" "Want To Have The Best Sex Of Your Life?" "Are You Depressed?"

Spam was the offer that seemed too good to be true. Hope was an evergreen commodity, Roman told me. By the middle of the decade, spam had come to represent 85 percent of all emails sent worldwide. Tens of trillions of spam emails were dispatched every single year. As far as Roman was concerned, this granted us supermajority status. Whatever the original intention of email might have been, it now ceased to exist. Spam had taken it over.

"Spam doesn't discriminate," Roman Holliday told me proudly. "That's the beauty of it. Everyone is invited to click."

Still, it was hard for me to imagine anyone with a brain actually bothering to do that. It wasn't until Roman explained to me the microscopic hit rate we were actually targeting that I understood what was happening at all. As long as one in every twelve million people clicked on my email, he said, we made money. This was staggering to me. After my first month on the job, Roman Holliday had disseminated more than 350 million copies of my emails. This resulted in a paltry twenty-eight hits, a number that Roman was ecstatic about. Abundance is the mother of neurosis, I marveled.

"The Government Is Coming For Your Guns!"

Spam was nothing if not a call to arms. "Don't Let Them Take God Off The Dollar Bill!" This was broadcast at a special frequency for the shut-ins and reactionaries among us. I was trolling the trolls. "Global Warming Proven False!" I was playing on people's loudest, most bombastic selves. "Help Stop The War On Christmas!"

Roman was particularly taken with an algorithm he had written himself, which allowed us to distribute my emails through a network of "zombie" computers. More to the point, he was hacking into your old AOL and Hotmail accounts and ripping through your contacts list. Boy, oh, boy. You wouldn't even believe how many people could be thrilled to get a message from *you* out of the blue.

"Where Have You Been?"

Sometimes this was all it took to make somebody click the link. "Are We Still Friends?" There was an incredible intimacy in using email, Roman told me. "I Never Had The Guts To Tell You I Love You!" People were desperate for a real connection. It didn't matter if it sounded trivial or banal. "Do You Believe In Miracles?" "Angels Exist!" They were all thinking of someone specific. They all had a real person in mind.

The charm of working for Roman Holliday had begun to wear off, though. It was getting harder and harder to shake the idea that I was consorting with a known criminal. Worse, he had taken to leaving me maundering voice messages where he would threaten to fire me for using too much punctuation. It was *supposed* to be written badly, he scolded me. That was the whole point.

"Help Stop Spam Emails!"

This was my new personal favorite. This was my cry for help. I was desperately trying to turn this thing into an art project now. "Click To Make Sure Your Protected!" Roman was a stickler for enforcing the deliberate misuse of *your/you're*. "Get Registered In The Anti-Spam Database Today!"

I tried my best not to take the whole thing too seriously. Maybe people really *were* looking for penis enlargers and local sluts and off-brand medications. And, in that case, maybe I was a hero all along. Or maybe I was just spreading viruses. Abundance is the mother of neurosis, I worried.

Spam was just one of many diseases born of the Internet, I was sure of it. It was part of the general force-feeding going on in the culture now, and everyone was complicit. At its worst, the Internet was one giant snuff film. We were all adding content into the collective nervous breakdown.

Did I hate myself for this work? Probably not sufficiently. No. It was just work to me. It kept me knee-deep in alcohol and fucking around. Plus, it helped pay back my student loans, which my parents were thrilled about. That was about all I wanted at the present moment. I knew I was a hack, of course. I knew that this was not art. But at least I wasn't working in something truly ignoble, like advertising. The spam writer gladly acknowledges his own whiff of repulsion.

AIDS. That was the reason I was sitting in this waiting room. I had been battling the disease in secret since the seventh grade when they pounded it into our heads, in health class, that sex and death were the same thing. I was struck by a memory of Don telling me that the government had created AIDS in a laboratory. Germ warfare gone terribly wrong, he said. This was toward the end, after the OTB, after I'd stopped listening to Don. I didn't want to hear that shit anymore and I'd started cutting him off. I told him I didn't believe in that, and I didn't want to hear any more about it. I remember Don shrugging. Nodding. I felt like an asshole now.

I didn't actually believe that I had AIDS, but being

symptom-free, it seemed like the logical place to start. My real symptom was my guilt. Loneliness and confusion had turned me a little strange. I was better when I had someone, of course. Everyone is. On top of this, I knew I would be paying for this visit out-of-pocket. The euphemism for the uninsured, I had learned, was *self-pay*. Har-har-har.

I didn't even know what it was I was paying for. A fresh start? Peace of mind? My paranoia? It was money that I didn't have for such nice things as these. I daydreamed about a time when I'd have so much money that I could be taken to a hospital or a jail without a second thought. Strange luxuries, indeed. I thought about where I'd be living one year from today, and I came up blank. For some reason it still appealed to me that I couldn't know a thing like that.

I did actually want to talk to a doctor about a number of things, in fact. The poison in the tap water; the Teflon in our food; arsenic in the soil; radiation from cell phones. I wanted to ask a doctor about headaches. About blurred vision. My liver; my kidneys; my heart. I had imaginary lumps in my neck and my groin and under my armpits. I had questions about all these things I couldn't possibly see or feel. Potent, malignant cancers lying dormant in the body somewhere. What should I know, and how much should I worry? What did it mean when you woke up with sore throats or sore muscles? And what was the least amount of sleep a person could get away with anyway?

If a doctor in a white coat could just tell me I was fine, I thought, I might actually begin to recover.

But there was no time for any of that here. This was a

clinic, and I was here, ostensibly, to take an AIDS test I didn't need. Abundance is the mother of neurosis, someone said. I wondered if that could be a kind of prayer. I had not said a single prayer in almost fifteen years, and I wondered how God looked upon johnny-come-latelies and those who make their prayers in selfishness. *Save me, Father, and screw everyone else. I've come back again. This time it's serious.* Is that what people say when they pray for second chances?

A real change could do me good, I supposed. I had daydreams about serious employment, with health insurance and a 401(k). I could dress myself less shabbily and finally have an adult haircut. Standing around the water cooler, quoting lines from television shows with my coworker/friends. I could cut the grass and shovel the snow. I could check the oil and fix the flat. I could play golf, and tennis, and fantasy football. I could find myself a nice girl to go to the movies with again. I just needed to find one nice girl who liked to laugh and eat and fuck and have fun. Simple things.

The door buzzed again and a girl my age walked into the waiting room. Someone more like me, I thought. I watched her talk to the lady receptionist with a kind of self-assurance I was sure I'd never had. She was matter-of-fact and free from paranoia, and this made her very pretty, actually. I could almost place her face from somewhere, too, falling just short. I was intrigued, though. I wished stupidly that there were some way for me to kiss this girl today. I could never talk to her now, though. Not here, and not anywhere.

Still, I couldn't stop myself from stealing glances. I

wanted to know what her story was. What was her dirty little secret and why had she come here to the Planned Parenthood on a Wednesday? Maybe she was simply picking up her birth control or having some kind of annual exam. Or maybe she was hiding ugly blisters and sores, or worse, something invisible. Like me.

The girl looked out the window and down at the carpet and up at the posters, and she reached out for a pamphlet, which she read and quickly tired of. But she never once looked at me, waiting patiently to make eye contact. How could she not look over at me at all? And why was that a turn-on? I was either totally invisible or she was making this tremendous effort not to see me on purpose. I had no idea what this meant. Didn't she see we were the same here? Out of place among the teenage Latinas and the pizza-faced boyfriend who was yawning wildly now. Maybe this room was the reason we were doomed to never meet. We had been marked by the waiting room of the Planned Parenthood. We couldn't just ignore that fact. Eventually we would have to acknowledge what we were both doing here on this day. I thought that that could be a very funny moment, actually. Unless, that is, she really was hiding blisters.

I realized I'd been doing this for weeks now, making up stories for strangers. I secretly wanted to be in love again, and I'd been projecting the vague idea onto girls all over the city. Daydreams and missed connections. I saw these happy girls walking around with their boyfriends and I wanted to take them away. All these girls I would never even speak to. But I could again, and that was the point.

And just then, as I stopped waiting for the girl to look at me, a door opened. A nurse was calling her name, and I turned around, and back again. She stood up and I missed it. I missed the girl's name and then she was gone, too. The door closed and I smiled. I leaned back in my chair for a second. And then I got up and left.

A CATTLE, A CRACK-UP

I was unlocking my bike downtown when this girl walked by. I caught her eye and she smiled at me, I thought. But she was walking away.

"Hello," I called out, surprising her a little.

She turned back and waved her hand, unsure. "Hey," she said. "You don't remember me, do you?"

"I do. But I don't know how."

"In Washington," she said. "We were neighbors."

"Oh, right. You lived in Columbia Heights. You're Jamie."

"Danielle."

"Shit, right, Danielle. I remember you." I smiled at her like a moron. "You live here now? Where are you headed?"

Danielle hemmed a little, looking past me up the street. "Nowhere. Just running some errands. I have the day off today. You?"

"I don't know." I paused. "Maybe I'll just come with you. I might have errands, too. Things I haven't thought of yet."

"But I'm taking the bus," she said, looking at my bike.

"That's okay. I can lock it up." I snapped the U-lock back together and took the key. I looked at Danielle, forcing her to tell me no now. But she didn't, and the bus was already coming up Burnside.

"Okay," she said, not quite smiling. "Why not, I guess."

I did remember her, too: this girl from the ancient past. It wasn't that I thought I'd never see Danielle again; I'd forgotten there even *was* a girl called Danielle. But I liked the randomness of this. I liked sitting beside her on this city bus. I wanted the other riders to imagine us as a couple, the way I was trying to imagine it myself.

Danielle looked at her watch. "I'm supposed to meet my boyfriend back in front of the Whole Foods at six o'clock," she said, trying to sound casual. "Just so you know."

"This is so strange, running into you out here," I said, answering a different question. "All the D.C. kids I know moved to New York. And San Francisco."

"Right. Me, too. But I was offered a job, and I ended up liking it here, I guess."

I nodded. "Lane Tworek told me there's a Target and a Best Buy on Fourteenth Street now. Right by the Metro. And all kinds of condos and shit."

"Uh-huh," she said. "And that weird brothel near your old house, with the Fruitopia machine in the front yard . . . that's a Brick Oven Pizzeria."

"Ha!" I laughed, and then I groaned. "Jesus. Yuck."

"Yep." Danielle sat back, and I could feel her beginning to loosen up. "I've seen you out here, too, you know. Last summer. They were kicking you out of a bar for taking your shirt off inside."

"Huh," I said, acting puzzled. "Maybe it was unusually hot or something."

"Right." She nodded.

"I'm afraid I can be a bit of an unpredictable drunk, Danielle."

"Yeah. I remember that, too," she said with a smile. "You were having fun, though. People seemed sad to see you go."

"Good, then. That's the only thing I really care about."

Danielle laughed and I was startled by what a nice laugh it was. Really lovely and in pitch, like a glass bell. My entire memory of the girl came whole in this one moment. She leaned in and pulled the cord above my head.

"This is our stop," she said, standing up.

The truth was, I'd grown bored with drinking and acting out. I was buying books and making soups and getting ten hours of sleep (which my sister told me was obscene). I'd stopped eating fast food and checking my email every day. I was flossing regularly and doing push-ups in the morning. I was reading the Metro section of the newspaper and making plans to watch NBA basketball on TV. I was going to the bank and the grocery store and the post office, and having long conversations with strangers about the weather.

And I was living alone, for the first time in my life. I had a big bed and a nice desk and no furniture. I used to be able to share the smallest spaces with people: sleeping on a futon in a walk-in closet; storing everything I owned behind a stranger's couch. I could lie down in a coffin with a girlfriend, or more likely just a twin mattress on the floor. There was something about that forfeit of space that I always liked: breathing each other's air, and smelling each other's skin.

But more than anything I found I liked being alone now. I liked sleeping diagonally and having the whole bed to myself. I even liked the celibacy that it bred. I liked taking long showers and talking to myself out loud in paragraphs. I liked keeping the house too hot or too cold. I liked the spareness of my refrigerator and the piles of clean clothes on the dresser. I filled my days and got things done, and I convinced myself that this capacity to be alone might even make me well disposed to being a writer.

But I didn't share any of that with Danielle. It was too intimate for the city buses.

We walked a block, looking for an address, and Danielle asked about Lauren Pinkerton. Out of the blue. I looked at her and realized she wanted to take a shot.

"That girl was always so *mean* to me, you know? For no reason at all, really."

"Maybe you looked at her funny," I said, yielding nothing.

"Yeah, right." She smiled. "Whatever happened to her anyway?"

"Oh," I said, feeling a strange prick of melancholy. "I don't know. The last I heard she'd gotten engaged to some guy with money. A doctor or an architect or something."

Danielle yawned, losing interest. "Uh-huh." It didn't mean anything to her and I was grateful for that. She mentioned her own boyfriend again, in a passing way, which was kind of cute. Something about his job.

"Oh. Super," I said flatly, just to make her smirk.

Back on the bus, we showed our transfers and found our seats, and I caught myself thinking about Danielle as an idea again. What would it be like to date a girl like this? She was too nice; too neat; too mature for me. Where would the tension come from? What would we fight about? There was probably not one single picture of Danielle on the Internet with her middle finger up, I thought.

She was talking about her day off again, too, which was an attempt to fish out what it was that *I* was doing wandering out in front of Powell's on a Thursday afternoon. And finally she just asked me.

"What are you up to these days, anyway? Like for work." I could tell that these kinds of questions were important to a person like Danielle. So I screwed up my face as serious as I could make it.

"I'm a dogcatcher," I said.

"Mm." She smiled painfully. "The world always needs good dogcatchers."

"Amen," I said, nodding.

I could go on like this all day, making jokes, talking about nothing. But suddenly I didn't want to do that with Danielle. I didn't want to be defensive and sarcastic. I didn't want to bore and annoy her. I just wanted to keep hanging out, running errands with this girl who felt like a stranger to me, and not, all at once.

"Actually, I just finished writing a short story this morning," I said.

"Really?" she said, brighter. "What is it called?"

"'A Cattle, a Crack-Up.'"

This was true. I had rewritten my four-hundred-page novel as a thirteen-page short story. It was an act of total and utter fucking madness, which I was still riding high off of.

"I could read you some of it, if you want."

"Right now?" she asked, looking stricken. "You mean you have it with you?"

"I'm supposed to mail it out to somebody, maybe." It was Bettina Kleins, but Danielle never asked this, so I didn't tell her.

"Well," she said, a little coy, "I'm sort of a tough grader."

"Ha!" I said, appreciating this last attempt to discourage me. "Good, give it to me, then. I like a hard F," I said with all sorts of disgusting innuendo.

Danielle shook her head. "Oh, man. Just read it. Go ahead."

I pulled the story out of my bag, laughing. And then, of course, I froze. "Should I set it up, or just start reading?"

"I dunno. What's it called again?" she asked, looking at the title. "'A *Cattle*, a *Crack-Up*'? What does that mean?"

I smiled back, not sure what to say. "I'm just gonna read it . . ." I said, flipping to the first page.

"*August Caffrey banged the latch off the pen and led his forty black 'n' white Holsteins grazing out into the field in a slow, somnambulant stream. He hustled the last of the milking herd out and made his way back up to the farmhouse.*

"*Overhead the clouds were raked out across the sky. At the western border of the pasture was a stand of rock elms where the scavengers waited for the herd. Pieces of trees could be seen breaking off in the wind and flying away as State Birds. The wooden fence that ran rectangular around the field seemed unfit to keep anything, but it was good enough for cows. The grass grew a fast vibrating green in the early summer that the cows beat back with hoof and mouth. And everywhere you stood you saw the kingly American Elm that lorded over the open pasture. The American Elm was the skyline here.*

"*Gail had August's lunch waiting for him on the table, and she stopped with the dishes to sit down beside him . . .*"

I stopped reading.

"Maybe I should explain it to you."

"No, it's good. Keep going."

I nodded reluctantly and picked it back up, feeling strange.

"*August never said much. If his appetite was good he ate quickly, as a rule. He picked up his ice water and swallowed it in gulps. Setting the glass down, he turned to his wife. 'Where's the milk, Gail?'*

"'*Well,' she began, as though she were expecting this. 'I just figured maybe you were still havin' problems with your stomach.'*

"'*Problems with my stomach? Since when did I say I was havin' problems with my stomach? All's I ever said was that the milk tasted off to me. Haven't I lived here my whole life? Don't I know how cow's milk is supposed to taste?'*

"'Of course, August. I'm not sayin' that.'

"'Don't look for fights with me, Gail. I work too hard . . .'

"Gail stood up and brought back a cold bottle of milk, which she poured out into a glass.

"'You take away the boy's milk now, too?'

"'Course not, August, you know Kurt loves milk. We all do. I was only thinkin' . . .' but her voice trailed away as she turned back toward the fridge.

"August Caffrey put his head back down and brooded over his plate. It had been two long weeks since his stomach started rejecting the milk. It was the smell or the color or something else. He tried not to taste anything at all, but the milk coated the inside of his mouth and throat, as milk does. August pulled at it slowly and then threw back half the glass. He returned it to the table and put his hands down on his thighs, sitting stock-still, as his body worked at something unseen. August grimaced then and belched quietly into a closed fist.

"Gail watched him painfully, wishing he wouldn't do this to himself. She knew he would finish the glass and go back out to work in the hot sun to be physically sick behind one of the outbuildings . . ." I stopped again.

"Okay, so I'm just gonna tell you about it."

Danielle laughed at me. "If you want to. I mean, it's fine, I like it. I like the writing."

"I'm still working on it," I said, feeling frustrated by my unwillingness to keep reading. I was thinking about too many unrelated things. Everything I had taken out. All these invisible holes I had left there on the page.

"This is a story about cows?" Danielle asked with a be-mused look.

"Sort of, yeah. I mean, it's really about the farmer."

"August."

"Right. August. This is his family's dairy farm, where he was born. Fine, fine." I gestured with my hand. "Except that now his cows are triggering some kind of nervous collapse in him."

"They what?"

"Well, see, it's actually a kind of allegory about the Invasion of Iraq."

Danielle laughed when I didn't. "Seriously?"

"Dead seriously."

"Okay. Tell it to me, then."

"All right, let me think . . ." I hemmed. "No, just let me read about the farm first." I flipped ahead two pages and kept reading.

"*A dairy farm is run on a religion of routine. Deviation is damnation, and every day begins at four a.m. when Buck Karen—the only employee of the Amelia Dairy—begins milking the herd. At five, August joins him in the milking parlor to help move the cows. He feeds the young calves and dry cows from the round bales of hay. Manure is scraped, and the parlor floors are hosed. By ten o'clock August's neighbor Elvin Hale arrives to fill the Amelia's silos with feed, always removing the glove from his right hand before waving across to the two dairymen. At eleven a.m., Buck feeds forage to the milking herd, and pulls away in a cloud of dust in his rust-colored pickup. August puts the herd out to pasture, and the afternoon is spent*

repairing fences and maintaining equipment. Buck is back by
three to start the—"

"How do you know all of this?" Danielle stopped me,
grinning widely.

"I dunno. A guy just picks things up."

"You liar," she said, giving me a teasing shove.

"Okay, I did a little research."

"How much?"

"Off and on, I'd say, four years."

"*Four years!*" Danielle said. "You've been learning about
dairy cows for four years? To write a *short story*?"

"Off and on," I said, trying to sound defensive. But I was
smiling with her, too. "I was in a weird place then, okay? It
seemed important."

"Okay," she said. "Tell me about the cows, then."

"See, that's the thing. There had to be the cows because
all I had when I started was the ending."

"You started the story so that you could write the ending
about the cows?"

"Right."

"So read me the ending."

"No. I can't read you the ending. The ending is terrible.
It makes no sense."

"Why not?"

"Because the ending is the part of the story that's *true*.
That part all really happened. I read about it in the news-
paper. It was horrible and I couldn't stop thinking about it.
That's what started this whole thing."

"The cows."

"Right."

Danielle was intrigued. "So tell me what happens!"

"Ahhh, all right . . ." I agreed. "See, the milk starts to make August Caffrey extremely ill—"

"Lactose intolerance?"

"No, no. Worse. Way worse. Some sort of nervous condition that I invented for him. It's all very psychosomatic and paranoid, but also totally debilitating. It's all very real for August, and it's all inside his head, too, which is why he can't stop it. And it keeps getting worse. So August starts to blame the cows. He develops these crippling sensitivities to light and temperature and smell, and he has to stay in his bed with the curtains closed tight . . ."

"This all really happened?" she asked eagerly.

"No, no, none of this happened," I said. "I made all of this up. This is just the story. Only the part with the cows at the end really happened."

"Okay."

"Right . . . so there's this storm—a big old midwestern tempest, right? And Gail, the wife, and Buck, the other dairyman, have been trying everything they can to hold it together— to keep the herd milked; to save the farm—while August has been shut up in his bed having these terrible fever dreams about his dead father, and about his son . . ."

"Kurt."

"Right. His *corn-fed, hay-haired boy* Kurt," I offered wryly. "And, anyway, this storm comes, and there's no one there to bring the cows back in. So they're all just freaking out, stranded in the pasture. And the only thing they know to do is to crowd themselves under this giant elm tree for protection . . ."

"The American Elm."

"Right, the *American Elm*, exactly. Except I keep changing the way that I'm describing this giant family tree, throughout the story: the Grandfather Elm; the Ghost Elm; the Fortune Elm; the Sorrow Elm . . ." I stopped, unsure. "Because the elm tree has become like a character in the story."

"Yeah, I get it," she said, as though this were obvious.

"Right, right." I smiled, feeling both annoyed and impressed by her attentiveness. "Because *really* the American Elm *is* the farm, you know? It's been there longer than the farm. Longer than the town or the state or even the country." I stopped and suddenly picked up the story again, reading from the ending.

"Out in the field the cows felt the weather in their arthritic joints and dropped to their knees, long before the storm was present in the sky. Through a hot sleep, August heard Gail's wind chimes calling in the clouds like church bells. The sky went ink-black and started to drip. When it all finally cracked open it was enough to stir August bolt upright in his casket-bed. He could hear the pellet-rain pinging off the windows in staccato. And he could hear the banshee lowing of his cattle, willing their heavy bodies upright with no small difficulty.

"August swung his feet out onto the floor, in a cold sweat, unsure whether it was night or day in his blacked-out bedroom. He knew he had to bring them in, though he could hardly make his body begin. It raced with everything that he must do. He fought through the fug of bed rest, knowing exactly where they

were now, pushing together in a craven huddle under the massive Deliverance Elm. Shoulder to flank, with mooing impatience. They forced themselves in with the butts of their heads.

"August limped through the downstairs with his hands trailing along the walls. Even the muted stormlight was painful in his eyes now. At the precipice of the house, the family dog howled at the storm without mercy, but was struck dumb at the sight of its master in shambles. It backed up meekly, with its tail between its legs, giving August a wide berth to pass. But the farmer stopped cold, frozen by the gray apparition of his wife running toward him from the field.

"'August! For God's sake, get back into the house. You're not well. You'll catch your death out here!'

August said nothing, fastening to his zombie-resolve.

"'Please! It's hopeless; the cows can't be moved! Just leave 'em,' Gail pleaded. 'Come with me. I'm going to call Buck.' She reached for his hand, but he took it away.

"'No . . . I have to bring them in,' August insisted in a hoarse voice.

"Gail's face went white with panic, and she hurried into the house.

"In his heavy jacket and boots, August walked out into the teeth of the storm. The sky filled with lead as the thunderstorm invoked its Midwestern Gods. August rushed forward, lunging for a pitchfork on the ground—a sick, comic prop planted by the Devil himself. Up the hill, he carried it out in front of him, in two hands, like a rifle. A sickly sweet taste gathered in his mouth that he could not spit away. The speed of the storm and the strain on his empty body made his head throb. He trudged

on, leading forward with the crown of his skull. And then there was just a single crack!

"*The first clear thing that August saw, after that, were the smoldering flames hissing off the Murder Elm. He lost his drowning grip on the pitchfork and started running up the hill, with his boots sucking in the mud and shit . . .*" I stopped again, feeling like I had been reading too long.

"Don't stop," Danielle said, hanging on the story.

"This is the part that happened, though."

"What happened?" she asked in earnest.

"Well . . ." I hesitated. "The elm tree was struck by lightning and the cows died of electrocution."

"Oh," she said, dropping back in her seat.

I'd just ruined the entire story with this death knell, but I wanted to tell her the truth. I wanted someone to see where I'd begun. I wanted to try and untangle it all in my own head, too.

Danielle tried not to look disappointed. "It's sad. The cows all died."

"A lot of them." I nodded. "A few lived."

"Read it to me," she said hopefully.

"Okay." I cleared my throat artificially and kept going.

"*Black and white, death was laid out in front of him. One single bolt of lightning had inexplicably killed forty-three of his fifty dairy cows. This, he would later learn from Guinness's London office, was simply unprecedented . . .*' That part is true, by the way," I offered solemnly, and kept reading.

"*August was shell-shocked by the scorched earth and carnage that he saw. He sent the live cows ambling backward with his unsteady movements. He picked up the head of a dead Holstein and shook it to make it real, but the emptiness he felt knocked the wind out of him.*

"'*What a waste, what a waste . . .*' *he said in a hollow voice.*

"*The living cows circled and stared, in reproof, while August sank down among the humiliating dead. He felt a weight that crushed involuntarily. He tried to rise to his feet again and couldn't. He felt the ground disappearing and suddenly rushing up to meet him. August's rope had just been cut from the top branch of the Gallows Elm. He looked at the curdling udders with frenzy as he felt himself sinking into the soft earth. His head spun. Death of the cattle is death of the farmer is death of the farm . . .*'" I stopped.

"And it goes on and on, a little," I said quickly, as I turned the whole thing back to the front page. "It's not right yet, exactly. I'm not convinced I've earned this big kind of biblical ending-thing."

"Gosh." Danielle exhaled. "I feel a little dizzy now."

"Right. Sorry."

"No, it's a good thing. We missed our stop," she said with a laugh, looking around. "It's good. It's weird, really weird." She smiled, imparting something strong in her silence. "I can't believe you got all of that into ten pages." She laughed again, breaking her own tension.

I started to say something about this, but I stopped myself. Nodding mutely instead.

"Here," she said, taking the story away from me. "Let me read it for real. I'll take it home. I can give you notes."

"Oh. You don't have to do that."

"No, let me," she said, pulling out a pen. "Write your email address on the front. I'll send you my notes. I like it, I do. It's good."

There was something charged in this proposition, like she'd just caught herself sounding insistent and was surprised. I smiled at her and she looked away. I wrote my email onto the top of the story and I gave it back to her.

"Thanks for not asking if I'm on Facebook," I said dryly.

Danielle laughed, and her eyes got big and shiny. "Have you ever read Michel Foucault?"

"Who, the philosopher?" I smiled, thinking this a particularly strange question to ask on a city bus. "Wasn't he the guy with the circular prisons . . ."

"Right, yeah. *The Panopticon*," she said excitedly. "And I was reading that last summer—for something totally unrelated—and I had this epiphany about Facebook."

"Facebook?" I asked, not understanding.

"Right, right, so listen. The purpose of the Panopticon is to induce a conscious and permanent visibility upon the inmates, right? You never know who's looking at you, or when. You give up your privacy and you behave because you never really know who's watching. So, with Facebook, what happens is that the population begins to self-report. And then we all start to surrender our privacy in order to indulge in the loss of everyone else's privacy. Right?"

"Holy shit," I said, a little startled. "Facebook is the new Panopticon!"

"Fucking Facebook!" she shouted. People looked up at us

from their seats. "It's Facebook," she said more quietly. "The prisoners are the guards and vice versa."

I laughed because I had no idea Danielle had it in her. Who knew this pretty girl from the suburbs was capable of making these kinds of advanced paranoid connections? All of a sudden I thought I might be falling in love with her.

"That's dark, Danielle. I like that one a lot."

She sat back and demurred. "Yeah. Well, I don't pretend it's any kind of earth-shattering conclusion. It's all up on the Internet already. It just struck me when I thought of it."

"No, it's yours. Own it," I said, charmed. "So did you quit Facebook then? After you figured out you were—what's the word—*self-reporting*?"

"Oh, yeah, of course. Are you kidding? I had to," she said. "What about you?"

"A while ago," I offered solemnly. "I had no idea I was in a penal colony, though. I just didn't think it was that much fun."

Danielle smiled at me, and I took away her pen to write *Foucault/Facebook* on the top of my hand. She laughed and looked away, out the window, before reaching up and pulling for the next stop.

"Facebook is nothing. Give it more time, they'll think of something way worse."

We got off the bus, and back on again, as the dull sun began sinking into six o'clock. Danielle stood closer at each next stop, using me to block the wind, she said. This was the end of our day out in the city. We were having fun just watching the people on the buses, with their strange comings and goings. We made jokes behind their backs, but never mean jokes, really. We just wanted to keep talking.

We showed our transfers and stood on the crowded #20 as it arced us back across the river at rush hour. The conversations became very easy, and I confessed that I had only just discovered Don DeLillo and I was taking the year to read every one of his books in order. It was always so strange to discover a thing that everyone else seemed to know so implicitly. Danielle nodded and admitted to doing something similar with Keanu Reeves movies. And then we laughed and gushed about the greatness of *River's Edge*.

Halfway up the hill, Danielle pulled the cord, saying that she wanted to walk the last ten blocks. But we mostly walked in silence. The whole day had been a dance this way. Our hands swinging, and nearly touching, like live wires. This was a danger to be fully conscious of. That was the fun we were having.

How could I say what my intentions with Danielle were? On some primal level I wanted to steal her away. I wanted her to fall in love with *me*, of course. But our errands were done and the day was over, too. We walked past my bike, past Powell's, to the Whole Foods. Danielle was looking around for her boyfriend, but I was not. His absence was a reason to keep going, to keep on walking. We went inside, out of the cold, out of the dark. We walked around the bright supermarket, trying samples and looking at the fancy foods.

Danielle pulled out her cell phone and told me he was there now. Outside somewhere, she said. We went back through the automatic doors and onto the street, where the night was suddenly threshed with neon lights. People were standing around and coming home from work. Some gutter-punk kid was yelling for his mutt dog to get out of the street, and Danielle made one last crack about dogcatching.

"Sorry," I said. "I'm off the clock." And we laughed in a hollow way.

She looked around the street, and back at me. She smiled with her nerves, I thought. We touched hands unconsciously and held on too long. I squeezed and let her go, feeling something unexpected. This happy rush of warm blood as we looked at each other without speaking. Danielle blinked first and turned away.

"Well . . ." she said nervously. "This was a lot of fun, actually." She was afraid to really look at me now. Afraid that I could make her lose herself, I hoped. I wanted her to hate me as she hated herself for wanting me to steal her away.

"Yes . . ." I said, smiling and waiting for her to look back up. That look that said that she'd enjoyed our secret day in the city. In the movies this would be the kiss-moment. We would lean in and I would take her at the waist and bend her backward, or something.

But we didn't take a kiss here. Or, rather, I didn't, maybe. I liked the tension too much to spoil it all now. I didn't even want to touch Danielle again in this moment where men and women always hug platonically. Just to let the pressure off; just to say goodbye. But we didn't.

"I guess I should let you go, then," I said. "He's probably waiting for you."

"Right." She nodded, turning to look again. "Yeah."

"Have fun," I said. "Have a good night."

"Okay."

I could tell she was bemused. Nodding and turning away from me, walking away again. I could see she had something else to say; I was supposed to stop her now. I was supposed to take the last word and try something dangerous in the halo of the streetlight. But I didn't do that because I didn't want to ruin it.

I let Danielle go, and I watched her body go blurry in the reflected lights as she turned the corner and came together with a different body altogether. Gone.

BALENTYNE

People don't just disappear anymore. You would hear someone saying this. Everyone was talking about John Francis Balentyne. This was the kid who disappeared. Just out of the blue, gone, and no one could say what had happened to him.

We didn't know Balentyne, but we talked about him, too. There were friends of friends, and all the loose degrees of separation in a small city. People felt like they could've known him, at a party, in a bar, just casually, wherever. Balentyne's roommates were talking to the free weeklies, and we would look for his name in *The Portland Mercury*. Everyone felt certain he would come back. Everyone was sure that the whole thing would turn out fine. John just did this sort of thing sometimes, and no one gave much cause to worry yet. It had only been one week.

The story of Balentyne was simple enough: he drank too much one night and had a bad encounter with a girlfriend, or somebody, at a bar. People said that Balentyne made an ugly little scene of it and got himself kicked out. They all remembered him leaving the bar, drunk and unhappy. Walking out onto the street to unlock his bike.

Balentyne came home around midnight, grumbling how sick he was of all this Portland bullshit. His roommates laughed and ignored him as they watched TV in the other room. Balentyne dropped his bag onto the floor and took a beer out of the fridge. He went into his bedroom and came back out again, banging his bicycle down the hallway, letting the screen door slam. He didn't say goodbye.

And that was the last time anyone saw John Francis Balentyne.

His cell phone rang and rang, and eventually went straight to voice mail. His roommates looked through his bedroom but found only unwashed clothes. There were no notes or explanations. No directions or intentions or clues left to follow. There was nothing on his computer but fragments of artwork. His truck was unlocked in the yard, but the only thing they found out there was a stack of overdue library books.

Overnight, a photocopied poster went up all over the city. Stapled to telephone poles and taped up inside of convenience stores. We looked at Balentyne's face now as we waited for the bus or a cashier to make our change. This missing poster became a stand-in for the real thing. It *was* the disappearance after a while, and it kept people talking about this kid they hardly knew.

After a week, the *Mercury* gave a small public recounting of the life and times of John Francis Balentyne. His friends reported misadventures and personal oddities. John might simply have gone home to see his parents, they thought, though no one seemed to have a number. Balentyne used to hop trains and hitchhike, they all recalled now. He once rode his bicycle down to L.A., which had taken him weeks. He was famous for walking around the city at night, taking photographs, and showing up at work the next day without sleeping. But he never missed a day of work. They were all certain of that. He was always working: two, three jobs at a time. Balentyne had a history of leaving in the summer for seasonal work, and that could be what this was. He used to have a job on a farm outside of Olympia. He used to harvest pot for some old hippie in California. A year ago he took a job on an Alaskan fishing boat and came back with a scar on his face.

Balentyne was just prone to these breakdowns in communication, they all said, almost defensively. Even in the best of times, he would miss a bill and have his phone shut off for a day or a week. It just wasn't that unusual. Balentyne could be a bit of a loner, yeah, but he always came back around.

Together we all told the ballad of John Francis Balentyne. There could be only two possibilities now: either he had taken off on purpose, or something bad had happened to him. People found themselves attracted or repelled accordingly. Even in the rush to rumor and conjecture, it was hard not to acknowledge some dark appeal in simply taking off. We felt threatened and excited by the disappearance of this young man. In a world of false connections, John Francis Balentyne had found some quiet mystery here. He had a secret, and like it or not, it was making a kind of folk hero out of the kid.

After ten days, someone on the Internet found a photo of Balentyne from the night he disappeared. This grainy still-frame capture from an ATM outside a Wells Fargo. The image was time-stamped 12:41 a.m., and it showed John Francis Balentyne leaning over his bicycle and withdrawing one hundred dollars, before disappearing into the night.

The photograph was online before the police even had a copy, and this was strangely thrilling. Finally there was a clue. We stared at the fuzzy blue monochrome, desperately trying to decide what it meant. Balentyne's tired face, staring past the security camera, as he waited for his money. One frame later, he was gone.

Still, this one photo helped jump-start the search for John Francis Balentyne. It restated the plea for people with any information to please come forward. His friends got the story back up on the nightly news. Phone calls were made to bars and chain restaurants in the area. Requests were made to view surveillance tapes from businesses large and small. Strangers constructed elaborate Google maps, with lines and concentric circles running off in every conceivable direction, to show the limits of how far Balentyne could go, in one night, on a bicycle. Whatever else it meant, this picture planted a third flag on the map for real. After the bar, and after his house,

John Francis Balentyne had taken out one hundred dollars cash in Northeast Portland.

By the end of the second week, the public imagination had started to turn on Balentyne, though. People knew that he had not gone to his parents' house. He was not in Olympia or Alaska or Los Angeles. Everyone knew that he hadn't hopped a train in over three years. No one in any part of the country had heard any word from John Francis Balentyne since the night he took off on his bicycle. And where was the girlfriend from that night at the bar, anyway? How come we never heard any more from her? Was it possible we had projected her into the story ourselves? Or maybe she just didn't feel it was right to talk about John this way.

Either way, Balentyne was still missing, and it seemed to make people anxious and resentful. The Internet took up this story in a kind of backlash. Message boards and forums that had felt so constructive the week before felt like echo chambers now. People said ugly, impulsive, hurtful things, and they didn't sign their names to them. Balentyne was framed as a misfit and a con man. Where was his Facebook page, and why hadn't he posted more pictures of himself or his artwork online? How could we be asked to trust a kid who had disengaged himself from the culture of self-promotion anyway? People found it baffling and amusing that someone could exist in the world without the paper trails of his generation. This was what made John Francis Balentyne so unusual to everyone. People don't just *disappear* anymore.

————

This being the Great Northwest, people's minds took to wandering. Everyone suspected foul play in one way or another. People joked about the one-armed man and satanists in the woods. Others were legitimately fixated on the hundred dollars, insisting it was a drug deal gone wrong. Or maybe just a botched robbery. Wasn't that a shadow, just off-camera, in the picture from the ATM? People said, in earnest, that John Balentyne had gone off his meds and didn't *know* where he was. They said he'd been hit by a trucker and buried in the woods. Others argued that sudden disappearance was the hallmark of organized crime. Or was that UFOs? Or maybe we were all just scratching at the idea of a serial killer on the loose now. It hardly mattered. People found ways to connect the disappearance of John Francis Balentyne to unsolved crimes all across the country.

The sheriff's office was forced to release a statement, saying that, without a single hard clue as to the whereabouts of John Francis Balentyne, they wouldn't even know where to begin a search. Furthermore, they wanted it put on the record that, despite the many rumors to the contrary, John Balentyne had no history of mental illness of any sort. He did not have a criminal record. He was not believed to be a drug user or a depressive or any overt threat to himself or anyone else. He was just missing.

Eventually Balentyne's roommates pulled everything out of his room and found some journals in a closet. But the writing was abstract and indecipherable, as these things usually go. They were just private conversations Balentyne was having with himself, and nothing more. Worse, the notebooks were all six months old anyway.

But the *Mercury* still printed excerpts, out of context, just the same, and it depressed us that they would do that now. Everyone was claiming squatter's rights on the life of John Francis Balentyne.

In quieter conversations, among friends, we found ourselves making grim jokes about death. People had some need to revel in a shared disaster. It was a way to begin to forget. Something terrible had happened to John Francis Balentyne, the same as it could happen to any one of us. So what could be done for it now?

There were rumors that Balentyne's sister was around now, too. People said she had paid her brother's rent and was living in his bedroom on a temporary basis. She had come because she wanted to help; she was looking for answers, and who could blame her? Someone pointed her out to me in a bar one night, but I couldn't make myself go up and talk to her. Not even just to nod and say something friendly. I couldn't risk the idea that she might burst into tears. Or that I might, maybe.

Is it too obvious to say that I was thinking about myself in all of this? I've been blacked out on my bicycle. I've been that drunk and fought with girls and friends. We were all self-pitying and self-destroying sometimes: taking the long way home; climbing over the wrong fences; lingering up on steep rooftops. I've trespassed in buildings, and jumped off of bridges, and crashed into the street. I've thrown punches at strangers and been knocked down for my big mouth. And who hasn't taken a ride from a drunk driver before? Or given one, too. All these fucking drunk drivers!

Once a guy walked into a party with a gun. He pointed it at me and told me I'd better turn the stereo down, *right now.* Me! Jesus Christ, it wasn't even my house. I hadn't even been *invited* to this fucking party! But everyone went dead silent just the same. A kind of horror-of-the-moment, with the stereo screaming out of the wall, as this guy walked me across the living room at gunpoint. I turned the music down, and he nodded and looked around the room. And then he left. That was it. We all just laughed and turned the stereo right back up, because *fuck* him.

This was a thing that really happened! I have no idea what it means, but I must've told that story a thousand times. I drank out on it for weeks! And it didn't do anything to change me, either. Even now, I still fight against that strain of recklessness. Every time we didn't die we laughed. It had to be this way. I could have died a thousand times by now, but I didn't. I was still alive.

So where was John Francis Balentyne, and what were we to make of his famous reluctance to reappear? He was more than just a name being drilled into my head. Balentyne would show up incongruously in my dreams at night. He had taken on a kind of weight in the full three-part name. John. Francis. Balentyne. His friends called him Balentyne, and his sister called him John. But the newspapers and strangers all called him John Francis Balentyne. We projected ourselves onto his life. Balentyne should have been a writer, I thought. This was the name that a novelist has. John Francis Balentyne would know how to rewrite his book. Even if it was about cows.

Eventually Balentyne's sister disappeared, as well. Gone home to Milwaukee or Pittsburgh or Toledo, someone said. The roommates were forced to rent out Johnny's room, and life went on. Until, one day, a picture was posted on a bike blog. Someone had found a fixed-gear locked to a tree, down by the Willamette River. Way down by the science museum, totally out of place. People wrote to say that the bike was Balentyne's, they were certain of this, and we all got excited again in spite of ourselves. But this was fleeting, too, of course. This was not good news. Balentyne was dead, I thought.

The next morning, I decided to go down there. It was a gray and ugly day, and I didn't tell anyone what I was doing. I wouldn't know what to say, besides. I just wanted to see the bare spot where Balentyne had locked his bike. I wanted to see the river there. I wanted to know what made him stop in that place. Why there?

I locked up on the street, outside of OMSI, and I followed the spiral sidewalks to the end. I left the path and went down into the weeds where the ground was soft and patched with moss. I could feel the heavy, metallic grind of the trains lumbering through the switchyard in the distance. I just wanted to see the bike and go, I told myself, as I fought deeper into the tangle of weeds.

But when I finally found it I wasn't sure. I had to stop and stare at the thing, so white and colorless it was absorbed into the landscape. I had to force myself to connect this bicycle to the picture I had looked at on the Internet one hour before. Something had already happened here, something very obvious. Balentyne's bike was just a shell of its lock and frame. Picked apart by looters. People had already come down here, claiming pieces off the wreck. The back wheel; the seat; even the handlebars were gone.

It was clear that there was nothing left to save. I had seen it, and I didn't want to linger. This bike was no more a symbol than Balentyne himself. And one day someone would find a way to take the whole thing apart entirely. It all felt so random now, as I exhaled and looked out across the river where the drawbridges were suddenly rising. I turned away and walked back up the hill to the street.

By the end of the week it was over. An OMSI worker found something washed up on the banks of the river, nearly a mile from John Balentyne's bike. The police identified the body of John Francis Balentyne, age twenty-six. There was no sign of foul play upon the body. There was no evidence of accident or intent. There was no categorical way to say how this boy's body had come to rest inside of the river. Only that Balentyne had been found now, missing one month to the day.

TEXAS LANDLADY BLUES

Maritza picked up Bruno off the floor and put him down in her lap, letting him settle there. I watched as she opened the front of her shirt and pulled out her breast to give it to the baby. I saw Maritza's dark tan line where the skin went suddenly and startlingly white. Her breast was the same color as the baby's face.

This happened right in the middle of our conversation, as we sat there in the living room. I paused, trying to meet Maritza's eye, trying to remember what it was we were talking about. Not that it bothered Maritza any. This was just one more thing that she did for the baby, all day long, out of need.

"Do you want to hold him?" she asked, misplacing my curiosity.

"Oh, no. Thank you," I said, sitting back. This was not what I wanted.

"Of course you do. Here." And, just like that, little Bruno's meal was over. Maritza held him out to me with his mouth still dripping. "Don't worry. You'll be fine."

I reached up reflexively as she pressed the wriggling child into my chest. Maritza stepped away and smiled, the way that all mothers revel in seeing their children held.

"There. See? You can't hurt him. He likes you."

I held Bruno close like a small, captive animal. Balancing him against my body. "He's so little," I said, looking up at her.

"That's not what Lane says. Lane says he's getting big and fat now," she said with a laugh. "He says that comes from my side of the family."

I smiled and gave the baby back to Maritza. Relieved to have my arms free again.

I found Lane in the backyard swinging an ax into a tree stump in a loose and unprofitable way. "Where did you come from?" he said, looking up, flushed with sweat.

"Nowhere. I left some things at Shawn's house. She asked me to pick them up."

Lane nodded and slammed the ax back down, reducing this poor dead tree to splinters. It was ninety degrees at nine thirty in the morning, and no one in their right mind was chopping wood. There was a statewide burn ban, besides.

"Where did you get that thing?" I asked.

"Lady next door traded it to me for a painting," he said.

"Wow." I smiled. I had one of Lane's paintings. It showed George W. Bush on the deck of an aircraft carrier dressed in full fighter-pilot regalia. Lane had painted this picture from a dream I'd once described to him. One more thing I had neglected to take away from Shawn's house, I realized now.

Thwack! Lane buried the ax into the old tree, chipping off another piece. It was clear that this stump had once existed as a table for splitting logs. But Lane had rendered the flat surface so completely crooked now as to make it almost entirely useless.

"Is this going to be some kind of sculpture?" I asked.

"This? No. This is just a thing to hit with my ax."

"Right," I said, watching him drive the bludgeon home again.

Lane stopped and wiped his hands on his chest, sucking at the thick morning air. "You wanna try it?"

It's important to recognize a question that no one has ever asked you. I smiled and took the ax, and was pleased to find that it was every bit as sturdy as it looked. I raised it up over my head and slammed it down into the wood with a grunt.

"You know what I was thinking?" Lane asked.

"Not a clue," I answered, bashing the stump again.

"We're alive and living through the first decade of the twenty-first century. Do you understand what that means?"

"I think so," I said, not at all sure what it might mean to Lane.

"It means that history is going to judge us as the most primitive and depraved people that live for the whole next hundred years. They're not going to understand a goddamn thing about us. They're going to think we were disgusting."

"Who's disgusting? Me and you?"

"Everybody," he said, considering the mutilated stump. "I should make a video of this. Keep going. I'll get my phone."

I was living at Lane's house on a temporary basis. This wasn't the plan, it just sort of happened. I had moved down to Austin with a girl named Shawn. Shawn was the first girl I met in Portland, really. You remember Shawn. This was the girl with the dog. She loved that fucking dog, man. She would feed him straight out of her mouth and then try to kiss me on the lips. The whole thing was terrible, honestly. I didn't even like going over to her house.

But the dog had died, and Shawn had been accepted into the University of Texas. This was the first thing she said to me when I ran back into her: Shawn was leaving town. We smiled at each other stupidly. This was fantastic news, of course; it relieved us of the pressure of starting over—this was just a fling.

There was something loose and uncomplicated about this girl, the second time around. Nothing against her poor dead dog, but Shawn had shed a lot of baggage. She was lighter; she was present. And, without realizing it, I began to fall for her in spite of myself. Shawn and I rode high on the madness and infatuation of new love, letting it carry us all the way to Texas. It was never even a conversation, really. Somewhere along the line she began including me in her plans. And I found myself telling people I was leaving. It was important not to overthink it—the whole thing had been pulled out of thin air anyway. Shawn and I were making a jailbreak.

———

The reality of Texas set in quickly, though. We were met by a brutal and otherworldly heat. Austin was in the midst of a historic drought and you could feel the weather in everything. It stayed hot in an unholy and interminable way. Even the grackles began to weep in the trees. These bony little deathbirds that would stack themselves on the power lines and scream for mercy. I couldn't help but take the whole thing personally. The weather had a strange effect on my psychology that way. It was bad for morale.

And then, a month in, something else happened. Shawn came home with a brand-new dog. And the writing was on the wall for me.

Lane, for his part, though, had made himself right at home in Texas. He would put on George Bush's twang, or John Wayne's walk, at the drop of a hat. These three men who couldn't help but play along, pretending they were born and bred.

"Shoot," he said to me with a grin. "If I'd known that Peloton was getting back together, I never would've sold my drums to buy all these fucking diapers."

Lane was in a good place, though. There was a change running through him that was hard to miss. I mean, the kid was somebody's father now. He looked leaner in that posture. Older. His skin was tanned, almost wizened. The whole thing just hung together on Lane somehow. To see him there with Bruno was to lose all doubt.

Lane would drive us out to Barton Springs, to go swimming in the heat of the day. I would watch as he zipped Bruno up in a full wet suit, which was easier than trying to slather him in sunscreen. It was a thrill just to watch the way the baby took to the water. This beatific smile coming over him as Lane set him loose—trusting his son to kick and paddle.

"How did you teach him to swim like that?"

"You don't have to teach him," Lane said. "You just throw 'em in. Babies already know what to do." I nodded dubiously, thinking of my sister's son, who was petrified to even *sit* in the bathtub alone. Meanwhile, Lane was managing to keep both the baby and his iPhone above water, as he and Bruno shot a swimming video.

"You know what the best thing about all of this is?" Lane announced afterward, as we sat out in the grass. "I've become a father without becoming my father."

"Who was your father?"

"Who knows," Lane said bluntly.

"Right."

I had been speaking with my own father a lot lately. He'd started calling me on his cell phone, in the middle of the day. On a Tuesday or a Wednesday, just out of the blue. I would see his number come up on the screen and it would freeze me. *Oh, god,* I'd think, *something terrible has happened. He's going to tell me he has cancer.*

"Hello?" I'd ask, in a voice filled with foreboding.

"Hey," he'd answer me elliptically.

I'd never even seen my father *use* his cell phone. No one had. He was famous for leaving it in the cupholder of his car, where it was impossible to reach him. The battery was dead half the time besides. The only time my father and I spoke on the telephone was when my mother handed the receiver to him directly. *Oh, no.* I winced again. *He's going to tell me that she's dead.*

"What's wrong?" I asked.

"Nothing's wrong."

"Okay."

"I was just thinking. Did you know Dick Cheney never apologized for shooting that guy in the face?"

"What?"

"His hunting friend. Harry Whittington. I just read the whole Wikipedia page."

"You did?" I asked, feeling my heart rate level off.

"Yeah. But lucky for him the Secret Service keeps an ambulance on call whenever Cheney leaves the grid. On account of his defective heart."

"Jesus."

"What a country, right?" And then he would laugh.

Every conversation was like this. My father was retired now and still learning how to fill his days. There was always something he had seen on TV, or read on the Internet, that made him think of me. He loved to hit me in the chest with these wild non sequiturs. Nobody was dead, after all. Not even poor Harry Whittington.

School started, and Shawn disappeared. She'd been accepted into a master's program at the University of Texas to study Public Health. Public Health was the reason we were here. Public Health was the reason for all of it, actually. I had no ax to grind against Public Health, I swear. I just wanted to know what it was.

"Everything is Public Health," Shawn assured me.

"*Every*thing?" I asked her.

And it was true, I suppose. Public Health was the broad umbrella that allowed Shawn and her cohort to embrace the larger platform of saving the world.

"The world?" I would inevitably end up asking. "Like the whole *world*?" Because they all talked this way, it seemed, and I wanted to understand it. I was trying very hard just to listen. But I couldn't figure out what was going on.

Public Health was nothing less than a worldview in this circle. It was a gift that these kids had been given at birth. It was a burden they'd been carrying for as long as they could remember. They recognized this mark in each other instantaneously. These were the children who grew up calling adults by their first names, and sending their allowance money to Greenpeace. They all wanted to make the world a better place, and who could quarrel with that?

But they had a way of carrying on. And at first I was sure that this was just the way that they unwound. God knows that the school expected them to work for it. But no one seemed to take a breath long enough to stop talking about Public-*goddamn*-Health. It was incredible. I was surrounded by kids who were obsessed with water safety and infectious disease. They could ramble on for hours about Universal

Preschool or the Midnight Basketball Program. I had watched
two young men pound the table and raise their voices over
gerrymandering in the exurban ghettos.

"Right," I would say patiently. "But is all of that really
Public Health?"

"*Everything* is Public Health," they would answer me in
earnest.

I eventually made a point of sitting in the middle of these
tables and embargoing the conversations as they passed,
sending them back as something new. Something I could
be reasonably certain *was not* Public Health. Football, for
instance.

But Shawn didn't like this. She told me I was being rude.
She accused me of picking fights. Shawn was convinced that
I was making fun of her friends, but I wasn't. I just wanted
them to acknowledge certain hard-line truths. Like the fact
that the game was rigged against us. We must consider this
first and foremost, right? It was incumbent upon us to speak
truth to power by calling out the fraud that *is* power. And
then, by all means, yes, let us begin to talk about Public
Health. Rah-rah. Let's lock arms and save the world.

But these philosophical differences had a way of opening
larger cracks in my relationship with Shawn. I felt like I knew
her less than ever now. The intensity of her graduate program had activated this entirely *other* part of her personality.
And the truth was I kind of liked this other Shawn. She was
smart; she was outspoken; she was engaged. These kids all
listened when she spoke. And I was proud of that. I just had
a threshold for talking about infectious disease.

———————

Honestly, I was sure I was just jealous. I wanted to make this work for Shawn. I wanted to be supportive of the thing she had found here. That's why it was so important for me to find my own thing. I needed to uphold my end of the bargain in this couple. Because, strangely, that's what we were now. In the eyes of everyone around us, we were a set unit. We were partners. We were a team.

This was how I ended up working as a substitute teacher in the Austin public school system. It was nothing if not steady and adult work for me. I even wore a necktie. But I had no business being a schoolteacher. I was brooding. I was quiet. I was disinterested. I'd never felt qualified to teach anything to anyone, and especially not children. Not that they were asking me to do anything like that, obviously. My job was to take attendance.

The real teacher would leave me a note with a short list of uncomplicated instructions. I might be charged with the distribution and collection of some mindless little ditto, say. Or the proctoring of a pop quiz. Nine times out of ten my job was just to put the DVD into the machine and press play. Teaching was a desk job for me. I was stuck there, staring up at the clock, with the other kids. Tracking the second hand as it ran its laps around the dog track, all day long.

My real job was to hurry home after work and take the dog out before he shat the living room. With Shawn at school, the majority of this dog care had fallen onto me. Walking him through the neighborhood, through the endless swell of heat. People wanted to stop and talk. They wanted to fawn over my pet dog, while I stood there sweating. Waving as we passed their houses; watching as I stooped down to pick up his mess. Everyone just assumed the dog was mine.

These were the same people who were convinced that Shawn was my one true love. Strangely, it was this fact of being accepted so fully as a couple that left me most bewildered. I wasn't even aware of having referred to Shawn as my girlfriend, back in Portland. But now we were a couple, and everyone was certain it was meant to be. I mean, look how happy our dog was.

Even Lane and Maritza seemed to meet us on these terms. I had an image of the four of us sitting around the table with a bottle, telling stories, while the baby slept in the other room. Like characters in a Raymond Carver book. Not that we ever did that, of course. But there was always this element of smoke and mirrors. It was flattering how easily the whole thing could be put over on people. There was a power in simply playing along. Because Shawn and I *did* want to be a couple. It was the reason we had moved two thousand miles across the country. But we had skipped a step; we had rushed the whole thing. And I couldn't help but feel like we were living someone else's life.

Lane helped me find a second job writing script coverage for a local production company. As work goes, it was really only marginally better. But at least I was being paid to write again. And, best of all, I could do it while I sat there at my teacher's desk.

Everyone, it seemed, was hell-bent on writing the Great

American Screenplay now. All I had to do was read the thing; write a summary; and offer up my professional opinion. Buy. Consider. Pass. These were the options at my discretion. Almost everything was a straight pass, of course. I was warned up front to never propose a buy. That was miles above my pay grade, and a fireable offense besides. Therefore the gold standard was a firm and serious "consider." And so I gave out a few of those, too, because, why not? I already had two jobs.

It was Danielle, of all people, who seemed the most intrigued by my entrée into the movie business. Somewhere along the line we had started texting again. This didn't come out of nowhere, but it was true that we had stopped speaking. I'd tried to kiss her over the summer, in the back of a taxicab, in Portland. And she kissed me right back, too. But Danielle was never going to leave her boyfriend for me. And that was that.

Still, I was lonely in Austin, and Danielle had a way of making me feel like myself. Plus, it was fun just to flirt. I felt a connection with her that I did not feel with anyone in Texas. There was a rush in commanding her attention.

Danielle encouraged me to write a screenplay of my own. Something about the medium made her believe that I could do it. But I didn't know the first thing about trying to write a movie, and I could never seem to take the whole thing seriously, besides. I made a game of pitching Danielle a laundry list of unproducible film concepts. A screenplay about *consciousness*, for instance.

"Hmm," she texted back. "Have you ever thought about writing one about a jewel heist instead?"

"I just think people want to see their own metaphysical reality projected a hundred feet high on a movie screen."

"But who's going to play the bad guy?" she asked.

"Capitalism," I answered.

"Right, well. Maybe you could try one about a prison break, too."

The joke itself was entertaining, and, more to the point, a reason to keep talking to Danielle. But I had no interest in writing the Great American Screenplay. The truth was I had already begun to double down on my book. In the midst of all this hand-wringing down in Texas, I had discovered the first good reason in years to carry on with *A Cattle, a Crack-Up*. I was determined to turn this book into a one-thousand-page novel. This was a number that could not be ignored. Credibility had always been an issue, and what was more incredible than a thousand fucking pages!

Danielle, to her credit, was against it. She had read a myriad of drafts over the last nine months, and she was convinced that it still worked best as a short story. She said that I should publish that, and cut bait for a while. It was time for me to start something new. But I was certain she was wrong. I had come too far with this book to abandon it in a dozen loose-leaf pages. No one reads short stories, besides. And while it's true that the readership for one-thousand-page novels might be even smaller, at least that audience was *elite*. And if no one was going to read the thing, then why not go for broke? I wanted to give people a book that they could defend themselves with in a fight. I wanted to write a novel that you could crack somebody's skull with.

But this ugly and ferocious desire for *more* did not manifest itself out of nothing. I was embarrassed to admit that I was almost twenty-three years old before anyone bothered to tell me that Joyce Carol Oates was a native of Lockport. Joyce Carol Oates, who had published more than forty novels and won the National Book Award. Joyce Carol Oates, who had taught writing at Princeton University for over four decades. Joyce Carol Oates, who had once graced the cover of *Newsweek* magazine as a writer of *fiction*!

Joyce Carol Oates was from the same nowhere town as *me*. The lapse in this detail was astounding. I felt angry and exhilarated to find it out only in adulthood. It was as if they had conspired to keep it away from me, for my own good. Not that it would've changed anything, obviously. But it's the fact of not being told something so seminal about the place where you are from that feels so galling. It was like trying to imagine a world in which no one bothered to tell you that Timothy McVeigh was from Lockport. Which, of course, he was.

Lane, for his part, claimed to have no idea who Joyce Carol Oates was, or why it possibly mattered. Lane was interested in Timothy McVeigh. He was fascinated by the fact that the Oklahoma City Bomber could be from my hometown. He'd begun badgering me to make a video with him about this. Lane had the idea that we could visit this monster in his super-max cell, in rural Indiana. He wanted me to interview McVeigh on camera about his memories of Lockport. Just Lockport and nothing else. Every little thing that this man might remember about the place we had in common. The smaller the detail the better, Lane told me.

"Dude," I said. "Timothy McVeigh is dead."

"Dead?"

"Yeah. They executed his ass."

"When?"

"I don't know when. A long time ago."

I watched Lane take this in. "Huh. Well, good fucking riddance, then."

"Yeah."

"We'll just think of something else."

I was amazed to find that Lane wasn't simply bugging out on his iPhone. He knew exactly what he was trying to do. He was watching scenes develop in the world. Encounters, really. Everything seemed to revolve around a moment of conflict for Lane. Couples fighting; babies crying; a group of teenagers swearing loudly in a parking lot. But these pieces could get altogether scarier, too. He had videos of dogs barking, and buildings burning, and paramedics loading dead bodies into ambulances.

Lane, I was amused to find, was turning into something of a big deal as a video artist. He'd been showing me segments from an unfinished piece on PTSD, which he had sold to *Vice* magazine on commission. There was one particular image of a young soldier in a grocery store that I could not shake. This plainclothes GI who was berating a middle-aged man in the frozen foods aisle. The civilian, it seemed, was guilty of touching the soldier lightly on the back, in order to squeeze behind him into the refrigerated cooler. I could still see the GI pulling up like a scared cat, as he snapped around on the other man, asking point-blank why he had touched him.

And in this moment it seemed clear to me that the two men knew each other. I thought for certain that they were playing out this scenario as a joke. The gray-haired man froze for a beat, before smiling in recognition. But this was no joke.

"Is something funny to you?" the soldier asked.

"Excuse me?" the befuddled man asked, waffles well in hand now.

"You put your hands on me, without permission, and now you're laughing at me."

"Hey. Take it easy, buddy."

"Who the fuck do you think you are? You touch me without my knowledge, without my permission?"

The older man seized up, refusing to answer. He was imagining the worst now, you could see it. He was desperately looking for a way out of this situation.

"You're some sort of fucking tough guy, huh? Is that it?" The soldier was becoming increasingly frantic. Puffing himself up for a fight. "C'mon. Touch me again. I fucking dare you."

But the older man was gone. Keeping his eyes on the floor as he hurried away. This was the guy that Lane's camera followed. Tracking him down the aisle, before the phone jostled and cut to black. The whole thing was less than a minute long and it made me sick to my stomach.

"Wow," I said.

"Yeah." Lane nodded. "I have tons of these. It happens all the time."

I had started getting tired of coming home to an empty house, though. The dog didn't count. There was something pathetic and demoralizing about having to hurry home to take Shawn's dog around the block and pick up his shit. I complained about this one time and the dog disappeared. Shawn was just as happy to take him with her, I learned. Letting him sit in on classes. Bringing him along to lectures and workshops.

And so I got what I wanted, and I was left all alone again. But I couldn't tell if I was better off or not. Shawn and the dog would disappear for days at a time now; coming home late at night, and sneaking in, long after I'd gone to bed. The whole thing took on the framework of an affair.

But Shawn and I had bigger problems. We found it impossible to live together. I wanted a space where I could spread out and work, but she could not seem to grant me that. Shawn, I learned, was sneaky. She was nosy. From the moment we moved in, I would find her rifling my desk or opening files on my computer. She had no compunction about leafing through the notebooks on my nightstand, demanding to know what it all meant. Shawn was convinced that I was writing about her.

"I'm writing about cows," I said mildly.

"What is that supposed to mean?"

"I don't know. It's a bad joke. It doesn't mean anything anymore."

"I don't understand what you're trying to tell me."

"Nothing. Don't even worry about it. You wouldn't like the book anyway."

"How do you know? I wanna read it," she demanded.

"It's not fucking done!" I said, losing my patience.

These fights were always meant to escalate. Shawn and I didn't know what to make of each other now. It felt strange to find ourselves occupying the same house, the same bed. There was a fixed feeling of claustrophobia that pervaded our apartment. We were almost never fighting about the things that we were fighting about. There was something else below the surface, always. Something curdling. Something that made us pity and resent the other person. And then one day Shawn admitted that she was feeling insecure about Danielle.

"Danielle?" I asked. "You don't even know Danielle. What is there to possibly feel insecure about?"

"You tell me," she said, laying it down in front of me like a devastating playing card. I couldn't help but feel exposed.

"What are you talking about? Are you reading my *texts*?"

"Can you blame me?" she asked, without shame.

"Are you insane? You're fucking spying on me!"

Shawn got teary-eyed then. "How am I supposed to feel? You won't even let me read your book, but you send it to *her* a dozen fucking times!"

"Jesus Christ! Are you reading my *emails*, too?"

"You're the one who leaves it open," she said pityingly.

I could barely process what was happening here. I didn't even know what she had on me. Shawn could've gone through ten years' worth of emails, for all I knew.

"I just want to know what's going on. I just want to

understand what I've gotten myself into. I mean, I'm not even sure that I can trust you."

"You can't trust me?" I laughed.

"I never lied!" she screamed.

"I'm not having this fucking conversation," I said, desperately trying to walk away. I was furious. But Shawn kept following me from room to room.

"You're in love with another girl."

"Fuck you."

"Admit it!" Shawn seemed determined to corner me in this lie. If only I would admit that I was still in love with Danielle we could end this whole charade and walk away. But I didn't want to do that. I didn't even know if it was true.

"Do you know what your problem is, Shawn?" I asked, turning on her now. "It's that you secretly want to fuck your dog."

Well, that pretty much did it. She practically shoved me through the door. Out onto the front porch, and into the heavy insect-heat of night.

I was pretty sure that I was done with Austin then. I had tried and failed, and the world had cut me loose one more time. Except that I didn't know where I was supposed to go instead. Danielle, for her part, seemed strangely underwhelmed, and almost disappointed, by the fact that I could not hold things together with Shawn.

"You're not coming back here, are you?"

"I don't know," I answered. And I didn't.

"Okay," she said warily.

Danielle only liked me in a box, I thought. Miserable and alone. With a terrible girlfriend. Two thousand miles away. This was the only way she was prepared to deal with me. And so we stopped texting once again.

The only person who took any of this in stride, at all, was Lane. He couldn't care less if I got back together with Shawn. He didn't even remember who Danielle was. He just wanted me to stay in Texas. And the truth was, I was scared to death of rushing back into something stupid. Besides, I sort of lived here now. Austin was a place I knew. I had stopped fighting the heat and made my peace with it. My body had adjusted.

Maritza, in particular, was insistent that I stay. "Lane likes you, you know."

"I know," I said. "I like Lane, too."

"No, but he really likes you. And Lane doesn't like *anybody*," she said with a smile.

"Good," I said. "That makes me happy."

I had come to appreciate these afternoons spent swimming with Lane and the baby. The water had a kind of spiritual effect, I thought. It was an answer, even briefly, to the incessant question of leaving. Sitting there on the scorched lawn, watching the girls pass by in their motley bikinis. Watching Bruno, the *Amazing Swimming Baby*, as he picked out the pretty ones and smiled at them. Freezing them, just long enough to stop, and laugh, and talk with us.

"Is there anyone else we know who has a kid?" I asked.

"Just Lauren," Lane said, tossing it off.

"Lauren who?"

"Lauren who-do-you-think?"

"Lauren Pinkerton?"

"Not anymore. She changed her name."

"Changed her name to *what*?"

"Whatever her husband's name is," Lane said, shrugging.

"Oh," I said, trying to process all of this. "Right. And they have a baby now?"

"More or less. I mean, she's definitely pregnant."

"Uh-huh," I said, nodding slowly. It never even occurred to me that Lane and Lauren would be in contact. But why wouldn't they be, of course? They had a lot in common, really. "You still talk to Lauren, then?"

"Yes and no. We're friends on Facebook," Lane offered blithely. "Do you wanna see a picture of her?" He was already bringing it up on his phone.

"No. Not really," I said, looking away. And I didn't.

I had actually received an email from Lauren Pinkerton the previous Christmas. I didn't know what to make of it, honestly. She was reaching out to me in a state of distress. *I'm writing this with tears in my eyes*, the first line read.

But this wasn't really Lauren Pinkerton. This was just a piece of spam. I recognized the template immediately. The tortured syntax. The dormant Hotmail account. Even the subject line, announcing "Very Sad News," tipped me off to its fraudulence. I knew all of these tropes by heart. But none of that stopped me from reading it eagerly just the same.

My family and I have come here to London, United King-
dom for a short vacation. But unfortunately we have been
mugged at the park near our hotel. All of our cash, credit
cards, and cellular phones have been stolen from us. Luck-
ily we have retained our passports.

We have visited the embassy and the police station, but
they are not helping matters. Our return flight is leaving
soon, and we are still facing many difficulties. The hotel
manager says he will not allow us to check out until we can
settle these bills. We are stranded here in London, UK
without our finances. I am freaked out at the moment, as
you can see. Please help me. Love, Lauren.

I laughed out loud the first time I read this. Speaking
purely as a connoisseur of the form, this email was a thing of
beauty. But reading it again left me feeling strange. And, if
I'm being honest, it was this last line that gutted me. This
declaration of love that made me feel something real. And,
all of a sudden, I was tumbling, on the verge of tears with this
image of Lauren Pinkerton reaching out to me. To me. Now.
After all of it.

I was ready to drop everything and put this flight on my
credit card. Part of me wanted nothing more than to simply
go. We could be together now; I could save her. I had not felt
this kind of tenderness toward Lauren in a very long time,
and it made me feel unhinged. Where did she get off reaching out to me now, after so long, anyway? Who the fuck did
she think she was? It made that *other* part of me want to leave
her there in raining, rotting London, UK. I would write back

immediately to say, swiftly and firmly, no. To say that I couldn't. To tell her that I *wouldn't* now. Enough was enough already. I wanted to tell her we were done with all of that.

But I didn't write back anything, obviously. I didn't have anything to say. I didn't know a single thing about Lauren's real life. I didn't know where she was or who she was with. All I knew was that I couldn't help her now. We didn't need each other anymore. And for all I know, Lauren Pinkerton is still stuck there, somewhere in London, stranded without her finances.

CHRISTIANS IN A RAINSTORM

had had three nondescript rides since Texas, but the last one ended badly. Something this man said or did that made me get out of his car. I wasn't scared, exactly; I just knew that going on with him would be a bad idea. I looked around the Okie gas station parking lot where I left him, and I decided I would walk for a bit. That was hours ago.

I was stuck walking through Kansas now, unable to find another ride. I walked through counties named for cowboys into counties named for Indians, and back again. The landscape could be remarkable and endlessly repetitive, by equal turns. I had seen incredible wild animals like snakes and armadillos and foxes. And I knew the putrid smells they made when they cooked on the blacktop as roadkill. I saw a wake of vultures at work on a meal, and I crossed the road with the powerful feeling that they could overtake me if they wanted to. I had been stared at by goats, and lowed at by cows, and chased a quarter mile by a three-legged dog, laughing my head off as I ran. And though I wasn't ready to admit it yet, I knew I wasn't looking for a ride anymore. I was happy just to be walking, happy to have control of that.

Everything in this place seemed to slow down to meet me. Kansas was flat and featureless, and the buildings were low and spread apart so that the eye drew up to the massive sky. I began to feel this landscape wrapping itself around me as I walked. Losing track of myself in the act of purposeful movement. I felt a quiet and a calm in my brain, and I forgot that I was walking at all. Snapping to, on my feet, several miles down the road. Almost laughing. I kept walking, walking through Kansas, walking.

But as the swirling sky began to darken, I thought of night and where I might sleep. There were blisters on my heels, and prickers in my muscles. I was thinking about my back and my neck. I was painfully aware of my hips and my knees. I had been following the name of a town, blindly, for hours. Hollywood, Kansas: written on the road signs; numbers punctuated with arrows. I had already passed three different high schools whose mascot was a funnel cloud with boxing gloves. What would the dark sky look like in the moments before it started to twister? What exactly should I be waiting for, and when would my last warning come?

All at once the sky opened up. Little rocks of ice were pinging off the road like marbles. I hustled into downtown Hollywood with the crashing rain all around me. People were scattering into buildings, into cars, whatever they had. I saw a woman and child standing under the awning of a general store, and I crossed the street to join them. Smiling crazily at God's great destruction.

"I wonder if there's a motel around here?" I asked, after a minute. I was tired from walking and wanted a shower and a bed. "Do you know?"

"Hmm," the Woman said, considering the whole of downtown Hollywood in a glance. "You're on foot?"

"Yes, ma'am," I said, careful not to let my voice fall into a mimic.

"Well. Nothing real close, I don't suppose. We're waiting on my husband with the minivan, though. Why don't you let us give you a ride."

"Okay," I said. "That would be great. Thank you."

"Where you walking from?" she asked without suspicion.

"Texas."

"On foot from Texas," she said, seeming to accept the idea easily. "And where to?"

"Minneapolis," I told her. "I have a brother up there. He runs marathons." This wasn't strictly the truth, but I liked the way it sounded.

The Woman smiled. And when the Man came around with the minivan, he smiled, too. He shook my hand as the Woman folded up her stroller.

"Michael's on a no-kidding pilgrimage," she said. "Traveling on foot to see his brother."

"No kidding," the Man said, and we all smiled.

This repurposing of my walk as a spiritual act felt important. I liked the encouragement of these Christians. I liked their easy excitement, and we fell into a friendly chatter as they drove me to the motel.

"They'll take care of you here, son," the Man said. "Good rates. Clean beds. Cable TV, too, I think."

"Good, good," I said. "That all sounds great."

I liked being a walker then. I didn't want the Man and the Woman to know that I'd been hitchhiking. That sounded dangerous and unsteady, and I was afraid they wouldn't approve. There was no reason to worry them unnecessarily. It was better just to stick to the truth of the day. I had walked more than fifteen miles, from the tip-top of Oklahoma into Kansas. I was dirty and aching and red from the sun, and that was real.

They were kind to me, too, never questioning the idea that I had been on the road for weeks. I explained away the fact of carrying next to nothing. I told them about motels and friends-along-the-way, whatever. I told them I was on my second pair of sneakers and third different ball cap. They could see I had a backpack and a sleeping bag. What more could there be?

"It's a kind of experiment in traveling light," I said, and they seemed to recognize the virtue in this. "It's surprising how little you really need."

"Jesus used to travel tremendous distances on foot," the Woman said. "Probably when he was about your age, too." She laughed and said that I was in good company that way. It made me think of all the great figures in the Bible making pilgrimages. Traveling hundreds and hundreds of miles on foot.

"It's faith's great loss, I think. The fact that these kinds of pilgrimages have been taken out of worship, I mean."

I nodded with her, smiling. The Woman had a way of making my life suddenly sound meaningful and richly plotted. I felt compelled to offer something of my own.

"*By chanting the names of the Lord / And you'll be free,*" I said, grinning like a moron. "George Harrison wrote that."

"Well, I think that's just wonderful," the Woman said, turning around from the passenger seat. "A *Beatle* sang that, huh? I thought they played for the other side."

She smiled and it froze me.

"No, hon, that's the *Rolling* Stones," the Man said.

"Oh, right," she said, and they both laughed happily. I smiled, thinking they were making fun of me now. But what did I care? I liked them both enormously. I felt safe in the back of their minivan, with their mute, happy Child. I looked at him again and couldn't decide if he was a boy or a girl. Whenever he smiled it reminded me of both.

We pulled into the driveway of the motel, and I could practically feel the hot shower and the cold air-conditioning inside. I thanked the Man and the Woman effusively, and I tried to say goodbye. But the Woman wouldn't hear of it.

"No, no, no, we won't leave you yet. Just go inside and make sure they're giving a fair rate."

"Oh, I'm sure it's fine," I said, not understanding this.

"No, no . . . Just go see," she said. "We can always take you somewhere else."

This was confusing, but I didn't want to argue with her. I went inside the little glass lobby, where the manager told me that a single room for the night would cost $39.99, just like the sign out front said. I nodded and came back outside to say thank you, one last time. But the Man stopped me.

"Say, Michael. We'd like to invite you to stay at our house for the night. We could get you some dinner and it'd save you a little money for your traveling."

"Oh, wow. Really?" I said. I never even saw it coming. "Are you sure?"

"Yeah, of course, of course. C'mon. Hop back in."

I got back into the minivan and smiled at the Child, who smiled back. These good people who wanted so badly just to help me. They wanted to make themselves of use, of service. I could almost see the appeal of a simple Christian life then. Living in a fixed place with a God, and a Mayor, and a nice red set of stop signs. Why not?

The Woman ran a bath for me, apologizing for the broken showerhead. But I didn't care. It was the first time I'd taken a bath since I was the Child's size, and it felt good to soak my body, so raw from walking in the weather. I lay back in the warm tub and thought about a level of trust that existed in these Christians, so off-putting and refreshing, both.

The Woman insisted on washing out my clothes in the machine. And when I got out of the bathroom, I saw that the Man had laid a fresh set on the bed for me. I felt strange about this at first, but they fit, and I decided that I liked the gesture. Studying myself in the full-length mirror, and trying to stand a little straighter in the Man's outfit.

I found him out in the backyard, barbecuing chicken on

the gas grill. We ate our dinner out here, on the back patio, like a Family. The Woman bowed her head and offered grace to the Provider, and the meal was served. I hadn't eaten meat in five or six years, but I didn't want to say no. I had come too far to be here, and it didn't feel right to make a fuss now. I picked apart my chicken self-consciously, pulling out the bones and generally scattering it around the plate. I chewed and chewed to break down sinew and muscle and tendon, and I still nearly choked with a hasty swallow. I admired the simpler mechanics of the Man, who sucked the bone clean and even ate the fat. A method that was pleasurable in its thoroughness.

I watched the Woman cutting tiny pieces for the Child, who smushed everything into happy little handfuls. I was glad to be here at this table, and I took another ear of corn to show that my appetite was healthy and not peculiar in any way.

After dinner, the Child got sleepy or cranky, and the whole house turned in early with him. The Woman gave me the wooden bed that the Man had built special for the boy to grow into. I protested, saying I was happy on the couch, but the whole family insisted.

I lay there in the dark room, staring up at the ceiling, counting all the lies I'd told today. Lies to smooth things over. Lies to stitch things up. Lies to pad the truth. But wasn't I also giving these people something that they wanted? The simple story of a traveler in need. This weary character undertaken on a whim. The act of walking itself was always totally sincere, of course. Everything else, perhaps, was not.

The thing that troubled me most was the fact that I was

hardly troubled at all. I was only asking for a ride to the motel. Smiling and playing along as the Christians began to improvise. I never could've imagined any of this. Naked in the tub, and dressed in the man's clothing, as I pretended to eat meat. I was just trying to keep my bearings.

I listened to the crickets and the bullfrogs chirping out beyond the shadows of the yard, and I let out a breath that had been sitting in my chest all day. I felt my eyes flutter and begin to close. And, all at once, my head drew a total and fantastic blank.

I woke up early the next day feeling stiff but determined. I dressed in my own clothes, and stuffed my clean-smelling laundry back inside my bag. I had the idea that I might be able to leave quietly, to slip out of the house unnoticed. But the Man and the Woman were already awake in the kitchen. Already drinking coffee and smiling. And I smiled, too, hurrying through my eggs and toast. I was conscious of overstaying my welcome now, but the Woman wouldn't hear of it. She made a big deal of packing me a lunch, and slowing me down. And the Man, too, made sure to give me a wide straw hat to protect against the sun. There was even a first-aid kit waiting by the door, where I could see forty dollars folded neatly inside its clear plastic walls.

And, truly, I was touched by all of this. But too much generosity has a way of making me feel inadequate. I was troubled by my inability to repay these strangers anything. It embarrassed me to stretch the lie out today. I just wanted to say goodbye, and figure out where I was. This would certainly be another long day, I knew. Even if I caught a good ride straight off, it would still take me the rest of the week before I reached Minneapolis.

I started packing up and saying goodbye all over again, when the Woman touched my arm sweetly. "We still have to pray over your travels, hon."

"Right. Of course," I said, but I didn't really know what this meant. It was just me and the Man and the Woman, standing in the kitchen. They each took my hand, and we made a circle, bowing our heads as the Woman began to pray. And not just some boilerplate blessing, either. Her voice was suddenly real with emotion. She was talking to me, *about* me, and that was strangely thrilling.

"Lord Jesus, we ask you to stand over Michael's journey now. Make him clear of mind and fleet of foot. Be the wing under which he seeks his shield and shelter along the road. Clear the difficult path for him in safety and in light. And keep your hand always at his shoulder as he makes this long pilgrimage to be reunited with his brother . . ."

And she kept going. I was not expecting any of this, and it moved me. I stared at our feet on the shiny linoleum, trying desperately not to smile. This may be the most singularly strange and wonderful thing I've ever experienced. To be blessed by strangers in the middle of Kansas. It felt tremendous.

"Do not fear what they fear; do not be frightened of the uncertain road ahead. For we Christians walk by faith, and not by sight alone. For no one can harm the man who is eager to do good in the world." The Woman inhaled. "Amen."

"Amen," we answered. I lifted my head and I knew, all at once, that I must keep walking. It was out of my hands. Only a fool would think to stop here.

I hugged the Woman, and I shook the Man's hand, and I finally left. I was truly a walker then. Everything was lighter, and I was lighter, too. The Man's hat was like a straw halo upon my head, imparting its conviction. This was a thing I could do for the Man and the Woman, I thought. This was the drumbeat that I felt inside my bones: *Just keep walking.*

And I did, for hours; but it was hard. Much, much harder on the second day. All the idiot joy was gone. It was hotter and drier, and I felt everything now. The pebbles inside my shoes; the spiders at the backs of my knees. I was sick and sweaty and lethargic, and my head just swam in the blurry heat. My legs felt rubbery and foreign to me as I walked with this snarl of distress painted all over my face. I could not believe how slow I walked today. Plodding, really. It was not the pain so much as the mental and emotional fatigue of not allowing myself to stop. I walked and walked, waiting for the pain to break.

Why did I keep walking, I wondered. Walking through Kansas, walking. It was for the Christians, of course. But that was a lie. This was an act of vanity now. Folly. Boredom. It was a morbid curiosity. An aesthetic masochism. This was the fallacy of misplaced romance. It was young legs. Pink lungs. An animal heart. And, all at once, it was a *spiritual act* again.

It was personal. It was inarticulate. And that was enough to just keep walking.

As I went, I daydreamed about turning around and affecting that enemy pose. Walking backward with my arm out. And in my brain I did this. Smiling at the cars as they passed me. Rushing by in a blur. Objectively, I understood it. I knew how I must look today. Run-down and washed-out. I imagined myself inside one of those vehicles: passing a walker on the roadside. *No, thank you, please. Not today, friend.*

But wouldn't it be strange and incredible if I did it? What if I just kept walking? I'd made it ten miles, through the morning, into some westerly Kansas county where they were Denver Broncos fans. I recovered my rhythm and I laughed out loud at my own fool ambition to walk two thousand miles, because I was doing it. Disappearing into Kansas. Hours turning into days; towns turning into states. There is a numb kind of thinking born of small repetitive acts. A slow anesthetic. I was losing track for miles. Losing time entirely. I disappeared into the walking like I was coasting on a bike. This was not me. The body has its own locomotion, and it was willing itself so now.

So much so that I hardly noticed the pickup truck that pulled off the road in front of me. Waiting there, idling, and it froze me. I knew, of course, that I must say no. I was supposed to tell the driver that I couldn't; to say that I didn't *want* to. I knew exactly what I was doing out here on the road. I was walking.

But that's not what I did at all. No. I jogged after the

truck quite willingly, almost laughing. I was giddy with my own good fortune again. This heathen absolution with its long hair and dirty smile. Rumbling metal and the soaked smell of gasoline. I nodded to the stranger as he unlocked the door, and it was over. Quick and dirty. I had done my walking and I was finished then.

GREAT EXPECTATIONS

was staring at a tower on the television above the bar, waiting for it to fall. This sudden, intrusive thought that came rushing back to me. I used to stand on a high floor and imagine this same building folding inward. Shuddering down toward the street in a sudden, violent collapse. And as I sat there, staring at the screen, I was watching it happen now. Only not in a way that anyone could've imagined. JPMorgan Chase had just purchased Bear Stearns for pennies on the dollar.

"Put all the bankers in jail," Cokie said, as she sidled up behind me.

"I used to work there," I answered, feeling strangely exhilarated.

"Of course you did," she said with a laugh.

"No, really, I'm serious."

And I was. This was my first job out of college. My first anything after moving to New York. Copying and shredding documents for the ignominious Bear Stearns. I answered to a frowsy, frowning woman named Judy. With her mussy muslin sweaters and her frizzy black bob. Judy was a force of nature in this office.

"What are you doing?" she would ask as she pressed a set of documents into my arms. This question that would set my hairs on end. Stealing its way into my dreams at night. "What are you doing?" Judy would ask me, over and over. It was the only thing she said to me, most days. Strangely, though, my clearest memory was of Judy asking this of someone else. Cowing one of her coworkers; a man of some esteem, I thought. He was standing over my desk with a thick yellow binder. "What are you doing?" she asked as she took the work away from me, putting her fellow countryman on the spot. It was everything I could do not to smile. The only person who was confused in this situation was the gentleman. I was Judy's bitch, motherfucker. You better step back.

And he did, too. Snapping up his folder as he grumbled down the hall.

"What did you do there?" Cokie asked me.

"Do?"

"What was your job?"

"I knew where all the bodies were buried."

I had run into Cokie on the subway. She was sitting on the bench seat of the R train, with her big draping coat splayed open. Looking tired, looking bored, as she stared at the in-car advertisements for plastic surgery and night school. I marveled at the air of inaccessibility that this girl exuded just simply being. A hardened New York cool that warned all comers, *Do not fuck with this.*

All I really had to do was start smiling, though. I watched the sternness fall away as she glanced up at me. Forced to look again.

"Oh, my god," she said. "Dude. What are you doing here?"

"I live here," I answered.

"Shut up."

"No. It's true." And we were both laughing then.

"Oh, my god," Cokie said again, as she pulled me into the seat beside her.

"Where are you going?" I asked, feeling suddenly excited. "We should get off the train. We should go get coffee, maybe. Or breakfast. Where are you going?"

"Borough Hall," she said, sounding genuinely disappointed. It was only three stops away. "I have to work."

"On a Saturday?"

"On *every* day," she answered dryly.

"Why?" I couldn't help but smile. "What happened now?"

"The same thing that always happens. Some kid grabs a cell phone and takes off running."

"Do people still steal phones?"

"Are you kidding me? It's like seventy-five percent of all my cases."

"Maybe he didn't do it," I offered glibly.

"Of course he did it."

"What are you going to say in his defense, then?" I was enjoying this.

Cokie's face went slack. "If it pleases the court, I would like to ask for leniency in this case, Your Honor. Jermaine is a good kid in a bad neighborhood . . . and circumstances have *blah, blah, blah* . . ."

"Right."

"Which he is. And they *have*. I mean, it's just a fucking phone. Don't dangle it out in front of your face like an idiot. You know?"

"Noted," I said as we got to our feet. I couldn't stop smiling at her. I had no idea how important it was to see Cokie until she was standing right there in front of me. We were holding hands now as the train pulled into the station.

"I'll call you," she said as she stepped out onto the platform. "We'll hang out soon, I promise. I'll call you," she said again as the doors slid shut.

That was two months ago.

We'd been making and breaking plans ever since. This is the latitude of old friends. It was easier sometimes just to push each other off. To delay. To wait for next time. Cokie would wake me up at one in the morning with a half-cocked text message entreating me to meet her at a bar in Manhattan. I would squint at this, in the dark of my bedroom, typing out a one-word reply: "Unsubscribe." This was guaranteed to rile her up, and we would spend the next forty minutes texting vulgar jokes back and forth.

It was strange. Just the simple fact of knowing that we *could* meet up again made me feel closer to Cokie somehow. Even so, it took an actual event to bring us together in the end. Patrick Serf was turning thirty.

"Thirty?" I asked as we carried our drinks to a small table at the back of the bar. "He's really only thirty?"

"How old do you want him to be?" Cokie asked with a laugh.

"I don't know. Just older, I guess."

"Well, I mean, when we were twenty-two and he was twenty-five, he kind of *was*, you know."

"Right," I said. "And now it just feels like we're all the same age."

"I sort of feel that way with everyone." Cokie smiled. "Anyway. We'll just have one drink and go over. All the old D.C. kids will be there. It'll be fun."

I nodded. There was something inevitable about this conversation. This was the conversation that we always had. These were the things that came flooding back when we looked at each other. Houses and bars and backyards that we'd shared.

"When was the last time you were there?" Cokie asked.

"God. Two years ago, I guess. The last time I saw you."

"New Year's Eve?"

"Right."

"That was the weekend that you and Lauren broke up," she said, almost reverently.

"Well. I mean, technically, we were already broken up. But we were still fucking like cats and dogs right through the end."

"I don't think that's the expression," Cokie frowned.

"Sure it is."

Lauren had moved in with Cokie and left me alone in the apartment in D.C. This was supposed to make us fully broken up. But we were still on the lease together, still paying rent through the end of the year. And there were things we needed to hash out between us. Like what to do with an apartment full of *stuff*.

I went through a period of hoarding. Everything that Lauren left behind was mine now. In total, abandoned, claimed. Beyond that, I had no plans for any of it. And, to be perfectly honest, it took less than twenty-four hours for me to change my mind completely. I became meticulous about getting rid of everything. All this dead weight tied around me could go.

The girls drove down from New York, on the morning of New Year's Eve, to collect the last of it. The empty apartment was nothing then if not an excuse to throw one last party. This was to be our great valedictory, our one final going-away.

"That was the last time everyone was together," Cokie said, almost wistfully.

"Yeah. What a nightmare," I said drolly.

"Horrible," she answered.

"But so much fun."

"Oh, my god. It was the best."

Cokie laughed. To hear her laughing now, as we said these things, made them funny. Funny for the first time ever, really. The whole fucking thing was hysterical.

"I just remember you standing on the table, counting down to the ball drop, at eight o'clock at night. And then you did it again at nine. And ten. And eleven."

"Well, I mean, once you've started . . . you're bound to land on it eventually."

"I must've kissed four or five dudes, thinking it was midnight."

"Yeah," I said. "You're good at parties, Cokie."

"And then, the next thing I remember, some kid started freaking out because the doors were locked. And nobody could find you anywhere. You were just *gone*."

"So you broke my front window."

"Hey. False imprisonment is a Class H felony in the District of Columbia, dude."

"Yeah, well, either way." I smiled. "We never did get our deposit back."

Cokie shook her head. "All of that was two and a half years ago?"

"Almost, yeah."

"And now Lauren has a kid," she said brightly. "You know that, don't you?"

"Lane told me. I think it's great."

"I guess so," Cokie offered mildly, in a line I could imagine she had delivered more than once. "Sometimes it feels like she loves that baby more than me."

I laughed.

"I'm serious. Without a baby, they'd still be living in New York."

I nodded as Lauren's life hung there between us. "And what about you?"

"What about me, what?"

"Are you ever gonna have one?"

"You mean *kids*? No."

"No?"

"Unh-uh, no," Cokie answered flatly.

"Why not?"

"Dude. I'm a *juvenile* defender. Why do you think?"

I laughed again.

"Plus, I mean, I live in New York City."

"You could always leave New York."

"Leave New York!" she practically scoffed. "And where would I go?"

"You could go anywhere."

"But I already live in *New York*," she sneered, owning this posture.

"Right," I said, giving up. "I always forget that."

Cokie laughed and finished the rest of her drink. Picking up her phone off the table. "What do you think? Should we go?"

"We can't go now. We just got here."

"All right. Buy me another drink, then," she said as she boosted herself up on the arms of her chair. But something made her sit back down.

"You did the right thing, you know. Leaving."

"Leaving Texas?"

"No. Going to Portland. It's the only thing that ever made anything change."

"Oh," I said, understanding now.

Cokie smiled tightly as she stood back up. "Anyway. I just felt like I needed to say that to you." I nodded and watched as she disappeared into the dark of the bar.

It was true that I had bought a plane ticket to Portland without telling anyone. After hanging up with Lauren, after one more endless fight. I went online and I did it.

It wasn't just me, though. Everyone had changed their mind about Washington, D.C. The people with the good jobs, and the people with the shit jobs, were all suddenly over it. Everyone was moving to New York City. A decision we all went to great lengths to pretend we had arrived at on our own, independent, and in spite, of everyone's identical decision. This tidal shift attached itself to all our friends, and was suddenly sucking hard on me. I wanted to get out of the city as badly as everybody else did. I just didn't want to go to Brooklyn now to do it.

I waited to tell Lauren I wasn't coming, though. I waited because I knew how she'd react, and I was finally done with all of that. I was sick and tired of having to defend myself in everything I did. *Why did I move to Portland?* Because it wasn't New York, and it wasn't D.C. I hardly knew a single soul there. All I knew was that it didn't look anything like any place I had ever lived. And that was enough to start.

But all of this felt perverse to Lauren. It felt hostile. It felt random and jarring. And she wasn't wrong, either. But I was determined to make a break now. This was an act of self-preservation. I was finally pulling the rip cord.

By the time everyone started showing up for New Year's Eve, Lauren and I weren't speaking. Unfortunately, this level of suffering barely registers on a night like this. With a house full of kids running wild with obliviousness, this party was happening with or without us. That was the reason for the fake countdowns, in the end. I was desperately trying to speed the whole thing up. I wanted to end the year, over and over. In room after room. Counting down from ten and celebrating *nothing*.

But Lauren didn't like this. She tracked me through the downstairs of the house, watching the whole thing unravel. Eyeing me uncertainly, with her arms at her sides, as the party counted down in farce. *Three, two, one . . . Happy New Year!*

Splash! Lauren threw her drink in my face.

I looked up and took a staggering step forward, as the whole room filled in between us. Cutting us off, like they were heading off a fight. This was hilarious, of course. But Lauren and I were the only ones left laughing. In tears, we were laughing so hard. Laughing our heads off, as the music came back up, and the party pushed us apart.

Cokie set her phone down on the table as I came back with our drinks. "I told Patrick that you're coming," she said brightly. "He's excited that you're back."

"Oh," I said. "Huh. That's sort of funny."

"Yeah." Cokie smiled. "Why is it funny?"

"I don't know. I sort of feel like I don't even really know Patrick Serf."

"What are you talking about? Of course you know him."

"Yeah. I mean, I *know* him. But only in the way that I know any of those kids now. Only in this superficial sort of way. It doesn't really mean anything."

"Do you not like Patrick?" Cokie asked.

"No. It has nothing to do with Patrick," I said with a smile. "All I'm saying is that I think of him as your friend. And Lauren's. The only time I ever saw Patrick Serf, in my life, was when I was with you."

"You're with me right now." Cokie laughed, clearly amused.

"Right." I nodded, letting it go.

But this was really how I felt. I'd never known where I stood with any of those kids, and now it didn't matter. I had nothing against the famous Patrick Serf, but his name alone rattled like a joke that had been told to death and was no longer funny. I just could not pretend to care about one more meaningless birthday, or the friends of friends who were waiting at the next bar. I was here because of Cokie.

But this had been going on forever. These were the circumstances through which I even came to *know* Cokie in the first place. She was my friend, yes, of course, but she was always Lauren's friend, too. And, more to the point, she was Lauren's friend first. Even now, I couldn't help but feel like an interloper. It was part of the reason I pulled back from the D.C. kids in the first place. I moved to Portland *because* they were all moving to New York.

"Do you think you'll still be living here a year from now?" Cokie asked me.

"I hope so. I mean, this is the happiest I've ever been in New York."

"Huh," she said, sounding surprised. "I feel like you have this whole secret life."

"Is it a secret?"

"It is to me," she said pointedly. "I don't even know where you live. I'm not even entirely sure when you got back."

"It wasn't really planned, I guess. I had some friends from Portland who were looking for a roommate. The timing just sort of worked."

"And what do you do for money?"

"I have a job building film sets out in Red Hook."

"Oh, wow. Really? What does that mean?"

"Breathing toxic chemicals."

"That's it?"

"No," I said. "There's also a series of small, repetitive tasks."

"Ha-ha-ha," Cokie said snidely. "Why are you doing it if you don't like it?"

"So that I can write."

"Oh." She stopped herself again. "Really?"

"Yeah. I mean, I go in every day for three weeks, and then they don't need me again for ten days."

"So you're still working on your book."

"No." I shook my head. "Not really. I sort of reached the end of that book."

"Fuck," she said, sounding guilty. "I really meant to read it, you know."

"I know you did. But you were in law school. You actually had an excuse."

A *Cattle, a Crack-Up* was everything I thought a "novel" was supposed to be. It was big, it was dense, it was ambitious. And, at one point, it was maybe even perfect. But I had long since passed that point. Eclipsed it. Obliterated it. Transcended it. A *Cattle, a Crack-Up* had ceased to mean anything to me. I was writing about things I could not possibly know or understand. The novel had evolved into a pantomime of something real. It was all one big performance, in the end. And, weirdly, that was my favorite thing about it. I couldn't write that book again, even if I tried!

"But a lot of people read it, right?" Cokie asked.

"Sure. I mean, I have a literary agent. It got sent out."

"You have an *agent*?" she asked. "And he knows you're building film sets?"

"First of all, it's a *woman*. And, yes. She's aware I have a *day job*, thank you."

Cokie laughed. "Tell me what happened."

"God. Who knows what happened. Nothing happened."

"Nothing?"

"I mean, she couldn't get it placed. No one had any idea what to make of it. The book was totally and utterly rejected."

"Oh," Cokie said, sitting back. "That sucks."

"It's not so bad. Lane told me some artists just aren't

recognized in their twenties." Cokie laughed. "Besides. I've already started something new."

"What is it?"

"I dunno yet. Something that's in my own voice, hopefully. The voice I actually speak in. The one I use in an email. Or a joke. That's the way I'm trying to write."

"Oh." Cokie nodded. "Good. Keep doing that."

I had taken the train into Manhattan, to visit with Bettina Kleins at her office in the Flatiron District. Bettina and I were going out to lunch to talk about "next steps." This had been my idea, in the end. I was eager to distance myself from *A Cattle, a Crack-Up* and express to her the ever-evolving state of my novel-in-progress. A book built on the acknowledgment that all memory is episodic memory, and every narrator is an unreliable narrator. Exactly as it must be, I was convinced now. This is what it actually feels like to know another person. I wanted the book to express those negative spaces, between two bodies, where the relationship breathes. I was interested in the gaps and discordances of experienced time. I was working through the role of memory and imagination as it functions, in its fullest capacity, to fill those empty spaces with meaning. Because what *was* this construction, after all, if not fiction? I even had a metaphor worked out to communicate this signal change in philosophy.

I wanted the next novel to be assembled like a mixtape. With all of the emotional modulations of an object that is constructed with an order and intention. Or its opposite, even. A seemingly random series of Polaroid photographs, spread across a tabletop. In each image you would see the protagonist. You'd recognize the changes in his face, and the shifts in his bearing. The tenuous state of his relationships, and the limitless discoveries of self. And suddenly you would find yourself internalizing the passage of time in each next image. You would begin to make all of these connections for yourself. The cities that he lived in; the apartments that he kept; the jobs where he worked. And you would shed all of these skins, one by one. Forgetting them completely once they were gone. Friends and lovers going in and out of focus, as you flipped through the pictures, fast, then slow. And, almost without realizing it, you would begin to *see* the narrator, right there in front of you. You would finally take his voice into your head. Because it is this transfer of consciousness that is your one and only constant in the novel. The narrator's story must keep moving forward.

"Mm," Bettina said, after a long, and slightly agonized, pause. "Polaroids and mixtapes are good, of course. But can't it be more *digital*, maybe?"

"Can what be digital?" I asked, feeling stricken. "You mean the *metaphor*?"

"Exactly!" Bettina exclaimed. "You need to start thinking more about the Internet. Your first book seemed to whitewash the whole world of technology. The world that actually surrounds us. The one that we *live* in. And I *get* it . . . they were living on a farm, and blah, blah, blah. But, I mean, you wrote *A Cattle, a Crack-Up* like the Internet never even existed."

"Huh," I said, sitting back in my chair, feeling stunned by

this. "I never thought of it that way. I think that's a really good point, Bettina."

"Well. It's just a thought," she said, waving it away as she signaled for the check.

It was midnight, and Cokie was standing up from the table, asking how it got so late. Laughing as she tried to find her arms through the holes in her coat. I couldn't help but think of Lauren and the last time I saw her. Every single part of me assumed that we would follow up once I got to Portland. But Lauren never did, and neither did I. Long past the point of waiting each other out. Past the point where there was even anything left to say. And there is no going back after that. The best thing for everyone, then, is to just do nothing.

It was inevitable that we would find each other at midnight, I knew. Kissing out of fear of kissing someone else. We kissed because we knew that it was over. With the room spinning around us like a mirror ball, and our friends screaming "Auld Lang Syne" in derision. Shouting it into the void of the year gone by. Lauren and I swayed back and forth in the center of the room. Holding each other up, with all the movements of a slow dance. Belly-to-belly, with all the intimacy of a stabbing. We stared into each other's eyes as we lifted each other up by the hilt.

Ours was the first kiss of the year Two Thousand Six.

It was Lauren who locked the doors at midnight, trapping everyone inside the house. We hid ourselves in the bedroom, where we kissed in the dark. Laughing like the first time. Lauren and I stripped each other bare, and fucked on the hard and unforgiving mattress. The only real part of us that was left inside the room.

This was where I woke the next morning. With the dazzling sunlight shining off the hardwood floors. I got out of bed, and I stood there, watching Lauren sleep. I couldn't bear to wake her now. I couldn't risk another fight. There was nothing left to say, besides. This was the end.

Cokie and I stood out on the street, searching for a cab. Watching three different cars pass us, in succession, with their lights off. I turned around again and realized she was staring at the sky.

"That's where the 9/11 lights come up."

"What?" I asked, certain I'd misheard her.

"The memorial lights. This is where they are. Right over that building," she said, running the blade of her hand up and down. I stared into the empty sky, seeing nothing.

"I don't know what that means, Cokie."

"The 9/11 lights. They put them up at Ground Zero for a week every September," she said. "You've seen them."

"No," I said, shaking my head. "I don't think so." I was sure now that I never had.

"Oh." She smiled as she set her chin against my shoulder. Cokie pointed to a gap in the clouds. "Right there. That's where the World Trade Center used to be. Not that you could've seen it from Fort Greene, obviously. But you could definitely see the lights. I mean, if it wasn't March." Cokie laughed to herself.

"Wow," I said softly, staring hard into this empty space. I

was surprised, and almost embarrassed, to find myself moved by it. When I turned back around, Cokie was standing out in the street with a taxi.

"You're not coming, are you?" she said with a sigh.

"No," I answered. "Sorry, Cokie."

"I'll pay for the cab, you know. I'll get you drunk at the bar."

"I'm already drunk."

"Yeah. Fuck. Me, too." We laughed stupidly, feeling dizzy on our feet. "When am I going to see you again?" she asked, as she tethered herself to the open door.

"I don't know. Soon, I hope."

Cokie didn't say anything. "Come here and give me a kiss goodbye, then."

She stood up on her toes and kissed me twice, on the mouth, quickly. These funny, happy little pops. A wry smile on her face as I pressed the door closed. And Cokie was gone.

I watched as her taxicab floated off and disappeared. I thought not of Cokie's columns of light, but of a dome. With a glow emanating off the fronts and tops of buildings. With a ceiling that was vaulted high above the bridges. An invisible skein of atmospheric gases that was buoyant on the surface of the night.

I watched a small mass of color coming toward me across the intersection. Bouncing and bobbing in the flexed light. A group of joggers was suddenly standing there, running in place. The lights changed and the runners came bounding off the sidewalk. Rushing toward me as I stepped out onto the avenue to meet them. Their bare legs and billowing breath, huffed and clutched, as they ran right through me. Changing sides, and disappearing. And, for a fleeting moment, I could swear that there was silence. Left alone in the great city tableau, once more.

ACKNOWLEDGMENTS

With gratitude for, and acknowledgment of, the help I received in finishing this book, I wish to thank: Soumeya Roberts; John Knight; Andrew Neel; Luke Meyer; Nait Rey; Jessica Arcangel; Laura Heberton; Sara Eklund; Adam Khatib; Ethan Palmer; Tom Davis; SeeThink Films; FSG and FSG Originals; Writers House; Hanly Banks; Annie McGreevy; Daniel Kine; Tracey Ennis; Matthew Schnipper; Kevin Donahue; Lindsay Nash; the Roberts and Purnell families; and last, best, most, Molly Purnell.